HELL ON WHEELS

HELL ON WHEELS

KAREN KELLEY

BRAVA

KENSINGTON PUBLISHING CORP.

http://www.kensingtonbooks.com

BRAVA BOOKS are published by

Kensington Publishing Corp.
850 Third Avenue
New York, NY 10022

All Kensington titles, imprints, and distributed lines are available at special quantity discounts for bulk purchases for sales promotions, premiums, fund-raising, educational or institutional use.

Special book excerpts or customized printings can also be created to fit specific needs. For details, write or phone the office of the Kensington Special Sales Manager: Kensington Publishing Corp., 850 Third Avenue, New York, NY 10022. Attn. Special Sales Department. Phone: 1-800-221-2647.

Brava and the B logo Reg. U.S. Pat. & TM Off.

ISBN 0-7582-1171-6

First Kensington Trade Paperback Printing: June 2006
10 9 8 7 6 5 4 3 2 1

Printed in the United States of America

Chapter 1

Cody Carlyle knew there were just some days when she wished she'd stayed in bed. She had a gut feeling today was going to be one of them.

She cautiously moved forward, hugging the alley wall, weaving between the large, dirty brown Dumpsters. The cold seeped into her skin like a damp blanket thrown on top of her.

Staying in bed would've been nice. A second cup of coffee, maybe read the paper. Instead, she'd tugged on ratty, knee-torn jeans, a second-chance vest, faded black T-shirt, and steel-toed boots. She'd slipped her gun inside the holster of her leather halter, tied back her dark hair, and pulled on a light jacket, effectively concealing her weapon. Her uniform of the day was complete.

She blended well with the riff-raff on Fort Worth's seedier side.

A hell of a way to spend one's life.

Okay, so maybe it wasn't *all* bad. On most days, she liked being a bounty hunter. There was nothing better than the adrenaline rush when she nailed a skip and brought him to justice, and picking up fat checks from desperate bail bondsmen didn't hurt, either.

They figured paying out part of the money was better than losing it all. That's why they called her or another bounty hunter to drag the skip back into custody—by whatever means available as long as the culprit was still kicking.

That's where the problem lay.

The law frowned on *dead or alive* and had removed the dead part. It made her job a little harder.

And today she had a bad feeling. Sometimes all she had to go on was what her gut told her. She'd learned in the past to listen.

Except maybe today.

She'd gotten a tip the skip was in the area and she wasn't about to let him slip through her fingers. Leonard Morgan, a mean son-of-a-bitch. He'd jumped bail—twenty-five hundred dollars at stake. Not a lot by the time she got her ten percent, considering what she'd had to go through, but the bastard liked to hit women. He'd broken his wife's jaw during their last fight. She really hated men who resorted to their fists, especially on a woman.

She'd been hunting Leonard for a week now. Into sleazy bars, flea-ridden motels—anywhere the dregs of society slithered off to. So far, all her leads had fizzled out, and none of his relatives were talking.

Probably scared.

Then she'd gotten this tip.

She straightened her spine and narrowed her eyes, moving farther into the alley with its myriad of twists and turns, the concrete and brick walls a musty tomb that seemed to press against her. A cold shiver whipped down her spine, sending goose bumps over her arms.

God, she had to quit watching late-night television. Pure escapism, that's all it was. There was nothing even remotely real about what she watched. Last night had been *The Vampire From Hell*. The vampire was a good-looking sucker, though.

She inwardly chuckled at her pun—until a rat as big as an overweight Chihuahua ran in front of her. For a moment, she couldn't move. Her gaze fixed on the creature as it stopped, glared at her with its beady little eyes, then scurried behind one of the Dumpsters.

Yuck! She hugged her middle. Yuck! Yuck! Yuck!

She hated rats. Hated them worse than anything. They were right up there with roaches on her list of things to avoid. She couldn't stand them. What she wouldn't give for her own apartment and a hot shower right now.

Maybe she should've kept to the streets, but then she didn't want to attract attention. Besides, if you were looking for a maggot sometimes you had to wallow in the garbage.

Just so long as the rats kept their distance!

"Hasn't anyone ever told you it's dangerous to walk the alleys at night?" A gruff voice spoke from behind her.

Damn it, she should've been paying attention. Shit, crap, damn!

You're a professional. Get hold of yourself.

She sniffed. Foul body odor, stale cigarettes, and rotgut whiskey. "Hasn't anyone ever told you that you won't die if you take an occasional bath?" She eased her hand upward, patting her gun to make sure it was within easy reach should she need it, then swallowed past the bile that rose in her throat before turning around. The light of the full moon made it easy to make out his features.

There was no doubt in her mind this was her man. Damn, he was built like a diesel truck . . . and looked like he'd been run over by one. What had the bail bondsman done? Airbrushed the fucking picture? The man outweighed her by at least two hundred pounds and had a face not even a mother could love. A big, hulking mass of ugly refuse.

She shrugged. What was a girl to do? She had to make a living.

"Hey." He grinned, showing yellowed teeth. "You're pretty."

She slapped a hand to her chest. "Oh, thank you! I've been waiting all day for someone to give me a compliment. Damn, now I can sleep tonight without worrying."

"You're makin' fun of me," he growled, plodding close enough to clamp a beefy hand on her arm.

"Ya think?" She pointedly looked down. "Remove your hand."

"I'd rather fuck you." A feral gleam shined in his dull eyes.

Like that would happen in his lifetime. "How about I fuck you instead?" she purred.

His brow wrinkled, then her words apparently sank into his feeble brain and he smiled again. "I like that idea even better."

She motioned for him to lean down, and when he did, she drew his head closer, then jerked her knee toward his groin with all she had. He grunted and doubled over, barfing up his supper. She brought her palm up, slamming it into his nose and felt the crunch of bone and ligament. A well-aimed stomach punch took him to his knees.

Breathing hard, she shoved him facedown on the filthy ground. His head thudded hard against the rotting earth. She quickly cuffed him before stepping away and scrubbing her hands on her jeans.

One eyebrow cocked upward. "Okay, you're fucked." No one could say she wasn't obliging.

"Hey, what're you doing to Leonard?"

Damn, who'd have thought Leonard had a friend. But then, maybe he had a bounty on his head, too. Her eyes filled with visions of a tropical paradise away from the smothering heat of Fort Worth in the middle of August.

This morning's rain made it feel like a sauna, rather than dropping the temperature to something she could live with. The second-chance vest didn't help, but better safe than sorry.

Still, she wanted to go somewhere she could actually see the sun instead of a haze of gray smog. A vacation would be wonderful. She hoped Leonard's buddy had a really nice bounty.

She slowly turned, her gaze sweeping over him. Only half his friend's size, and not quite as ugly or as mean looking. She could take him, no problem.

He pulled a gun.

Or maybe not.

Damn, she hated guns. They left really nasty holes, besides hurting like hell when you were shot, and she had a feeling he wouldn't hesitate to shoot if she reached for hers.

Plan B. She thrust her shoulders back and her chest forward, wishing for D cups rather than a small C. She'd have to take that matter up with her mother when she saw her next. If her mother was sober—and she doubted Pearl would be.

She'd have to hope the vest made her look better endowed. Okay, act two.

Cody batted her eyes. "Haven't you ever heard of kinky sex? Leonard and I were just about to have a little fun."

"It doesn't look like he's moving to me."

Leonard groaned.

Plan B wasn't working. "Of course he isn't. He's just waiting for you to leave so we can get it on."

Leonard tried getting to his feet but his bulk was too large to manage more than a belly-rock. He gave new meaning to the words *beached whale*.

"Goddamned bitch, unlock these cuffs," he growled in a nasally voice, kind of like someone with a bad cold—or a busted nose.

Okay, so maybe Leonard's buddy wasn't going to believe her if she told him that was only love talk.

The gunman squared his shoulders and narrowed his eyes. "Unfasten the cuffs."

After all the work she'd had to go through getting them on him? She didn't think so, but on the other hand, she didn't want to get shot, either.

Stall.

She turned, bending down as if she planned to do exactly as he ordered. If ever she needed to keep her wits about her, it was now. A little luck wouldn't be amiss, either.

Reaching into her boot, she slipped her knife out of the case. As she came back up, she threw it. The knife landed with a sickening clunk against the brick wall at the same time the little man jumped to the side.

"You bitch, you tried to kill me."

What little luck she had took a flying leap right out the window as he raised his gun. He wouldn't believe her if she told him that she was aiming to wound, not kill.

Damn, maybe she should've tried for her gun, but the knife was easier to get to, and she rarely missed. Now it was too late.

Nowhere to run. She wasn't supposed to die like this. Not in a dirty alley behind Tex's Bar and Grill. Her life flashed before her eyes. She blocked out the past. Hell, her life hadn't been anything to brag about and she damn sure didn't want to relive it.

What the hell. She didn't have anything to lose. She grabbed for her gun.

A shot rang out.

Too late. She closed her eyes.

Was this what it felt like to die? No pain?

Her forehead wrinkled. If she were dead, why did the jerk with the gun scream?

She opened one eye. Said jerk was sitting on his ass, holding his hand, the gun on the ground. She opened her other eye.

Josh Pierce stepped from the shadows, a wicked 9mm in his hand. Her insides tingled with awareness as her gaze swept over him. As always, he looked pretty damn hot. Thick blond hair brushed his collar, just long enough that she could run her hands through it or use it to tug his head closer to her mouth so she could taste his lips. He had the look of a surfer: tanned and muscled, as if he lived for the next wave to carry him into shore.

"What are you doing here?" she asked, reining in her thoughts, wondering if he noted the tremble in her voice. She could only hope he would think it was her reaction to almost getting shot and not the fact she'd been ogling him.

Damn, what was he doing here anyway? He was the last person she wanted to see her screw up. On the other hand, she guessed him witnessing her blunder and coming to her rescue was better than being dead.

He glanced her way and grinned. "Saving your ass—even though you nabbed my skip. Been after the bastard for three days now." His gaze slowly moved over her, pausing on her derriere. "But it's a very sweet ass if I do say so myself, and I don't mind a bit saving it."

"Funny. You're a regular fuckin' comedian. And I've been looking for him, too. Looks like the agency is mixing up their skips again. Turbo and I were after the same guy last week."

A bitter taste rose inside her mouth. There was no love lost between her and Turbo. Even less since she'd been the first one to nab the skip. Ahh, but seeing the look on his face when he slipped around the corner, gun drawn, and saw she already had the skip in cuffs—that had been priceless.

"Changing offices and getting married always wreaks havoc on a business," Josh continued. "Erik will eventually get his shit together."

Good point.

What he'd said finally sunk in.

He'd only been after Leonard three days? Not a bad turn-around time. Maybe she was getting rusty.

Her attention returned to the situation at hand when Josh strolled over, kicked the gun away, and knelt beside the man who was moaning and holding his hand. He looked him in the eye, but addressed his question to her. "Want your knife back?" He casually picked up the knife and examined the blade.

Apparently, the wounded man didn't like the tone of Josh's voice because he screamed and backed up as far as he could, which was against the alley wall.

"Stay away," the man croaked.

"Tell us your name and I might even call an ambulance." His words held no sympathy.

The man hesitated. Josh tossed the knife, deftly catching it, point aimed menacingly toward the other man.

"It's Ralph Carter."

Cody never forgot a name or a bounty. Her ears perked up. "Ralph Carter, the CPA turned embezzler?"

"I didn't embezzle! They fired me so I just took what was mine."

She raised an eyebrow. "Retirement plan?"

"Yeah," Ralph quickly agreed.

Josh glanced her way. "Bounty?"

She nodded. A little nicer than Leonard's. She'd read about Ralph on the fugitive recovery network about a month ago. The info had said he might be headed back to his home state of Mississippi so she hadn't pursued it.

Her gaze moved between the two skips. She expelled a long, deep breath. "You can have him, I'll take Leonard."

"Deal." Josh grinned, a lopsided smile that sent a flash of heat over her body.

When he looked at her like that, how could she not think about sex? He had the most intense, clear blue eyes she'd ever seen. He had a way of making women feel special.

And that was his problem. He could pick and choose his women. They never lasted more than a month before he moved on to the next.

Even though he'd hinted broadly they'd be good together, she wasn't about to become another notch on his bedpost. His bed probably looked like termites were devouring it from all his slash marks.

Her gaze swept over his broad shoulders, past narrow hips. A sigh escaped. She'd been tempted, though. Hell, she'd have to be made of ice not to have a few fantasies involving him.

And if she didn't want it to go past the drool stage, she'd better get her mind on something else. Like maybe cold, hard steel rather than hot, hard flesh.

The cold, hard steel was a sweet, restored 1964 competition orange Mustang. His car made her thighs tremble every time she saw it. He had the motor tuned until it purred like a cat with a belly full of cream.

Sheesh, sex, cars, and bail jumpers. What was her life coming to?

"You bring the Mustang?" she asked.

"I'm in the clunker," he said, referring to a beat-up, battle-weary Chevy he usually drove when he thought he was getting close to nailing a skip. He'd apparently thought his tip was a good one, and he'd been right . . . but a little too late to nab Leonard.

"You?" he asked.

"My bike. I was going to call a unit to haul him in if I got lucky. The cops owe me one or two favors. Since you're here, mind if my skip rides with your skip?" The situation suddenly struck her as being funny and she chuckled.

He smiled, and something passed between them. The air sizzled and crackled. Their gazes locked. Her laughter died, his smile vanished.

He was doing it again. Looking at her in that way he had. As if he slowly stripped her clothes away from her body, tugged her jeans over her hips, pressed his body against hers.

Her nipples hardened as the ache inside her grew. She leaned toward him, wanting more, needing his touch.

"I thought you were going to call an ambulance for me. I've been shot," Ralph whined.

Sweat beaded Josh's upper lip before he turned back to the skip, pulling a red bandana from his pocket. It was nice to know he wasn't unaffected by her any more than she was him. He tied the bandana around Ralph's hand and knotted it.

"You won't die from a graze. Hell, it's barely bleeding." He slapped a pair of cuffs on him and tugged him to his feet.

"Come on, big guy." She pulled on Leonard's arm. He lumbered to his feet. Man, he stunk. Josh would have to fumigate his rattletrap after he unloaded these two.

"Goddamned bitch," Leonard spat. "I catch you alone I'm gonna make you sorry we ever crossed paths."

She looked over her shoulder at Josh and winked before turning back to her skip. "Leonard, I hate to tell you, but we've already been alone and I kicked your sorry ass. But if you want me to kick it again, go ahead and jump bail and I'll be happy to oblige."

He grumbled something under his breath, but she didn't catch his words.

They walked the short distance to Josh's car and loaded the two men in the backseat before he shut the door. Josh had removed the door handles from the inside, making it almost impossible to escape, and the back was sectioned off from the front with wire mesh.

"So, I'll follow you to the station," she said.

In no hurry to leave, he leaned against the side of the car and crossed his arms in front of him. "You did a good job taking down Leonard."

Inwardly she smiled. Josh was an ex-cop . . . undercover. One of the best. She'd heard he'd gotten tired of all the bullshit and struck out on his own. He was one tough bastard. He didn't take crap from anyone. And he was damn good to have around when you needed him. Like tonight.

"Thanks for saving my ass."

His grin was slow, the kind that started in his eyes and worked down to his mouth, then only lifted one side.

"Like I said, it's a pretty nice ass. I'd have missed seeing it around."

"Well, don't get any ideas because you aren't getting a piece of it." She jutted her chin out, but he caught hold of it, rubbing his thumb across her jawline. She drew in a sharp breath as the heat of his touch caused a friction further down her body.

"So you say."

"So I mean." She forced herself to move away from him and went to her bike, which wasn't that far from his car.

When she straddled her Harley, she wished for a split second she straddled something else.

Thinking like that could get her into serious trouble. Josh was a heartbreaker and her heart couldn't stand another crack in it.

She inserted the key and turned. The bike roared to life. A surge of adrenaline rushed through her as she forced thoughts of Josh to the back of her mind. She liked having this much power nestled between her legs.

The bike was her baby. When the wind whipped through her hair, she felt renewed, as if the air cleansed her of the filth she dealt with each day. There was nothing better than flying down the highway. It was the only time she felt truly free from the harsh reality that was never very far away. She needed that escape to feel whole again . . . or at least as whole as she could ever get.

Chapter 2

Josh glanced in his rearview mirror, looking first at the two skips, then at the beam from the single headlight that followed behind him.

His fingers tightened on the steering wheel. He'd almost lost it when he stepped around the corner and saw Cody taking down Leonard. The skip was at least four times her size. Not that she'd ever seemed to care. Hell, she'd probably take on a grizzly if one ever skipped bail.

Then, before he'd had time to step into the open, Ralph appeared. That had been a close call. He didn't know what he would've done if anything had happened to Cody.

His fingers relaxed their death grip and he grinned. Like anything would. Damn, she was one tough cookie. He'd never seen her back down from anything, and there'd been plenty of times when some jerk tried to get the best of her.

A few months ago, he'd been at the police station handing over a kid he'd brought in. Just a penny-ante thief who didn't think the judge was serious about him showing up for his court date, but while he was talking with the dispatcher, Cody came barreling through the doors, her skip yelling, cursing, and struggling all the way.

Her chest had been heaving from exertion, one eye already swelling, and looking like she'd rolled a few times in the mud.

She'd stuck her foot out, tripping the skip. The guy landed with a hard smack on the tile floor, and apparently realized it was better to stay there. Cody had casually looked up and seen him. She'd cocked an eyebrow and said, "Hey, Josh, how ya doin'? You bring in a skip or reliving old times?"

As casual as that. As if she hadn't just had the crap beat out of her. Yeah, Cody Carlyle was something else. He'd heard she'd been raised in the worst part of town, running wild in the streets. He'd even heard that she'd been with a gang. That she didn't know who her father was, and her mother was dead.

Of course, he'd also heard she ate nails and barbed wire for breakfast every morning. All unsubstantiated rumors, but from the way she acted, he wouldn't doubt that most of them were true, including the nails and barbed wire.

Leaning forward, he grabbed a cinnamon candy out of the ashtray. He'd smoked his last cigarette four years ago, but sometimes he had the urge to light up. The cinnamons usually took away the craving.

The beam from her headlight bounced off his rearview mirror, catching him in the eyes.

He wished he had something that would take away the craving he had for Cody. She was one hot lady on the outside. Long black hair, and a body that was explosive—curves in all the right places.

He sucked in air and shifted the cinnamon to the other side of his mouth. The candy was so hot it burned.

Or maybe the heat came from the mental image of Cody as she'd stepped inside The Blue Eagle last Saturday night. She was a looker, all right. And she didn't just walk. It was as if she'd drifted over to the barstool and slid onto the vinyl seat. Her tight red skirt had hiked up enough to show sexy, lean thighs.

She'd owned the bar that night. No woman came close to looking as good as she had. Cody whet his appetite for more, but as hot as she was on the outside, she was like a chunk of ice on the inside. He'd used all his charm and she still wouldn't have anything to do with him.

If she wasn't careful, she was going to give him an inferiority complex.

He turned his blinker on and pulled next to the curb in front of the police station. Her bike roared in behind him.

One thing he could say about Cody, she had great taste in wheels. He'd heard she'd bought the broken-down Harley and fixed it up herself, doing most of the work.

'Course, that was only rumor, too, but it was enough to give a guy a hard-on thinking about her with a wrench in one hand and a smudge of grease on her cheek.

He climbed out of the car and waited for her to join him.

"This is the part I hate." She grimaced. "Paperwork."

"As surly as you always are, I thought you hated everything."

She frowned. "You think I'm surly? Hell, all this time I'd thought I was being sociable."

He liked her sense of humor, too, almost as much as he enjoyed teasing her. In fact, he liked most everything about her. "Want to go to The Blue Eagle after we deposit these two? I'll buy you a beer."

She hesitated. "I'm already planning on going, but I can take myself, and I can pay for my own drink."

Damn, she was as prickly as a porcupine. "I wasn't asking you to sleep with me, Cody, only if I could buy you a drink."

"And after that? Then you'd want to be my friend. You'd come over to my place and I'd let you in because we'd be friends. I'd be thinking Monopoly while you'd be thinking strip poker. The next thing I'd know we'd end up in bed together."

He leaned close to her. She might look tough wearing her ratty clothes, but she smelled sweet. Kind of like wildflowers in the spring.

Damn, she'd have him writing poetry if he wasn't careful.

"Would it be so bad? I mean, sleeping with me?" From the light of the streetlamp, he saw her pupils dilate. She could deny it all she wanted, but the attraction was there.

She moved back a step and raised her chin. "I don't intend to find out."

With a grin, he moved closer. "You say one thing, but your body is telling me another."

Her eyes narrowed. "Do you think we could just get the skips inside? I'm tired."

"That's what I'm trying to do, but you're blocking the door handle, baby."

"I'm not your baby." Her eyes glittered dangerously.

His gaze slowly roamed over her delicious curves. "You're definitely not a baby."

He enjoyed seeing her irritation as she moved to her right. Probably as much as she enjoyed his disappointment that he wouldn't be crawling into her bed tonight. Surely, she had to know what she did to him.

But then again, she obviously didn't care. Ah, hell, what did it matter? When it came down to it, they'd probably be lousy in bed together. Each one fighting for control.

As he opened the car door, he glanced her way. Now he was lying to himself. Cody would be a handful, but nothing he couldn't handle. He'd like to be the one who tamed her.

"Okay, boys, we're home," he said, motioning for them to get out.

Leonard wiggled and squirmed out first. He glared at Cody. "Bitch, I'm gonna come after you and I'll make you regret—" He stumbled over Josh's outstretched foot and began to fall. He missed the curb, his face slamming into Josh's knee. He went down with a grunt in pain.

"Damn, Leonard, you need to be careful. A shame you busted your nose . . . again." He met Cody's look of skepticism with one of innocence.

"Motherfucker," Leonard began only to have his words cut off by his scream.

"Was that you I stepped on? I'm really sorry." Josh took a firm grip on Leonard's arm and hauled him to his feet. "Maybe it would be better if you kept your mouth shut. You *are* in the presence of a lady."

"Lady," he snorted. "She ain't nothin' but—"

Josh tightened his hold and shoved Leonard's arm into an awkward position. Leonard clamped his lips together.

Cody clasped the other skip's arm as he exited the car. "You know, Josh, you should open a school of etiquette. You'd have everyone saying 'yes sir' and 'no sir' within an hour."

His forehead wrinkled. "Never thought about it, but you might have something."

He liked the way her eyes twinkled. A nice change from the usual hard glare she cast in his direction. "So, you changed your mind yet and decided to let me buy you that beer?"

She walked the skip up the steps toward the glass doors, tossing over her shoulder, "Maybe *you* should go to charm school first because you still haven't charmed your way into my bed."

He watched the gentle sway of her hips with each step she took. She might act tough, but she looked all soft and sexy.

"You think it would help?" he called to her.

"Doubtful," she said, and opened the door.

He chuckled. Spunky, sassy, *and* sexy. Maybe it was time he quit pulling punches and fought a little dirty. He wanted Cody Carlyle in his arms and in his bed. He had a feeling she'd enjoy herself as much as he would. He only had to convince her of that fact.

Cody sipped her beer, her legs stretched out with her boots propped on one of the four chairs circling her table. The bar was dim; only a few low-watt overheads kept the room from total darkness.

It was the middle of the week and not very crowded—two men sat on stools at the bar while three women on the prowl lounged at one of the scarred tables closer to the door. Cody had already seen them turn down the two men as they waited for something better to come along. Apparently, they were picky about who they screwed.

She couldn't fault them for that.

She rested her beer against her lips and tipped the bottle. The Bud Light was already room temperature. Hell, she didn't know why she was still there. A week of little sleep, living on crackers smeared with peanut butter and drinking flat soda had taken its toll on her. She should be at home in bed. Tiredness seeped out of every pore.

When she glanced up the reason she'd hung around strolled through the door looking dangerously attractive. Like her, he'd gotten rid of his vest. The deep green T-shirt molded to each sinewy muscle while his jeans hugged every inch of his sexy thighs. He could put Calvin Klein male models to shame.

He surveyed the room until his gaze landed on her, and stopped. The little half grin that always sent tingles down her spine appeared—as well as the tingles down her spine.

Crap, she should've left. But then, maybe he was worth a little self-torture.

Casually, she watched as he came toward her. The three women zeroed in on him, their antennae going up. She could almost see the drool running down the sides of their mouths.

One of the three stood. Apparently, the leader of the pack. A frizzy-haired blond bimbo with *fuck me* flashing on her forehead. She wore a tight black leather skirt up to her ass cheeks and a knit shirt so low her silicone-enhanced boobs practically spilled out. She went so far as to stand in Josh's path.

Cody had to give Josh credit—he walked around her as if she wasn't even there and didn't seem to notice when she flounced to the bar to order another drink.

He stopped at Cody's table. "You waited."

"Yeah, right, in your dreams," she said with a very unladylike snort. "As soon as I finish this I'm out of here. Sorry to disappoint you."

He pulled a chair out, flipped it around, and straddled it.

He didn't look a bit put out by her rudeness as he rested his chin on the top chair rung and stared at her.

What the hell had she been thinking? Hanging around the bar this long had been a terrible idea.

She'd reached her self-torture limit, and then some. Josh was one of the bad boys. The ones who enjoyed the chase almost as much as they did the victory.

Foreplay. That's all it was to them. She'd seen too many females fall prey to a man in low-slung jeans, boots, and a cowboy hat. Josh had left his hat behind, but he might as well be wearing it the way the three women had given him the once-over.

"Can't we just talk?"

"Your kind never wants to just talk," she countered.

"I won't even touch you." He straightened, opening his hands in supplication. "Talking, that's all we'll do."

"Talking?" She didn't trust him, but then, she didn't trust anyone.

"Yeah, don't you feel it?"

He continued before she could ask what exactly she was supposed to be feeling—other than sexually starved.

"You know, the rush of adrenaline that quickens your pulse when you bring down a skip. It takes me at least a couple of hours to unwind. Help me out. Just talk."

Bad thing was, she knew exactly what he meant. She might look calm on the outside, but on the inside she was wound tighter than an eight-day clock. She doubted talking would help, but he was right. She didn't want to go home to a cold, empty apartment.

She nodded toward him. "You talk, I'll listen."

"Fair enough. What do you want to know? Ask me anything and I'll tell you."

Yeah, right. Let's see how long it would take him to clam up when she got personal. "Why do you date so many women, but never stay with one longer than a month?"

He grinned. "So, you have been paying attention."

"Ass."

"Nah, just horny. Anyway, are you so sure I left them? Maybe they left me, but thanks for thinking it was the other way around."

"It wasn't?"

He shrugged. "Sometimes. Not many women like being left alone at night. You know the routine. How many late nights did you search for Leonard? Two? Three?"

As if she was going to tell Josh she'd been searching for Leonard a solid week after he'd told her he'd only been looking three days. Instead, she countered with another question. "Why'd you quit the force? I heard you were an undercover cop."

He crossed his arms, resting them back on the top chair rung. "I didn't like risking my life for low pay when I could risk my life and make a lot more money."

"So you're in it for the money?"

"Aren't you?"

"You're not allowed to ask, remember, you can only answer questions."

"Sorry. And no, it isn't exactly what you're thinking. I want to open my own P.I. agency and that takes time and money. Papers have to be filed. I'd like to rent an office without bars on the windows."

"A regular entrepreneur."

"An investment in my future is how I think about it."

There was a subtle change in the air. An almost comfortable feeling, and that was the last thing she wanted to feel around Josh. She downed the rest of her beer. "No more questions," she said as she came to her feet. "I'm tired."

He stood. She was five feet, seven inches, and he still towered over her. Someone put a quarter in the jukebox, breaking the sudden silence as an old Garth Brooks song began to play. She made a move to go around him, but he put a hand on her forearm. It was warm, not binding or tight.

"Dance with me."

She studied him for a moment, tempted. "It won't change anything between us. I won't let it."

"I'm just asking you to dance," he said, breaking into her thoughts. "Unless you're afraid you might enjoy it too much."

"Don't flatter yourself." That sideways grin was back on his face. She sighed. "One dance. That's all." Maybe because she wanted to feel his body pressed against hers, if only for this one dance.

He held her hand, leading her to the small floor, as if she might change her mind and go the other way. Maybe he'd read her thoughts because she'd already asked herself why she was letting him get this close. Hell, he only wanted one thing from her. Her stomach knotted when he turned, taking her into his arms. Damn it, she wanted the same thing. She'd fought the urge for months now.

Maybe that's what scared her the most, that tonight she might just give in to temptation, but for the life of her, she couldn't walk away. Not this time.

It's just one dance.

He pulled her close. Not even giving her the chance to keep a little distance between them. Hesitantly, she put one hand on his shoulder and the other on his arm, but he didn't allow her the luxury of even that small amount of a comfort zone. He dragged her hands upward until they were around his neck, then took his own sweet time returning his hands to her waist, grazing the sides of her breasts on the way back down.

Heat flared inside her, almost taking her breath away. Her body pressed intimately against his as they swayed to the music. Just stood there and swayed, not even taking a step. She raised her head, their faces so close they almost touched. His eyes were a deep, dark, passionate blue as they gazed into hers.

"Let me make love to you," he whispered, the warmth of his breath caressing her face.

"It wouldn't be making love, Josh. It would only be sex."

He shook his head. "Not between us. You know as well as I do that it would never be just sex. With us it would be rockets blasting into outer space."

She pulled her emotions close to her and raised an eyebrow. "Rockets? Sex *and* a trip to outer space? Sorry, but I don't believe it could ever be that good."

"But then, you've never been with me, have you?" He lowered his head, his lips brushing across hers.

End it now, her brain screamed, but how could she when he was awakening sensations inside her that had been dormant for too long? She'd been with other men, but none who could satisfy her. They'd left her wanting, needing more.

Just a kiss, just a taste of him. That would be all she'd take.

Her mouth opened and he entered. His tongue was hot and searching until it found what it wanted. He stroked her, then deepened his kiss. Shivers swept over her. Without conscious thought, she pressed closer to him. Her breasts crushed against his chest.

His hands slid lower, cupping her butt, edging her nearer, until she was nestled against his hard length. Her fingers twined in his hair as their bodies continued to sway to the music. She'd been right, his hair was just long enough to pull him nearer.

Thunder rumbled, lightning cracked as the song on the jukebox continued in a crashing crescendo of power unleashed, then softened, slowed, and when Josh's lips left hers, she felt more than a sense of loss.

She drew in a deep, shuddering breath, staring into his face. She untwined her hands from around his neck, but before she stepped away, she lightly touched the side of his face.

"We'd be good together. Can't you see that?" he said.

She shook her head. "We'd have good sex. There's a difference. We'd only end up hurting each other." He opened his mouth, but she hurried on before he could speak. "We wouldn't mean to, but we would."

She turned before he could say another word. A deep, cavernous ache welled inside her. One part of her said she was a fool while the other knew she was doing the only thing she could.

She wasn't good with people—never had been. Why else were all her past relationships so messed up? But she had a feeling Josh was right. They'd have been damn good in bed together.

And that was probably what was at the heart of her problem. Maybe they would be too good. When he said good-bye, and he would say good-bye, how much of her heart would he take with him? She didn't have enough left to spare.

He grabbed her arm before she made it out the door. "I need you," his voice rasped. His fingers caressed her arm.

Josh wasn't playing fair—not at all.

"One night alone with you," he said softly. "Maybe then you won't haunt my dreams."

She drew in a deep, shaky breath. Her whole body ached with need. One night. What would it hurt? Maybe then she could forget about him, as well. She closed her eyes, trying to resist, but treacherous visions filled her mind: the two of them naked, straining toward fulfillment.

Damn, when had she become so weak? "The Harris Motel. I'll meet you there."

"We could go to my place."

"No." Nothing personal. That's the way it had to be. Ah, damn, she was such a fool, but at least she'd be a satisfied one. Unless he was a lousy lay, but maybe then she might be able to forget about him. Either way, she'd win.

She pushed out the door and stepped into the night. It was only moderately cooler than it had been this afternoon. Her legs trembled as she climbed on the Harley. The motor roared to life when she turned the key.

Don't think about what you're doing, she told herself. *Just live for the moment.* Tomorrow morning she would wake satisfied and ready to move forward. No harm, no foul. Then why did she have a strong suspicion that this was not a smart thing to do?

But how long had she dreamed, fantasized, about sex with Josh? Too damn long. It was time to put the fantasy to bed so she could concentrate on her job.

She followed behind him through the dark streets. The traffic was light. She pulled into the motel behind him, waiting while he got a room, then followed him to the parking space. They didn't speak until they were inside.

"Lady, you've been torturing me with that sexy body of yours for months now." He pulled her into his arms and lowered his mouth.

She'd never thought about how a man tasted until Josh had kissed her the first time. Cinnamon and heat. She couldn't get enough of him. Everything she'd held at bay was suddenly unleashed. She tugged at his T-shirt, he tugged at hers. Their arms tangled. The tension melted away. Their eyes met and they laughed.

"It's your own fault for making me wait so damn long." He grinned and her world turned upside down.

"Well, I'm not making you wait now." She pulled her shirt over her head, tossing it to the side, then unhooked her bra and let it fall to the floor.

He just stood there, staring. "Damn, you're so fucking sexy." He reached out, cupped her breast, his thumb brushing across her already hard nipple.

Lord, it felt so nice when he touched her. Liquid heat pooled low in her belly. She tugged on the hem of his shirt, drawing close so she could pull it over his head. Her breasts brushed across the hairs on his chest, stealing her breath. Josh took his shirt the rest of the way off, but instead of removing all of her clothes, he wrapped his arms around her.

He ran his tongue lightly over her lips. "You taste sweet . . . and hot, like a woman ready for sex."

His words sent tingles of pleasure over her. She gasped when his teeth scraped her earlobe, taking it in his mouth and gently sucking before letting it go.

"I want you so damn bad I'm about to burst." His tongue delved inside her ear.

Oh, God, he started an ache deep inside her. She pressed her body closer, rubbing against his jeans-clad thigh. But rather than relieve her frustration, he lightly bit her ear and moved away. It took her a moment to regain her equilibrium.

So, that was his line of attack, tease her until she begged for mercy. Two could play that game, and she was more than ready.

"Think you can hold out longer than me?" she purred.

He grinned. "Yeah, I do. I'm pretty damn good at the art of seduction."

"We'll have to see if you like to paint by numbers, or if you're another Rembrandt," she said, running her hands over his nipples. They immediately tightened into hard little nubs. Leaning forward, she flicked her tongue over each, scraping across them with her teeth. He sucked in a deep breath. She smiled, letting her hands drift over his six-pack abdomen. Any woman would fall off the wagon for a chance to caress his abs.

When she slipped her hand inside his waistband, he groaned. "Still think you can last longer," she asked, tugging the top button undone and slowly sliding the zipper down. She brushed her knuckles against him, and he jerked forward.

Josh was definitely ready—his hard length was proof without him having to say a word.

"I just thought you fought dirty—you play dirty, too," he said.

"Does that bother you?" Her words were husky, wanting him free of his clothes. She'd denied herself far too long. She wanted him naked—now.

"Bother me?" He shook his head, his gaze capturing hers. "Not a bit. In fact, I kind of like it."

"Oh, I can get real dirty." She shoved his pants downward, then pulled at the elastic of his briefs. Her gaze lowered. "Nice," she breathed before pushing them down, exposing all of him to her view.

"Enjoying what you see?"

She shook her head and grinned. "I like closeups much better." She knelt in front of him, her hands gliding over his hard erection, her thumb tracing the tip. He rocked his hips toward her, his eyes closed. "Do you like that?" she innocently asked.

"Umm, yeah."

"Then you'll like this even more." She started at the base of his erection, finding the quarter-size area on the underside, lightly massaging while gliding her tongue over him. "Ah, nice," she murmured, closing her eyes as she took him into her mouth.

"Sweet Jesus," he gasped, grasping her head.

She freed him, circling his penis with her tongue. "You taste good," she said before sucking him back in her mouth. Salty . . . musky . . .

He groaned.

She slid her hand between his legs, letting his balls rest in her hand, gently massaging. She was so lost in her own enjoyment that it took her a few seconds to realize he'd placed his hands beneath her arms and was pulling her up.

"So soon?" she taunted. "I was almost certain you'd be able to last much longer."

"I'm not ready to stop the games, sweetheart. I'm just getting started. Turnabout is fair play."

"But I don't play fair, remember?" she said.

One side of his mouth lifted. "Yeah, but neither do I." He jerked the top button of her jeans out of the buttonhole and slid the zipper downward.

It didn't take him long to get her out of her pants. She stood before him in only a red thong.

"Lie down on the bed," he ordered.

She cocked an eyebrow. "Excuse me?"

He walked behind her, his hands cupping her butt. She could see him in the mirror above the dresser. His hands moved over her hips, then came back up to cover her breasts, tweaking her nipples.

"I want you to lie down so I can suck on your breasts."

His hands glided over her rib cage, over her flat stomach, down her thighs, close to the vee of her legs, but he didn't touch her. The mirror captured her gaze as she watched through half-closed lids. He caressed her body, slipping his fingers beneath the elastic of her thong. Oh so near the heart of her desire, then trailing away. He left her wanting . . . aching for more.

"I want you to lie on the bed so I can slowly strip these sexy little panties off you. Then I'm going to spread your lips and look at you for just a moment before I taste you. I want to lick you, draw you into my mouth."

Her knees went weak, but she didn't have to worry about falling. He scooped her into his arms and carried her to the bed. Then he lay beside her, his hands massaging her breasts before he leaned over her and captured one taut nipple, drawing it into his mouth, flicking it with his tongue.

She arched toward him, gasping with pleasure as sensations swirled downward. Closing her eyes, she bit her bottom lip and lost herself in his touch.

"You taste good," he said, moving so he could give equal attention to her other breast. "Do you like what I'm doing?"

"Yes," she groaned.

"Do you want me to move lower or stay right here?"

"Not fair," she groaned.

His chuckle filtered through the haze that had enveloped her. "Didn't I mention that I don't play fair? So what do you want?"

She arched her hips. "Lower," she cried. "Go lower."

He licked her abdomen, his tongue swirling around her

belly button before dipping inside. Her body was like a wire strung tight, and any minute she would snap.

"Please, Josh, please." She pushed his head downward.

"Spread your legs for me."

She obeyed without hesitation. The ache inside her was growing stronger with each passing second.

His breath fanned her sex before he kissed her through the red silk panties, his tongue scraping over the material already damp with her juices.

"You smell sweet," he said. "But I want to see all of you. I want to taste all of you." He moved to his knees and pulled her panties down her legs.

Her breath was coming in ragged puffs. She couldn't think; all she could do was let the pulsing sensations wash over her in waves. The need to have him take her in his mouth was growing stronger. Her body was on fire. One touch from his tongue and she'd incinerate.

And then his mouth covered her. He sucked, drawing her inside his mouth, then released her clit only to begin licking, thrusting his tongue at her sex.

"Come for me, baby."

She cried out, holding his head and straining to get closer. The first waves of her orgasm rocked her whole body. She barely knew when Josh quickly pulled on a condom and entered her.

Before her orgasm ended, he began thrusting inside her. The tension started to build once again. She grasped his shoulders, wrapping her legs around his waist, drawing him in deeper.

"Look at me. I want to watch you when you come."

She opened her eyes, their gazes locked. She met him thrust for thrust. His body tightened, but he didn't slow until she felt the spasms grip her body in wave after wave of heat. Only then did his body shudder with his own release.

His gaze continued to hold hers until he rolled to his side, taking her with him. She buried her face against his chest as they tried to catch their breath. She listened to the pounding of his heart until it finally began to slow to a more normal rate.

She'd known this wasn't smart, but still she'd given in to temptation. Damn it, how could she have known it would be like this? So fucking intense.

"Don't think about it," he whispered close to her ear.

But how could she not?

Chapter 3

Cody unlocked the door to her apartment and stepped inside. After locking the door behind her, she slid the deadbolt into place and dropped her keys in the dish on the small table.

A shiver washed over her, making her wonder how low she'd set the thermostat. She checked. Seventy-four. Not that cool. Maybe it was the apartment itself. Or that her body wasn't curled up next to Josh right now. She'd refused to spend the night, and instead pulled on her clothes and left the motel.

Having sex with Josh had been a mistake. She ran a hand through her hair. Tonight should've taken away her desire for him, not made it worse.

Had he thought her cold when she'd refused to stay the night? Why should she care? He was a player. And she wasn't cold—just cautious.

Her gaze slowly skimmed the open layout of her apartment as if seeing it for the very first time—and she didn't really like what she saw. Stark white, except for the wall that looked like a post office with wanted posters plastered all over it.

Cold.

Maybe it wasn't that bad. Her black leather sofa and chrome lamps sitting on black end tables were . . . sleek, with clean lines. Yeah, right. The place could've come right off a showroom floor. No rugs, no family pictures, no clutter. Nothing that would say this was a home. It looked very institutional.

Great, now Josh had her questioning how she lived.

Rather than go to The Blue Eagle, then the motel, she should've gone to the gym and worked off her frustration. Moji had given her a key to his gym about a year ago.

Moji. She shook her head. She only thought her life was screwed up. What kind of name was Moji for a short, middle-aged, gay white man, anyway? A smile lifted the corners of her mouth. If nothing else, Moji was flamboyantly entertaining, and she liked him. He was probably the closest thing she had to a friend.

She gave her apartment another sweeping glance. Did she really care what Josh thought? Hell no. They'd had—she swallowed past the lump in her throat—sex. Nothing else. It was over now. There was no big mystery anymore. Maybe that was her problem. There *was* no mystery. She knew exactly what she could expect if they had sex again.

Liquid heat swirled in the pit of her stomach. She drew in a ragged breath.

No, she wouldn't give tonight another second of her attention. Resolutely, she grabbed the black marker off the entry table, and strolled to her wall of wanted posters, drawing a big X through Leonard's picture. Job finished. On to the next one, tomorrow. And she would forget about everything else that happened. Even if it killed her.

She sat in the nearest chair and struggled with her boots for a few minutes. Finally, she got one off and dropped it to the floor. The other followed. Grabbing the remote, she turned the television on to the news channel. Anything to unwind.

They were showing a car bombing. Death and destruction, that's all she ever saw anymore.

She started to turn it off when they switched to another story. They showed a man walking into the courthouse. She didn't have to turn the sound up to know who he was— Adam Sinclair.

A damn shame. The man had had it all. He'd gone from the slums to the big time, but greed got the best of him and he was about to go to trial for the murder of his partner. Why the hell would he throw it all away?

She flipped the television off and stood, padding across the room in her socks.

And Josh was wrong. Her apartment suited her just fine. No fuss, no worry.

She yanked her T-shirt over her head, letting it drop to the floor.

All her life, Pearl had had cheap, dollar-store knickknacks all over their tiny apartment. Her mother crammed them into every available spot, in every corner, until there wasn't any room left.

Cody stopped long enough to yank her jeans and socks off and continued on her way to the bathroom wearing only her panties and bra.

Her mother was . . . odd. She refused to move from her apartment. It was home. Besides, she was still waiting for Cody's father to return. She'd never said as much, but Cody knew that was the reason.

She snorted. As if that was going to happen after twenty-seven years. Besides, if Pearl was so anxious for Cody's father to come home, why had she let men move in over the years? *Ain't love grand?* She doubted the real reason would ever surface. Speculation, that's all it was.

Cody walked inside the bathroom and turned the water on, tested the temperature until she had it at just the right degree of warmth, then went to the kitchen.

Hell, technically it wasn't even her mother's apartment anymore. Cody paid the rent, and if she stopped, it would force her mother's hand. The landlord was a bastard. He'd kick her mother out and then Pearl would have to move to a better place.

Maybe move in with her. Wouldn't that be a damn shame? Having to live in a decent neighborhood with her one and only child.

With her hand on the refrigerator handle, Cody paused, then jerked the door open. Pearl would probably get a cardboard box and take up residence in one of the alleys before she'd move away from the area where she now lived.

Cody knew that for a fact. How many times had she asked her mother to move in with her? Too damn many times to count. She'd finally stopped asking.

It hurt to know her own mother would probably rather sleep in the streets than move in with her daughter. Goddamn it. That hurt more than she wanted to admit.

Hell, maybe her mother was smarter than she gave her credit for. They'd kill each other after a week of living together.

She grabbed a soda and twisted the cap off, flinging it toward the trash but missing. She squeezed the plastic bottle so hard soda fizzed over the top.

"Son-of-a-bitch." She set her drink down and grabbed the dishcloth, wiping up her mess. "It doesn't matter what you do with your life. I don't fucking care. I don't fucking care about anyone." As she straightened, she tossed the cloth into the sink and made her way back to the bathroom.

By the time she stripped out of the rest of her clothes and sank down into the tub of warm water, she'd reined in her emotions. She was tired. It had been a long-ass week. Hell, her whole body trembled from exhaustion. No wonder she was dredging up painful memories.

But it had been so worth the long hours and total exhaustion to bring Leonard down.

The steam from the water swirled around her. She'd done it. Leonard was behind bars and tomorrow she'd pick up a nice little check. Small, but nice. Every penny counted. Her bank account was growing. Another year and she'd be set.

Her eyes drifted closed. Pearl said she'd never leave Fort Worth unless it was to a house on the beach. Florida, no less. Okay, if that was what it would take to get her mother away from her tiny apartment, so be it. She had no idea why she should even care, but she did. Okay, so maybe it sounded like a good idea to her, too.

She could see herself sunning on a pristine beach, listening to the sounds of waves gently rolling into shore. No problems, no worries.

A new start.

She could get used to the slow pace. Maybe open a little store that sold shells or something. Her mother would like that. She'd be surrounded by all the knickknacks she could stand.

She'd never been to the ocean. Only a few hours away, but every time she'd start to leave something would come up. Maybe she was more like her mother than she thought— afraid to leave her own backyard.

Yeah right, she wasn't afraid of nothing or nobody. If she wanted to, she'd pack her bags and be out the door tomorrow.

She leaned her head against the back of the tub and closed her eyes. Damn, she was tired.

So tired she'd let Josh kiss her, and that had led to the motel. Damned stupid. She'd played with fire—and he'd made her burn.

He was better than all her fantasies. He was the only man she'd ever met who could make her toes curl.

She stretched her foot out and bumped on the hot water. Steam rose around her as she inched her shoulders under the water.

For just a moment, she lost herself in the memories. His hands gliding over her body, his mouth following right behind his caressing fingers. She sighed with regret.

She'd never been good with relationships and Josh would be no different. Falling in love with him would be too damned easy and she didn't want another broken heart.

She sighed and bumped the hot water off. No, better to keep her distance from now on and not risk getting hurt.

* * *

Josh sat in his car, staring straight ahead at the motel, but he couldn't stop the memories from flooding his mind of another motel. Damn, he had to quit thinking about Cody. Having sex with her was supposed to get her out of his mind.

It hadn't.

Okay, he had to concentrate. He glanced at his reflection in the rearview mirror and tugged his cap a little lower down on his forehead. The pin-striped coveralls were a good idea. His own mother would think he looked like a maintenance man.

After he climbed out of his Chevy, he grabbed his tools from the trunk and slammed the lid. Now all he had to do was convince the skip to open the door.

The manager had said Roberta Smith was registered in room 208. He'd only caught a glimpse of her once, but he was almost positive her last name wasn't Smith.

He'd been following leads for a few days now, and they all landed right here at the Number Nine Motel, a one-story dump with all the rooms opening to the parking area.

The manager was a short, balding guy who didn't ask many questions if you had the cash to pay for a room—or for a little information. Why should he care? Most of the occupants were lowlifes: prostitutes, druggies, skips. Hell, the motel was a smorgasbord of waste.

Roberta Weston was one of them. A known drug addict and prostitute caught selling too close to a grade school. This time she'd do a longer stint in prison. She was on the run.

He strode to her room and knocked on her door. "Maintenance," he called out.

"Yeah, yeah, just a minute." She was pulling on a thin robe when she opened the door. "You'd better fix that goddamned air conditioner or I'll—" She glanced at him, her eyes widening. "Shit! If you're a maintenance man then I'm a fuckin' nun."

She tried to slam the door in his face but he caught it with his boot and shoved it open. The door banged against the wall. She made a run toward the bed, grabbing her purse, but he was right behind her. He tackled her. The air left her body in a whoosh. He tossed the purse over the side and out of her reach.

"You son-of-a-bitch!"

Baring her claws, she aimed toward his face. He grabbed her wrist before she could scratch him, but at the same time she brought her knee up. He twisted away.

"Will you be still before you hurt yourself?" he panted. Or him. Damn, she was like a starving wildcat that had been let out of her cage and he was a juicy piece of prime rib.

She snarled and jerked her knee up again. He moved just in time and she only caught the inside of his thigh. Too close for comfort. He threw his leg over her bottom half and pinned her arms to the bed.

That's when he heard a chuckle behind him. Great, he had an audience. He only hoped it wasn't one of Roberta's friends. He glanced over his shoulder and groaned. Well, damn.

"You have a thing about rolling around on motel beds this week, don't you?" Cody sauntered into the room.

"Instead of making smart-ass remarks, I could use a hand here."

"Now you're wanting applause, too?" She shook her head. "I didn't know you had an ego problem." Laughter spilled out of her.

This was all he needed. The woman straining against his hold seemed to have an endless supply of energy. He still had to figure out how he was going to reach the cuffs in his back pocket and get them on her. He had a feeling even cuffed this one wouldn't be close to subdued.

He really disliked picking up female skips. Women didn't fight clean and this one didn't look like she was going to be the exception.

"If you're not going to help, then get the hell out." He

damn sure didn't need her smart-ass remarks. Roberta wiggled a hand loose. He grabbed her wrist before she scraped her nails down the side of his face.

"I'll make a deal," Cody told him, casually crossing her arms in front of her and leaning her hip against the dresser. "Fifty percent."

"You bitch, I'm not letting you take me in, either."

"She's a damn contortionist." He couldn't hold her. She might as well have been smeared in butter for all the good he was doing. He certainly wasn't having much luck.

As if to prove him right, she slithered out from under him and onto the floor.

"Okay, fifty percent," he panted.

Roberta grabbed her purse as Cody stepped forward. She reared her fist back at the same time Roberta brought out a gun, but that was as far as the skip got. Cody's aim was sure, her fist landing on the woman's jaw with a loud crack.

Roberta stumbled back a step, dropped her purse and the gun, stared at Cody as if in a daze, then her ass slapped the yellowed linoleum floor with a resounding smack.

Josh cringed. "What'd you hit her for? Hell, I could've done that." He frowned as he grabbed the gun Roberta had dropped.

Cody rubbed her fingers across her knuckles. "But you didn't. Another minute and she'd have blown your head off."

"I don't make a habit of hitting women." He reached in his back pocket and pulled his cuffs out.

"Sometimes you have to use a little force."

"I have a feeling hitting her didn't bother you as much as it did me."

She grinned. "You'd be right."

God, he really liked the way she smiled. The whole room seemed to light up. It seemed like forever since he'd seen her. Had it only been a week? He had a feeling she'd been avoiding him, but it didn't matter, she was here now.

He slapped the cuffs on Roberta, who was starting to come around a little more.

"What are you doing here, anyway?" His glance swept over her. "And dressed like a . . . maid? I know business has been slow, but it's not so bad you have to moonlight, is it?"

Her mouth turned down. "Funny. I could say the same for you." Her gaze scraped over him. "Maintenance man? Sorry, but you don't fit the picture of someone who'd work in this dump."

"Damn." He caught a glimpse of his reflection in the dresser mirror. "I thought I did a pretty good job, especially with the coveralls." He looked in the mirror again. Yeah, maybe she was right. He shouldn't have shaved this morning. Scruffed up a little more.

They each took an arm and began to drag Roberta to his Chevy.

"So, what are you doing here?" he asked, changing the subject.

"You nabbed my skip." She stepped sideways so he could go through the doorway first.

"You've been watching Roberta?" How could they have missed each other?

They dumped Roberta into the backseat of his car and closed the door.

"Apparently Erik is still on his honeymoon. We were after the same skip again."

"Figures." He took a deep breath and leaned against the car. "Maybe we should go in as partners. We make a pretty good team. I save your . . ." His glance slid lower. She did have one sweet ass. He cleared his throat and returned his gaze to her face. "I save your hide and you save mine."

She shook her head. "I work alone, but I'll follow you to the station," Cody told him.

"Don't you trust me to give you half?"

She smiled sweetly, but it didn't even come close to reaching her sexy green eyes.

"I don't trust anyone. I thought you knew that."

"Then let me buy you lunch just so I can prove how trustworthy I am." He leaned toward her, inhaling the soft fragrance of her sweet perfume. The memory of what they'd shared filled him with thoughts of holding her close, tasting her lips, feeling her body pressed against his, sinking into her body.

Maybe he could talk her into having lunch at his place, but when he asked, she shook her head, dashing all his plans.

"I'm already having lunch with someone."

As she walked to her bike, he followed. Strange how the thought of her having lunch with someone else made his gut clench. Hell, he'd never seen her with another man. Turbo Manning had been sniffing around her skirts, but he didn't seem her type. The bounty hunter made some of the skips he dragged in look clean. He had no ethics whatsoever. A real jerk.

If not him, then who?

"So, meet you at the station?" Cody asked.

"Yeah, okay." He started back toward his car, but at the last minute turned around. He had to know. "Who are you having lunch with?"

She looked at him, seemed momentarily taken aback by his question, then a slow smile lifted the corners of her mouth. "Jealous?"

"Maybe."

Her eyes widened, as if she hadn't expected that answer. "My mother. I'm having lunch with her."

"She's not dead then."

"Not unless there's something she hasn't told me."

He frowned. Smart-ass. "I'll meet you at the station."

So maybe he had no business interfering in Cody's life. Damn, she probably thought he was hung up on her or something. Sure, he wanted her in his bed again, but that was all.

He certainly didn't want to get tangled up in her life. He didn't do tangles.

But he hadn't nearly gotten his fill of her.

He slid beneath the wheel and turned the ignition key, glancing in his rearview mirror, he met Roberta's glare.

"Don't take it personally, Roberta. I'm just doing my job." He grinned.

Her eyes narrowed. "You may be a good bounty hunter, but I know women and you ain't got a chance with that one." She rubbed her jaw. "I've heard about Cody Carlyle. You'd do better rubbing against a block of ice than you would her." She leaned forward. "Now, if it's a good lay you're wanting maybe we could ditch the motorcycle bitch and do a little trading."

He wouldn't tell her that Cody wasn't nearly as cold on the inside as Roberta thought. "Didn't you know . . . everyone has their melting point, Roberta?"

And he intended to make Cody melt at least one more time. It would be interesting to see what it would take to get her into his bed again. And to see just how fast he could raise her temperature.

Chapter 4

Cody shifted her weight to her other foot, bit her bottom lip, then determinedly knocked on her mother's apartment door. Long seconds passed.

Had Pearl drunk so much that she'd passed out? It wouldn't be the first time.

The door opened.

Cody quickly ran her gaze over Pearl. She looked fine—even sober. Her short, light brown hair was brushed and her clothes clean. Why did her smile always look forced, though?

And she was actually wearing the pants and top Cody had bought her for her birthday. Until now, she'd wondered if her mother had even taken the price tags off.

"Cody, how nice of you to drop by. Why didn't you call and I could've made us a nice lunch." She opened the door wider. "Well, no matter, come inside. I think I have some leftover roast. I can make us a sandwich."

"I'm not hungry." Her gaze darted around the room as she stepped inside. Everything looked the same . . . but something was different. Before she could figure out what it was, her mother began talking again.

"You look like you haven't had a decent meal in weeks. I swear you've lost weight every time I see you."

Great, she'd picked a day when Pearl's motherly instincts

were kicking in. It would be fine, except these times were rare.

"I can't stay but a minute. I wanted to make sure you didn't need anything. Groceries . . ." She shrugged.

"I'm fine. The last time you were here you brought enough to fill my freezer." She looked away, then squared her shoulders and met Cody's gaze head-on. "Stay a while. I have lemonade in the fridge."

"Lemonade?" Jeez, she sounded like a regular Suzy Homemaker.

Pearl frowned. "Yeah, just plain lemonade. No alcohol. Just lemons, sugar, and water."

There was a hard edge in her voice. This was more like the Pearl she knew.

Her mother quickly turned and walked toward the kitchen. "Stay if you want. Makes no matter to me."

She squeezed her eyes closed. Damn, why was it like this every time? They were always walking on eggshells around each other . . . and they were always cracking beneath their feet.

She drew in a deep breath. "It's okay, Pearl. I can stay a while, and lemonade sounds good. It's so fucking hot outside it'll steal your breath away."

"Watch your language. I'm still your mother."

But sometimes you make it easy to forget.

"Sorry." She went into the tiny kitchen and got two glasses out of the cabinet while her mother brought the lemonade to the table.

"It's okay. I know I wasn't the best mother to be teaching you. Hell, Rodney taught you more than I ever did." She went back for the roast and mayo.

Cody's hand stilled for a moment before she set the glasses and two saucers on the table. She didn't meet her mother's eyes. "Do you ever think about him? Rodney, I mean."

Her mother sat at the table and began spreading mayo on

the bread. "Sometimes," she said, a wistful expression on her face. "He was a good man. The war did a number on his head, but most of the time he was good." She looked at her daughter. "I guess he was partial to you. He had a daughter of his own, you know, but his wife ran off with her and he never saw his kid again. Same as your father did to us. Maybe that's what drew you two together more than anything. Two lost souls."

"Then he left. Just like Daddy." A vice tightened around her chest, making it difficult to breathe. She sliced harder than necessary into the roast.

"Rodney drifted out of our lives just like he drifted in. One day he was there, the next day he wasn't. I know you've always thought I had something to do with his leaving but I didn't. Everyone makes their own choices." She handed a plate to Cody.

"I never thought that. I knew it was his decision. It would've been nice, though, if he'd stayed." And it wouldn't have hurt nearly as much.

"Maybe so. The only fault I had with him is teaching you how to fight. A girl shouldn't know that kind of stuff. That's why you haven't hooked up with a man. They all know you can beat the hell out of them."

Cody laughed. "You think that's the reason?"

Pearl smiled, and for the first time in a long time, Cody felt a connection with the woman who'd given her life.

"Maybe that's not a bad thing," Pearl continued. "Sometimes men aren't worth killing."

"Like Dad?"

"Not worth killing, not worth talking about, either." Her lips clamped together.

She sighed. It was the same, always the same when she brought up the subject of her father. She could deny it all she wanted but there was a burning need in her to discover more about him. The only information she had was that he'd walked out of the house when she was a baby, and never returned. What if he'd been in an accident? What if he'd tried to get home, but something happened?

What if? What if?

"I can see those wheels turning." Pearl bit into her sandwich and slowly chewed.

This was the first time her mother had acknowledged that Cody might want to know more. She took a drink of her lemonade. It was tart, cool, and refreshing.

"Can you blame me?" she finally asked her mother, not willing to let it drop this time. "He was my father and I don't even know what he looked like."

She set her glass back on the table, running her fingers over the condensation that was forming.

Pearl hesitated, and Cody figured that she wouldn't find out any more today than she had any other day, but then Pearl surprised her by continuing.

"Oh, you see him, you just don't know it."

Cody frowned.

"Every time you look in the mirror he's staring back at you. You have his green eyes. I used to tell him he had the eyes of a leopard. When he looked at me, I couldn't look away. It was like his eyes captured mine, hypnotizing me, and they wouldn't let me go."

Cody held her breath, cold chills running up and down her arms. This was the most Pearl had ever said.

"And black hair . . . just like yours. Coal black, but with a dark blue shine to it." Pearl's hands fluttered toward her hair. "I used to love running my fingers through it . . ." She gulped down half her lemonade before setting her glass back on the table. "Enough. Sometimes the past is best forgotten."

The softness had left her voice, replaced by a hard edge. This was the mother Cody knew and that was the end of their conversation about her father. From experience, she knew Pearl wouldn't say more. If she pushed too hard, it would drive her mother straight to the bottle.

But she knew more now. Excitement quickened her pulse.

She knew her father had eyes the same color as hers, and dark hair. Someday she might even know why he'd left and never returned.

Maybe someday.

"You being careful?" Pearl asked, breaking the silence. "I mean at work and all."

"I'm always careful."

"Yeah, I saw how you're always careful when you came by with that black eye that time."

"Occupational hazard. Good with the bad."

"I don't like you going after scum. You'll get yourself killed if you're not careful."

"I'm always careful. But don't worry, I have a nice life insurance policy. If anything ever happens to me, you'll be taken care of." As soon as the words were out, she wanted to call them back.

Pearl stiffened.

"I'm sorry. I didn't mean it. I don't know why I even said that." She reached across the table for her mother's hand, but Pearl pulled it away.

"I'm grateful you're taking care of me like you are. Lord knows, you don't have to. I remember all the times I passed out drunk and you had to take care of yourself. Never did bring any friends home because you were ashamed of me . . ."

"It wasn't like that," Cody interrupted.

"Yes, it was. You don't have to sugarcoat the truth. I drank too damn much. I wasn't there when you needed me." When Pearl looked up, her eyes were swimming with tears.

Damn! Cody wanted to kick herself. Why had she done it? They were finally making a little progress and she'd gone and blown it. Guilt washed over her in waves as she stared at her mother.

Suddenly, it was as if a veil lifted from her eyes. When had Pearl begun to look so old? So tired? A tremble of fear weakened her knees.

For just a second she wanted to walk around the table and

draw her mother into her arms, hold her close, and tell her the past didn't matter. They could build on the future, but the words stuck in her throat.

She bit her bottom lip. She'd never hugged her mother, nor did she remember her mother hugging her. Abruptly, she came to her feet. "I need to be going." She paused when she was even with her mother and squeezed Pearl's shoulder, then hurried out of the room.

Once outside the apartment she leaned against the wall, her legs suddenly shaky, as if any second they might stop holding her up. Damn it, why couldn't she just say to hell with it and hug her mother? Other people hugged their mothers. But she knew the answer—she didn't know how.

From the other side of the door, she heard crying. Cody pushed away from the wall and hurried toward the staircase that would lead outside, into the fresh air and warm sunshine.

She slipped on her shades when the sun's glare blasted her as she pushed through the doors.

Were all families as fucked up as hers? God, she hoped not.

Damn, she needed to unwind. Maybe she'd drop by The Blue Eagle this evening, see what was going on there. Now she was lying to herself. She'd been avoiding the bar, avoiding running into Josh. She missed him. So badly it caused a deep ache inside her.

He'll hurt you.

No, she told the voice inside her head. *I'll be careful. I won't let him.*

The light over the pool table shone brightly on the green felt as Josh calculated what he would have to do to sink the eight ball. He blocked the noise from the crowded bar as he studied every angle.

When he glanced up, his opponent grinned.

Focus.

His gaze returned to the table as he slowly walked to the other side and leaned down, eyeballing the distance and angle between the two balls.

Shooting pool was second nature to him. Something he took for granted, like breathing. He'd been shooting pool since he could look over the table.

This shot would be difficult, but not impossible. He'd made harder ones.

"You can't sink it," Randy told him. "Why not just hand over the money now? Twenty green ones. Come to daddy." He brought his fingers to his mouth and kissed the tips. "The big man is going down."

Without answering, Josh straightened, chalking up his cue. Once again, he leaned over, took aim, and slammed the tip against the white ball. It crashed into the eight ball, spiraling it toward the corner pocket. He exhaled when it dropped inside with a sweet thud. The cue ball gently kissed the corner and stopped. He grinned as he looked up. "Not today, buddy. You owe me twenty."

"Son-of-a-bitch. You have more luck than any one man deserves." Randy pulled a twenty from his wallet and tossed it on the table. "That's all for me."

"Ah, come on, guys." Josh tugged his black Stetson back to a comfortable position on his head. He frowned at the other three men who'd been watching, but were now nodding their heads in agreement with Randy. "The night is still young."

"You already have all our money," one of the men said. "Hell, we don't even have enough cash to buy a beer. See what you've reduced us to." He downed his head, shaking it forlornly.

"Like you didn't take my money last week." He looked toward the bartender. "Joe, a round of beers for the guys. Put it on my tab."

"You got it."

"Now that's a true friend." Randy put his stick on the rack and they left, heading toward the bar.

"Yeah, yeah," Josh grumbled. "What are friends for?"

Josh leaned on his pool stick. Now what was he going to do for the rest of the night? He spent every evening at The Blue Eagle hoping Cody would show. Each night he'd left, a little more disappointed than the night before. He couldn't face going back to his empty apartment. Not right now.

"Does anyone want to shoot a game?" Laughter followed his words, but when it died down a deep, sultry voice floated toward him from a dark corner.

"I'll shoot a game with you. Heaven forbid you have to play with yourself."

A shadow moved, slowly coming toward him. He sucked in a breath as Cody stepped into the light. He'd known she wouldn't stay away forever.

His gaze drifted over her. The woman sure knew how to wear her jeans. She gave him a hard-on just looking at her.

And look he did.

She wore a white shirt that buttoned down the front and low-riding, body-hugging jeans. Only thing was the shirt and jeans didn't meet. About two inches of delectable skin showed, that and her sexy little belly button. It didn't help that he remembered the last time he'd seen it. The way he'd swirled his tongue around it before dipping inside. Ah, damn, this wasn't good.

"You going to stand there all day or are you going to rack 'em?" She sauntered to the corner and picked up a stick.

Josh couldn't have moved if he'd wanted. He could only stare as she slowly caressed the stick, sliding her hand up then down the polished wood, licking her lips.

His mouth went dry.

She put the stick back and reached for another. He groaned as she slid her hand over that one, her thumb brushing the tip.

He quivered.

She faced him once again, eyebrows raised. "You haven't racked the balls."

He mentally shook his head, and leaned his stick against the table before reaching down and pulling the wooden triangle out of the slot. "You've pretty much racked my balls already," he mumbled as he slapped the triangle on the table and gathered the balls. When they were set, he carefully removed the frame and put it back in the slot. "You want to break?"

He wondered what she was thinking as a slow, sexy grin lifted the corners of her mouth. No, maybe he didn't want to know what she was thinking.

"Sure," she said. "I'll bust your balls."

"Funny."

"I thought so," she said.

When she came around to the end of the table, he took her hand. It was soft and warm. He liked touching her. She stirred something deep inside of him that no woman had ever made him feel. It was probably just a super-sized case of pure lust, but she made him forget they were in a bar. Or what the hell they'd been talking about.

"Are we going to play or what?"

He really liked the way she said *or what*. Josh had a strong feeling she wasn't thinking what he was thinking, though, but maybe the night wasn't going to be a total loss.

"We haven't wagered yet." He met her eyes. Those sexy, penetrating green eyes that made it so damn hard to look away. How'd she do it?

"Wager? Aren't we playing for fun?"

He leaned closer. She smelled nice, a light, tropical scent. Coconut and something else he wasn't quite sure of, but it brought forth images of Cody lying on a beach towel with the sand and surf all around her, not a stitch of clothes on, sweat glistening on her skin.

He drew in a deep, ragged breath. "I never shoot pool for fun."

She tugged her hand free and dug into her front pocket. Her pants crept down an inch. He held his breath. Cody pulled a few bills from her pocket and her pants rode back up.

Then he breathed.

"All I have is a couple of bucks."

"Not enough," he said with a shake of his head.

"Okay, so what do you want to wager?" Her voice took on a silky quality as her lids half lowered, concealing her thoughts.

"Another night with you."

For just a moment, he thought she might agree, but he saw the subtle change, almost as if she'd closed herself off from him.

"I don't wager for sex."

"A kiss then." Before she could say anything, he continued. "Just one kiss."

She squared her shoulders and jutted out her chin. "And what will I win?"

"That *is* what you'll win, darlin'. I haven't figured out what you'll owe me when you lose, but I bet I can come up with something."

His grin was slow as his gaze swept over her. He'd been right about her—she'd been a handful, but damned if he didn't want her more than ever. He hadn't even begun to get her out of his system. Just once more, he wanted to touch her naked body, cup her breasts in the palms of his hands, testing the weight. He wanted to taste her . . . every delicious inch.

"Okay, let me get this straight. If I win, I get a kiss from you. And if you win, you get something else. Why do I have the feeling you wouldn't care if I win or lose?" Sarcasm dripped from her words.

"Oh, I can guarantee you'll enjoy the kiss as much as I will. You can't tell me you didn't like the last one or what followed."

"Do you really think I haven't had better?" She nudged him out of the way and bent over.

"No."

"You might be wrong," she said.

"I don't think so."

His gaze landed on her nicely rounded backside. He itched to reach out and caress it.

She propped the stick on her thumb, reared back, and hit the cue ball. Balls scattered. Two stripes fell into pockets. She straightened and smiled. "It looks like I have the bigger balls."

He leaned against the wall and grinned. "So it would seem, but do you know what to do with them?"

"Oh, yeah, I know exactly what to do." She moved to the other side of the table.

When she leaned over to size up her next shot, her top gaped open. Sweat beaded his brow. She wore a flimsy little piece of lace under her shirt. He was so damned jealous of her bra. It cupped and held two perfectly formed breasts while all he could do was salivate and fantasize about what it'd been like to squeeze and fondle them.

"Your turn." She straightened.

"What?"

A knowing grin curved her lips. Son-of-a-bitch, she knew exactly what she was doing to him. How many times had he heard that Cody Carlyle fought dirty? Too many. He pushed away from the wall.

"We still haven't agreed on our wager." He shot and missed.

She grinned, leaned down, and made the next shot. "Okay. So let's wager. If I win, you pick up my beer tab at the end of the night."

"Fair enough. If I win, I'll take the kiss."

"But you're not going to win," she said as she sailed past, moving to the end of the table.

That's what you think. Cody was good, but there was one thing she apparently didn't realize. He fought dirty, too.

She leaned over, lining up her next shot, pulling the stick back.

"I love the way you bend over the pool table," he said. "The way your bottom wiggles when you line up your ball. You've got the sweetest ass I've ever seen on a female."

She shoved the stick forward, missing the cue ball entirely. Her eyes blazed when she whirled around. "That wasn't fair."

"Yeah, I know." He tipped his hat further on his forehead and leaned in for his shot. He made it. Cody nibbled her bottom lip. He made the next shot and missed the next. He had five balls on the table to her four, but he wasn't worried.

She glared at him before leaning in for her next shot.

"I told you that we'd be good in bed. I bet we would be again." A grin tugged at his mouth, but he stopped it from forming. He'd beat her in the battle of wits.

She managed to hit the cue ball. It whisked by her ball without touching it.

He eyed the table, looking for the best shot. A piece of cake. She'd left him a gimme shot.

He caught a glimpse of her from the corner of his eye as she casually picked up the chalk. He blinked twice, trying to clear his mind and concentrate, but his gaze strayed to her hand and what she was doing with the chalk. There was something sensuous in the way she massaged it against the tip, sliding her other hand up and down the hard shaft of the pool stick.

A soft little groan escaped from between those sexy lips of hers. The kind of noise she'd made when they were making love. He remembered her lying on the bed, her legs slowly parting.

Blinking rapidly, he willed his mind to clear.

Focus!

He missed his shot.

Her grin was wicked.

Okay, so maybe beating Cody wasn't going to be quite as easy as he thought.

"I'm tuning you out," she warned as she stared at what he'd left her. "No matter what you say, it will not affect me."

Yeah, right. What was she pulling now? Reverse psychology? It wouldn't work. He moved in for the kill as she leaned over.

"I want to make love to you again, but then, you know that."

She made the shot.

Damn, he'd used the voice that no woman had ever been able to resist. It didn't seem to faze her at all as she straightened, moved around the other side of the table, and made another shot. The nine and fourteen were left on the table.

His eyes narrowed as she lined up her next shot. He stretched his neck to the right, then the left. He couldn't let her win.

He drew in a deep breath. "When I go to bed, I think about you." He moved to stand directly in front of the shot she was about to take.

"And what do you think about?" Boredom laced her words.

Her game wouldn't work on him. Cody thought she had him—by the balls. Not so.

"I think about how I tasted every inch of your body." His words were lazy, sensuous. A sheen of moisture glistened on her forehead. He ambled to the other side of the table, leaning closer to her, keeping his voice low. "Last night, I dreamed of sucking on your breasts, then moving lower, parting your legs and covering you with my mouth, running my tongue up and down you. God, it's all I can think about sometimes. What you tasted like the other night. How hot I could make you again."

She rammed her stick against the cue ball. The cue ball bounced off each side of the table and flew toward the opposite end. It came to a stop in the middle of the table without hitting a ball.

"You missed," he casually told her as he picked up the

chalk and passed it over the tip of his cue. "What a shame."
He shook his head in feigned sympathy.

"So I did," she snapped. "But it doesn't change the fact I
only have two balls on the table and you have five. I'll still
beat you."

"You think so?"

"Yeah, I do." Palms on the edge of the table, she leaned
forward. "And I'm feeling awfully thirsty so I hope you
brought lots of money."

"Cocky, aren't you."

"It goes with having the bigger balls."

"So let's increase the wager."

She hesitated.

"Unless you're afraid I'll win."

"I told you I don't wager for sex."

"I remember."

She straightened her spine. "Make it easy on yourself."

"Have supper with me. If I win, I'll get Joe to throw a couple of steaks on the grill."

"And if I win?"

"I'll have Joe put one steak on the grill for you, and I'll call
it a night."

"You're on."

Josh felt just a twinge of guilt. Okay, maybe not exactly
guilt. That was probably what he should be feeling, though.
He'd been champion pool shooter three years in a row back
in his hometown of Two Creeks, Texas. It would've been
four but his best friend, Wade Tanner, had grabbed the title
one year.

A moment of nostalgia washed over him. Maybe he'd call
his friend and see how he was doing since he'd become the
proud papa of twin daughters. The last he'd heard, Fallon
was keeping him on his toes.

Briefly, he wondered what it would be like for a woman to
love him that deeply. A moment of panic washed over him.

Nope, he wasn't even going down that path. His life was just fine like it was.

"You going to shoot, or stand there staring at the table all day?"

"I'm going to shoot." His gaze held hers until she looked away. Damn, but she was one sexy lady. It might be worth . . . No, it wouldn't be worth it.

He leaned over and dropped the next two balls. One in the side pocket and the other in the corner.

"Bet you'd never expected me to be such a wildcat in bed," she said in a voice dripping with lust.

He gritted his teeth and put the seven ball in the corner.

"But if there ever is a next time I'll . . . uh . . . massage your body in warm oil and . . . uh . . . "

The table blurred.

Focus.

She was reaching now, anything to make him forget his game. And it was damn near working.

His brow beaded with sweat.

This would be a tough shot. He'd have to bank it off the side, put enough English on it so the cue ball only caught the side of the five. A once in a lifetime shot. He could do it. All he had to do was tune out the images Cody was putting in his head. Lord, they were really sweet images.

He drew in a deep breath and made the shot. "Yes!"

She frowned. "You still have one ball and the eight ball. I wouldn't start celebrating just yet."

"Didn't I tell you, baby, I don't like losing."

"Didn't I tell you, I'm not your *baby?*"

He easily made the next shot, noting the worried frown on Cody's face. He should feel at least a little remorse. He didn't. He wanted that kiss from her. And he wanted supper with her. If he had to play a little dirty, then he didn't mind. Not in the least.

She leaned over, her shirt gaping.

Don't look!

His body tightened until he thought he might snap in two, but he didn't look up again.

He called his shot. "Eight ball in the side pocket." The cue ball nudged the eight ball. Almost in slow motion, the eight ball rolled toward the side pocket, bumped the corner, teetered for a full second, then fell with a clunk. He straightened and grinned. "What kind of steak do you want?"

She turned on her heel, striding to the rack. He flinched when she slam-dunked her stick back into the rack, then faced him with a brittle smile on her face. "Rib eye, well done."

"Don't tell me you're going to be a sore loser?"

"I'm never a sore loser." Her lips were clamped together. "And how long have you been shooting pool?"

"Eight . . . nine, maybe."

"You've been shooting pool nine years? No wonder you beat me."

He tugged his hat down on his forehead. "Actually, since I was about eight or nine *years old*." He tried not to laugh.

"Stop laughing. It isn't funny."

"I'm not."

"I can see it in your eyes. You're laughing your ass off."

He leaned toward her. "You're cute when you lose."

"Yeah, well, let's get it over with. You won your kiss." She closed her eyes, puckered her lips, and raised her mouth.

For a long moment, he could only stare at her. His gaze went straight to the throbbing vein in her slender, pale neck. All he could think about was how much he'd like to slip his hand behind that same neck and pull her close.

Damn, she was tempting. Just lower his mouth and her lips would be his. He could stroke her velvety tongue, taste her, have her body pressed against his. Not a night had gone by that he hadn't dreamed of kissing her again.

When she opened her eyes, they were filled with confusion. "You won a kiss fair and square. Don't you want to collect on the wager?"

"Yeah, I'm going to collect, but not right now. When I do,

it won't be in a noisy, crowded bar. I want to take my time. Enjoy the moment."

"Has anyone ever told you that you can be a real pain in the ass?"

"As a matter of fact, I believe *you* have on more than one occasion."

"Well, I wasn't lying." She swept past him and strode toward the bar.

He leaned against the pool table, watching the sway of her hips in those tight blue jeans. When he finally straightened, *his* jeans were a whole lot tighter. Hell, his jeans had grown tighter the minute she'd stood and sauntered toward him.

So, what did he have to do to get her into bed again? He'd better charm her pretty damn fast. Wanting her was killing him. One time was not enough to get her out of his system.

A few beers would loosen her up, then a nice steak.

How would she be able to resist him?

Chapter 5

What the hell had she been thinking of when she'd challenged Josh to a game of pool? That was the problem, she hadn't been thinking. She'd walked into the bar tonight hoping to see Josh. And she had. Her plan was to sit in a corner and salivate. She'd look her fill, then go home. He wouldn't have to know she'd even been there, except she hadn't been satisfied.

"Is your steak okay?" Josh asked.

"Yes." Cody cut into her meat and took a bite. She didn't want to talk. Not only had she seen him, but he'd cheated and won the round of pool. He'd only had to say that he'd been born with a cue stick in his hand and she wouldn't have made the bet with him.

And he hadn't kissed her. Why? To torture her? All she'd been able to think about was the way his mouth had felt against hers, the feel of his tongue stroking hers.

But he hadn't kissed her.

Torture—that was his goal. Well, she damn sure wouldn't play his game.

Yeah, right.

This was definitely torture.

"That's three. We're on a roll now." He took a long pull from his beer.

What the hell was he talking about? She placed her fork

on her plate, planted her elbows on the table, and stared at him. The man had lost his mind.

And it didn't look like he was going to explain. Curiosity got the better of her. "Three what?"

He smiled as if he'd beat her at something again. She'd never realized what a competitive streak he had.

"Three words. Yes made the third word you've spoken since we sat down."

"You're drunk."

"Not in the least. I've had two beers, same as you—over two hours. I don't even have a good buzz."

"Well then, stop looking at me like that."

"Like what?"

He leaned forward and stared into her face. Very slowly, one corner of his mouth raised. There it was again. That damned sexy smile. An ache started from deep down inside her and spread to her outer edges. She felt as if she were being wrapped in a chenille throw.

This was why she'd dropped by The Blue Eagle. Without any effort, Josh drew her like a moth to a flame, but the burns he caused only made her want to test the heat again and again.

For a few seconds, she languished in the warmth, then forced herself to look away. She didn't want to get drawn into his hypnotic gaze.

Grabbing her napkin, she wiped her mouth. "Your charm won't work on me this time so you might as well give up," she lied. She only hoped he didn't guess he had more of an effect on her than he knew.

Josh was like a narcotic: mesmerizing, hypnotizing. Just one look, just one touch, and she needed her fix, but she was afraid the next high would be one she couldn't come down from. She'd settled for just being in his company, knowing it was only a substitute for what she really wanted.

It was time she left and stopped torturing herself. Tossing her napkin back on the table, she stood. "Thanks for supper, but I'm calling it a night."

"Without dessert?" He motioned for one of the waitresses.
"I'm full."

"But when we made the wager we did agree to supper.
What's a meal without dessert?"

"Okay, fine." She plopped back into her chair.

As if on cue, the waitress set down a bowl of hot apple
cobbler with vanilla ice cream slowly melting on top.

Her stomach rumbled as if she hadn't just eaten what
seemed like half a slab of beef. She loved sweets. Hell, she
loved to eat, period. One of her weaknesses and apparently
her downfall tonight. Especially when she knew Joe's wife
had probably cooked the cobbler fresh today.

She glared at Josh. "This is so cheating, Josh Pierce."

He grinned. "Yeah, I know."

Some of her anxiety dissolved. Damn, did he have to look
at her like that?

She took a bite of her dessert to take her mind off him. Her
taste buds exploded. Heaven. Pure, unadulterated heaven. She
closed her eyes, savoring the burst of flavor. Josh was momentarily forgotten. "It's so . . . damn . . . good."

When she opened her eyes, he looked a little . . . odd, and
he hadn't touched his dessert.

"You okay?"

He picked up his spoon and shoveled in a large portion of
his dessert. "Great, just great," he grumbled, speaking around
a mouthful of food.

Josh Pierce was different than other men. She wasn't quite
sure how to take him. She cast a look in his direction.

And he was devilishly sexy. He was the only man who
could look at her in a way that made her body itch from the
inside out.

Okay, enough of that kind of thinking—and eating. She
was practically busting out of her skin now. She stood. "My
hands are sticky." Without any more explanation than that,
she headed toward the ladies' room.

Maybe she'd pour cold water over her head while she was

in there. She sighed as she weaved her way between the tables. It was definitely time for her to go home.

"Hey, sweet thing, you're about the prettiest thing I've seen since I got to town."

Damn, not tonight. She just wanted to go to the ladies' room, do her business, and go home. One glance at the man who'd spoken and she was afraid that wasn't going to happen. He could've been a cousin to Leonard. Big, ugly, and . . . big.

She kept her mouth shut and made her way around him, but he had other ideas and pulled her into his lap. Lord, he smelled like a brewery.

"Now, is that any way to be sociable, little lady?"

"Mister, I'd advise you to take your arm from around my waist."

The man was apparently hard of hearing because he squeezed instead. She really hated fighting right after a big meal.

She rammed her elbow into his stomach. A whoosh of stale beer air exploded from his mouth. Oh, lord, she was going to be sick and it was Josh's fault for insisting she have dessert on top of everything else.

His hold did loosen, though, and she took the opportunity to come to her feet.

"Now that"—he wheezed—"wasn't very nice, little lady."

He grabbed her by the wrist as he stood. She clasped his in return, surprising him, but before the stupid grin on his face could fully form, she swung her knee toward his crotch.

The hold on his wrist gave her just the right amount of momentum. She reared her fist back, but before she could take the swing, Josh beat her to the punch—literally. The big man let out a loud woof, and like a tree slowly toppling over, he went to the floor.

"I can fight my own battles." She frowned.

"Yeah, but—"

"Eyeeeeeee!"

They turned toward the high-pitched scream at the same

time the flame-haired, screeching banshee flew toward them. "You killed my Harold."

Before either had time to do anything, she grabbed a beer bottle and crashed it over Josh's head.

Cody slammed her fist into the woman's jaw. Red stumbled backwards, tripped over a chair, and splattered onto the floor.

Josh groaned, holding his head. "What happened?"

She whirled around, bracing Josh before he fell and aiming him toward one of the chairs. He sat down hard.

"She clobbered you with a beer bottle. Why the hell did you jump into the middle of my fight, anyway?" She examined his head, but couldn't see much in the dim light. She ran her fingertips lightly over his head. A goose egg was already forming.

"Stupid me thought you might appreciate an extra hand. Ow, ow, be careful. That hurts."

"Quit being a wuss, I'm just looking." She frowned. It was a really big bump.

"Sorry about this," Joe said as he hurried over. "I should've tossed the both of them out an hour ago. I had a feeling they were trash." He looked at Josh. "She thumped you a good one. Might want to have a doctor look at your head."

"I'm okay now—I think."

"Joe's right." She didn't like the fact that his face was pasty white.

"I just need to get home and lie down a bit and I'll be fine." When he stood, he swayed just enough that he had to grab the back of the chair to keep his balance.

Josh couldn't drive in his condition. She'd have to take him. Unless one of his buddies . . .

She looked hopefully toward the bar. Not a soul there. She hadn't even noticed when they'd left. Great. Why was she the designated baby-sitter? She'd sworn a long time ago she wouldn't be responsible for another person. Why the hell did she have to be the one left holding the bag?

On the other hand, she *could* walk away. It wasn't as if he was her responsibility. Hell, she wasn't married to the man. She didn't owe him anything. She bit her bottom lip. Technically, he *had* come to her rescue—even if she hadn't needed rescuing.

Her gaze swept over him. Even beat up, he looked pretty damn hot. He'd be easy to take advantage of and he might not remember—No, no, no! It wasn't even safe for her to think like that.

Lord, give me the strength and the will not to do something I'll later regret.

She drew in a deep breath. "Joe, I'm leaving my bike here. You still have that extra set of keys?"

He nodded. "I'll put her in the garage. Need any help getting him to his car?"

"I can manage." She tugged on Josh's arm, helping him to stand. Then with one arm around his waist, she aimed him toward the door. With every step she told herself he needed to keep his balance and that's why it was necessary he put his arm across her shoulders, but did it have to feel so good?

She even liked when he drew her closer. His body heat was nice. She could get used to this.

Better nip it in the bud. Feelings like this were superficial. There wasn't one thing real about them.

But damn, she'd enjoyed getting down and dirty—really dirty—with him the other night. His hands squeezing her breasts, his teeth tugging on her nipples, their bodies hot and sweaty as they fondled and caressed each other.

She drew in a shaky breath, but it didn't remove the burning ache that had begun to build in her lower regions.

Ah, hell, she'd known she'd regret having sex with Josh. A relationship with him wouldn't last. Josh was Josh. A player. All the women loved him and he loved all the women. She was afraid she wouldn't be the exception. She'd fall just as hard as all the others because he *had* been the best lay she'd ever had.

He stumbled as they stepped outside and she caught a firmer hold around his waist. Her whole damn body tingled with awareness as his body pressed intimately against hers, and he smelled so damn good—spicy. What was it about Josh that made her want to throw caution to the winds and have hot sex with him for the rest of the night?

Maybe that was the attraction. Women just knew—they sensed Josh Pierce was sinful. Women were naturally drawn to the forbidden fruit. He was a temptation they didn't even try to resist.

He'll hurt you, a voice inside her head chided. More than her father, more than her mother, more than Rodney, more than any man she'd ever dated.

He drew in a deep breath. "You smell nice," he said, breaking into her thoughts. "Like the beach."

Thank you, Josh. She'd needed something or someone to pull her thoughts back to the present.

Okay, she thought he smelled like an irresistible sin and he thought she smelled like the beach. Not good. Or maybe he meant the sand and surf? She could live with that. She'd always thought it would smell somewhat refreshing.

"I wouldn't know," she said.

Josh was just flirting. *Don't listen to his line of crap.*

He probably had more sweet words than she could ever imagine. She wouldn't let him break through her barriers. Besides, he was loopy. Red had really brought that bottle down hard on his head. He probably wouldn't remember a damn thing come morning.

"I've never been to the coast," she finished. Anything to take her mind off walking him to the parking lot or the way he felt against her. Talking travel seemed safe enough.

"Nah, really? You're shittin' me. Everyone has been to Galveston or Corpus." His words were slightly slurred.

"Not me. I've never made it down that far."

"Would you like to go?" He squeezed her arm.

His touch was nice, but he probably did it so he wouldn't fall down.

"We could go tonight. Just take off."

Josh was so full of it, but she couldn't stop her smile from forming. No wonder he could pick and choose the women. The ache inside her grew. Ah, temptation.

He stumbled on the uneven sidewalk and leaned heavily against her for support. She drew in a deep breath. Accident or on purpose, she wondered. No, she'd give him the benefit of the doubt. This was the best bar and grill in Fort Worth, but it wasn't in the nicest part of town so the sidewalk and streets weren't in great shape.

Maybe for a moment, though, she could pretend his touch meant something. Tomorrow would be time enough to face reality.

Lost in her own thoughts, it took her a moment for the enormity of her situation to sink in as her gaze landed on the parking lot. Then it hit her in the face like a bucket of cold water that had been thrown on her. Her mouth went dry, her legs trembled, her pulse quickened.

He'd driven the Mustang.

She almost let go of Josh and hurried to the car, but at the last moment stopped herself. It didn't keep her insides from trembling, though. God, the Mustang was so sweet.

Competition orange was waxed to a high sheen, and in the glow from the streetlight, it stood out from the rest of the vehicles. A bright topaz amidst colored glass. Her gaze skimmed over the car. Not a dent, not a scratch marred her magnificence.

"I know that she-witch popped me pretty hard, but are we moving forward or standing still?" Josh asked.

"You drove the Mustang," she stated in a breathy whisper.

"Yeah?"

"You can't drive it in your condition." Hell, she'd kill him before she'd let that happen.

"I thought you were going to drive me?"

"But it's . . . the Mustang."

"Don't you know how to drive a standard?"

Her brows drew together. "Of course I know how to drive a standard."

"I don't see the problem then."

But he might in the morning. Man, Red had knocked him a good one. As far as she knew, no one drove the Mustang except Josh.

She grinned. He shouldn't have beaten her at pool. Sweet, sweet revenge.

As they made their way toward the car, he stumbled again. At the last minute, she remembered to catch him to her so he wouldn't fall. When they finally made it to his car, she ran her hands over his butt before leaning him against the back door.

He had a nice, firm ass. Her hands lingered a little longer than necessary.

"I knew you couldn't resist my body."

"Don't get your hopes up." Her pulse had to be at least a hundred and twenty beats per minute. Outwardly, she was calm. At least she hoped so. But then, he was loopy so what did it matter?

"I wasn't feeling you up, only making sure your pockets didn't have any metal on them. I'd hate for you to wake up tomorrow and find a scratch on her."

"Did you?"

"Did I what?"

"Feel any metal."

"No."

"Maybe you should check again."

Her heart caught in her throat. "I don't think so. Give me your keys."

He reached into his pocket. "Damn, my head is really

pounding." He grabbed his head. She caught him to her so he didn't fall over. One of her legs slipped between his, her body pressed intimately against his, her thigh against his crotch. The heat from his body begged her to explore, to touch, to taste, to fulfill her every desire.

She quickly put a few inches between them. This was just great. The man could be dying and all she could do was lust after his body.

"Maybe you should let me get the keys," she told him. She'd retrieve the keys, get him inside the car, and stop thinking about sex. Yeah, like she could really make herself stop thinking about sex with Josh.

"Good idea. You get the keys."

She straightened him a bit more before reaching into his front pocket. For a moment, she was sorely tempted to move her fingers a little further over. Her thighs quivered. Her nipples tightened.

Damn it, she had to stop before she threw him down on the ground and had her way with him. Just deliver him to his home and get the hell out of there.

"I don't feel them." She raised her head; their noses were only inches apart. The heat of his warm breath tickled, and for a second she could've sworn he looked as lucid as the next person. So how much of his condition was fake, and how much was real?

She couldn't be sure.

"Like I said, they're not there." She pulled her hand from his pocket.

"Other one."

"Why didn't you tell me that in the first place?"

"Felt good."

"Not funny. If you're faking this I swear you'll regret it for the rest of your life." She watched him for some sign that he was making more out of his injury than was there.

"Ow," he moaned, closing his eyes.

It was hard to tell. Damn it, he did have a good-sized lump

on his head, but if he was pulling her leg, she'd put another knot on his head that would make the first one seem small in comparison!

She jerked the keys out of his other pocket and unlocked the car before helping him slide into the passenger side. Once she had him in the seat, his head resting on the back, eyes closed, only then did she take a deep, cleansing breath.

After shutting his door, she went to the driver's side and climbed into the seat.

She forgot Josh as the car caressed her senses.

The black leather cupped her bottom. Ahhh . . . nice. The seat fit her butt perfectly. She'd have thought it was made especially for her. This was good . . . so good. She closed her eyes for a moment and inhaled the scent of leather.

Nothing else could compare. She'd always wondered if she might be a little . . . strange. The scent of leather or a man with a little grease on him turned her on quicker than all the fancy colognes or vested suits. As the scent curled around her, she knew this was no exception.

Butterflies fluttered inside her belly. *Start the car,* she told herself. Ask Josh where he lived and get the hell out of there. Her gaze fell on the steering wheel. Too late.

Just one touch, one sweet stroke, then she'd concentrate on driving.

She ran her hands over the hard steering wheel, feeling each ridge, each bump. Deep breath, she told herself. Calm down. How could she? This was the *Mustang.*

She opened her eyes, taking everything in. The visors, the dash . . . the gearshift. Her legs trembled as her hand closed over the round knob, pushing the smooth surface against her palm. She bit her bottom lip to keep from moaning.

Josh coughed, or maybe it was a gurgle, but it drew her attention away from the car and back to him. Damn, he'd been watching her. His mouth had dropped open and he looked a shade paler, somewhat sickly.

"If you're going to toss your cookies tell me and I'll help

you out of the car." God forbid he puke in here. It would be sacrilegious.

His mouth snapped shut. "No, I'm fine." He leaned his head against the back of the seat and closed his eyes once more. "I've just never seen a woman have an orgasm feeling up a car before. It turned me on."

Heat spread to her face. "I didn't have an orgasm. I just appreciate the fact that you have a very . . . nice car."

She frowned as she inserted the key and turned the ignition. The car roared to life, practically vibrating the seat beneath her. Her panties grew damp. She closed her eyes and let the sensations wash over her.

"What . . ." She cleared her throat. "What do you have under the hood?" The engine had to be at least a three-fifty.

"A four-sixty," he murmured without opening his eyes.

Oh God, a four-sixty? She clamped her legs together.

Soft snoring came from the other seat. He was asleep. She ran her hands over the steering wheel, across the dash. Damn, this was so sweet.

Stop thinking about the car. She should be concerned about his injury, not his blasted car and what he had under the hood. Wow, a four-sixty. Too cool.

And he shouldn't be sleeping.

"Josh, where do you live?"

He opened his mouth, then closed it.

"Your address?"

He frowned. "I'm thinking." He shook his head, then grimaced.

"Maybe we should go to the hospital after all?"

"I have an aversion to hospitals. I've always come out of them feeling worse than when I went in. Home is fine. As soon as I remember where I live."

She could drive around the city until he remembered. Ripples of excitement ran up and down her arms.

As tired as she was, maybe that wasn't a good idea. She

could take him to her apartment. Her gaze trailed over him. The same feelings she'd just had for the car washed over her as she stared at his magnificent body.

Nope, not on her life, wasn't going to happen, no way, no how. But memories plagued her. Sensuous, hot memories.

She drew in a deep breath. She'd promised herself only one night with Josh, and she'd had it. End of story. She'd drive him home and say good-bye.

His driver's license would be in his wallet, but it would take him forever to get it out of his back pocket. She slipped her hand behind him. He really did have a great ass. Damn, she was practically on top of him.

He opened his eyes. "I knew you couldn't resist me." He kissed her lips.

Short and sweet, but so damn hot she felt it all the way to her toes. And he hadn't even used tongue.

"I was trying to get your wallet so I'd know where you live. It's kind of hard to drive you home if I don't have an address."

"Around you, baby, it's always hard." A wicked gleam entered his eyes.

Her own narrowed. "Har har. And I'm not your baby, and I didn't give you permission to kiss me."

"Sorry. I couldn't help it, though. You taste good." He closed his eyes.

Shaking her head, she slipped his wallet out and opened it. Lots of greenbacks. He shouldn't carry so much cash. He'd be too easy to roll.

He had pictures.

She looked at him. It would be wrong to snoop, but he'd closed his eyes again. She couldn't resist. Professional hazard.

The first picture was of a dark-haired man. Nice. Sexy. The next was of a dark-haired woman. She frowned. A dark, mysterious woman. Kind of bitchy looking, in her opinion. A lover?

She flipped to the next picture and breathed easier when she saw it was a picture of the dark-haired woman with the dark-haired man. The woman had her arms around the man and she looked very pregnant. Anyone could see they were in love with each other. Okay, maybe not as bitchy as she'd first thought. Not that it would've mattered to her one way or another.

Josh shifted.

She quickly moved to the other side of his wallet and found his driver's license. He didn't even take a bad DL picture. Her gaze moved to the address. Terrific. All that trouble for a post office box. It was doubtful she could stuff him into a mail slot, no matter how tempting the thought.

"This is a post office box number. Why don't you have a regular address like normal people?"

He yawned. "It's a commercial license. Not required if you register your address. Safe that way in case a skip gets hold of your wallet."

"I knew that," she mumbled. She had been going to get a commercial license but hadn't gotten around to it. It didn't help her current dilemma. She studied Josh. He'd saved her butt when Leonard's friend had pulled his gun. Then tonight he'd attempted to help her.

Damn.

Last resort—her apartment. She really didn't want to wake up in the morning with him underfoot. For the first time in her life, she wished she had a lock on her bedroom door. One that would keep her in. Josh Pierce was too damn much of a distraction.

Nothing would happen. Not in his condition. She'd leave the apartment early the next morning while he slept. Maybe prop a note somewhere he could find it.

She might not have sex with him again, but at least she'd get to drive his Mustang. She crammed his wallet in her back pocket, not about to return it to his, and she didn't feel comfortable leaving it in the car. He could have it back in the morning.

She clutched and shifted into reverse, backing out of the space. She hadn't even gotten out of the parking lot and her insides were quivering. The Mustang was almost as good as her Harley.

She shifted into first, and felt the roar of the engine beneath her before backing off the gas. She wondered what the car would do on an open stretch of highway. She was tempted to find out.

Maybe someday, she sighed, but for now she had to get home and get Josh bedded down. No, she didn't want to think about Josh and bed in the same thought.

But a mental image flashed across her mind just the same. Josh naked and sprawled across her cotton sheets, her head resting on his chest, listening to the sound of his heartbeat, feeling the texture of his skin beneath her hands, inhaling his scent, her mouth trailing kisses over his naked body.

This was such a bad, bad idea.

She drew in a shaky breath and concentrated on getting home.

The drive to her apartment didn't take long. It would've been nice to drive his car a little more. This was probably the last time she'd even get to ride in it.

She pulled into the parking garage attached to her apartment building and whipped into the space closest to the entry that would take them to the elevator. With a sigh of regret, she turned the ignition off. One last caress, one last look, and she stepped outside. Going to the passenger side, she opened the door.

"We're here." She nudged his shoulder. Great, he'd fallen asleep. She knelt down and nudged again.

He turned toward the open passenger door and groggily opened his eyes. A smile lifted the corner of his mouth when he stared into her face. "I knew I'd get you in my bed."

"Not quite, but you did get me into your car. Nice car, by the way."

He sat up and looked around. "Where are we?"

"The parking garage of my apartment building."

"Planning to have your way with me, huh? Good thing I woke up."

"In your dreams." She stifled a laugh. He made it difficult to remain serious around him.

Maybe all wasn't lost now that he was somewhat awake and sort of alert. "I don't suppose you remember your address?"

"Of course I do." He frowned at her as if she'd just asked the dumbest question he'd ever heard.

Hope rose inside her chest. "Where?" Maybe she could get him home after all.

"Post office box three-one-five."

She might have pursued the issue except he'd gotten his post office box numbers backwards. She had no desire to drive around Fort Worth for the rest of the night. It would be just her luck if he led her to the home of his last skip. Wouldn't that cause a stir if they ran into the skip's pissed-off friends?

She tugged on his arm while he slid around in the seat, feet landing on the concrete garage floor.

"You smell so damn good," he said. "Have I ever told you that?"

"Once or twice." She tugged him to his feet, then braced him against the car until he had his balance.

"You've always been in my dreams . . . in my fantasies . . . my every waking moment. Don't you want to put me out of my misery?"

She chuckled. "Sorry, I left my gun in my nightstand, but I can get it out when we get upstairs."

"You wound me." He clutched his heart and began to slide sideways.

She grabbed him, and he pulled her close, staring down into her face. Her heart caught in her throat.

"You have pretty eyes. It's hard to look away. And you have sexy lips, too." His head began to lower.

Automatically, she raised hers. Damn it, she jerked away. "And you probably tell that to every woman you want to go to bed with." No wonder he went through women like water through a sieve.

"Just you, darlin'. Just you."

The spell was broken.

"You're so full of it." She put his arm around her shoulders and began walking him toward the glass door. "Just try not to step on my toes."

Thankfully, she didn't run into any of her neighbors before she got Josh inside her apartment. They already looked at her as if she were from another planet.

One reason might be that she was coming and going at all hours, and maybe because she'd been dressed in every imaginable and outlandish disguise, from a maid to a derelict. They never asked about her job and she'd never had the inclination to tell anyone she was a bounty hunter. Hell, most of the tenants were so old they didn't care as long as she minded her own business. That suited her just fine.

She unlocked her door and they went inside. Kicking the door shut with her foot and leaving the entryway light on, she aimed Josh toward the sofa, except they stumbled along the way and landed in a heap on the sofa, him on top of her.

"Sorry about that. Everything is still a little fuzzy."

He moved off, but his hand stayed on her bare waist, pulling her closer. God, how could he make her feel this good with just a touch?

"Have I mentioned how great you smell?"

She would've laughed, except his hand felt incredibly sensual against her bare skin and his lips against her neck were causing a reaction much further down on her body.

Drawing in a deep breath, she wiggled away from him and off the sofa. A little distance between them made all the difference.

"Your couch is hard," he grumbled. "I promise not to touch you if you let me sleep in your bed."

She did laugh then. It bubbled right out of her—more so when she saw the disgruntled look on his face.

"Can I at least have a pillow?"

"A pillow and a blanket, but that's all you'll be getting from me. Remember, you're injured." She went to the hall closet and took down a blanket and pillow, tossing them to him when she returned.

He pulled the pillow close to him and closed his eyes. Before he could get too comfortable, she brought an icepack for his head. She hoped the movies were accurate about ice to stop the swelling. There was one other thing she vaguely remembered.

"I don't think you're supposed to go to sleep. Not with a head injury."

"Then talk to me or I will." He frowned, staring at her wall. "And why the hell do you have pictures of fugitives on your wall?"

She glanced at the wall. "It's my job."

"It's mine, too, but I don't have to live with the bastards."

"Could we change the subject?"

"Okay, talk about something else."

What the hell was she supposed to talk about? The weather? It was hot yesterday, it was hot today, and it would more than likely be hot tomorrow. No, that would put the most wide awake person to sleep.

"You're not talking," he mumbled.

"I'm not the talkative kind."

He rolled onto his side and opened one eye. "A woman who doesn't like to talk. You know, if you're not careful they might want to clone you."

"Funny."

"So, what made you want to become a bounty hunter?"

A fairly safe topic. She sat down in the chair and propped her feet on the ottoman. "It was the only kind of work that I thought I would be really good at." The years rolled away. "I was twenty-one and thinking I could take on just about anyone."

He chuckled, then moaned. "Remind me not to do that. I know what you mean, though. I was the same way. Invincible. Nothing could touch me."

"I grew up fast, though," she continued. "My first skip knocked some of the wind out of my sails when he got the jump on me. He laughed the whole time he was tying me up. Damn, I was pissed, and so embarrassed I wiggled my hands until I got loose, too stubborn to call out for help. Then I tracked the skip. I had him in cuffs and sitting in jail before he knew what had happened."

"Why didn't you become a cop?"

For a moment, she'd forgotten Josh was in the room. She blinked her eyes to clear away the past. "Too much structure. I like being my own boss."

How long was someone with a head injury supposed to stay awake? All this chumminess was starting to wear thin.

"Who taught you to fight?"

"You ask too many questions." She stood. "I'm beat. If you start feeling . . . sick or whatever, call out."

She hurried out of the room before he could say another word. Once she was safely behind her door, she leaned against it. No, bringing Josh home with her hadn't been the best idea she'd ever come up with.

For just a little while, she'd been comfortable sitting in the dimly lit living room and talking.

Too comfortable.

She pushed away from the door, stripping off her shirt. Josh's wallet was still in her pants pocket. She tossed it in her bedside drawer. He could get it in the morning. She damn well wasn't going back in the living room.

Lord, she hoped he didn't croak during the night. The last thing she wanted to explain was a dead body in her apartment. The neighbors already thought she was weird. Besides, she sort of liked him . . . a little. At least enough that she didn't want him to come to harm.

He'd probably be sore when he woke up in the morning, too. Especially after sleeping all night in his clothes. She should at least go back in there and help him take off his boots.

Maybe unbutton the top button of his jeans, slide the zipper down so he'd rest easier. In fact, it wouldn't hurt to remove his pants. He'd certainly sleep a lot better. All she'd have to do would be to shove them over his hips . . . Her mouth began to water. Over his hips and down his legs, and if she accidentally brushed against anything . . .

Oh, you are so sick, Cody.

She quickly stripped off her clothes and climbed into bed before she could change her mind, pulling the sheet under her arm as she lay on her side.

Maybe the itch she had would be gone by morning.

Josh would make a good itch scratcher, and if she were entirely honest, then she would admit no other man had satisfied her like he had. But she wasn't quite ready to be that honest with herself.

It was going to be a long damn night.

She yawned and closed her eyes, praying for a dreamless sleep.

He couldn't stop them. Why in the hell couldn't he stop them? No matter where he ran, they kept coming.

Josh flung his arm out; it connected with something cold and hard. His gun? He needed his gun. He reached forward, felt along the hard ground, but he couldn't find his revolver and it was so dark that he couldn't see a damn thing.

"Josh?"

Her voice. Run! He wanted to scream at her to run, but the words wouldn't come. It was so damn dark. Where the hell was she?

God, they were getting closer. He could hear their foot-steps tromping through the underbrush. He had to find her . . . get her to safety.

"Josh, wake up. You're having a bad dream. Please, wake up."

Chapter 6

Josh dragged himself out of the dregs of his nightmare. A small light cast shadows about the sparsely furnished room. He blinked several times. These shadows were different from the ones in his nightmare. These were cold, stark . . . but safe.

The room swam in front of him, his head pounding as he sat up. He grabbed the edge of the sofa to keep from falling flat on his face on the hardwood floor. A small hand touched his shoulder, adding support.

"You okay?" a soft voice asked.

His stomach settled as the last vestiges of his nightmare were swept away by the sweet sound. Nice. He didn't want to think about the dream. Her voice pushed it back to the far corners of his mind.

He never wanted to think about the dream. Someday he would have to face what had happened, let all the pain and anguish sweep over him, but he couldn't do it right now. Just the thought scared the hell out of him, made him vulnerable.

So he pushed it away and pretended it had happened to someone else—wished it had happened to someone else.

But it hadn't. The awful truth was always there, just around the corner, waiting to pounce whenever he let his guard down.

He drew in a tired breath and looked at the face wavering above him. A few seconds passed. The face came into focus. Cody? What was she doing here?

Had he gotten lucky again?

He snorted. Not likely. If he had, he wouldn't have had the nightmare.

"Where am I?"

"You're in my apartment."

"My throat's dry." He reached up and massaged the back of his neck. "I feel like someone hit me with a two-by-four."

"Actually, it was a beer bottle." She stood. "I'll get you something to drink." She glided from the room like a specter in a silky, mossy green robe.

He blinked several times to clear his vision. Was he still dreaming? Not a nightmare this time, that was for damn sure. More like a fantasy.

He took stock of his situation. He was in her apartment, it was the middle of the night and she was wearing a thin robe, and from the way her nipples had pushed against the material, he had a feeling she was naked underneath. At least, damn near it. His body began to throb.

Not now. All he needed on top of everything else was a world-class boner. His head *and* his dick throbbing. What the hell was he even doing in her apartment? Especially when he was on the couch and she'd apparently been in her bed and they'd both been sleeping.

He rubbed his forehead as if that would clear away the cobwebs. The last thing he remembered was shooting pool with her.

A smile curved his lips.

She'd looked damned hot. It had been all he could do to concentrate on the game. She'd lost.

He closed his eyes against a sudden, sharp pain. When it eased, he tried to remember what happened next. Oh yeah, supper. Great steak, lousy conversation.

Ah, it was starting to come back to him. The man who'd grabbed Cody. Anger built inside him. The bastard had his nerve. Just as quickly, his anger dissolved. She'd gotten in her two cents. That was one man who would think twice before he pulled a woman onto his lap again.

Josh rubbed his knuckles. He'd gotten in one good punch. Everything was fine until that crazy woman hit him over the head. Ah, right. That's what had happened to him, why his head continued to pound and why everything after that was fuzzy.

How had he gotten home? Or at least to Cody's apartment?

Cold chills ran up and down his arms.

Crap! Where was his car? He stood. The room spun. He caught the arm of the sofa and sat back down with a hard thud. As soon as his head stopped pounding, he looked down at his feet. He couldn't go anywhere. No boots. Vaguely, he remembered tugging them off during the night.

The light was dim so he felt around on the floor. His hand brushed the worn leather of his boot just under the edge of the couch. He found the other one at the end. Damn it, how could he leave the Mustang parked at The Blue Eagle? He began yanking his boots on, even though his head was splitting in two.

"Going someplace?"

Cody stopped in front of him with a glass of water in one hand and two white tablets on the palm of her other.

"Tylenol," she explained.

Pain killers first, then his car. He scooped the pills up, popping them in his mouth before reaching for the water. "Bless you."

"That's a first. I don't think I've ever been blessed before. Damned a few times, but never blessed."

What was she talking about? It didn't matter. He swallowed the pills with half the water. God, water had never tasted so good.

"My car," he explained, setting the glass on the end table and sticking his foot in one of his boots.

She sat in the chair. "It's very cherry."

"What would you know about it?" He grabbed his other boot without looking up.

"I drove it here."

It took a few seconds for her words to sink in. He could feel the color drain from his face. No one drove the Mustang. No one. His best friend Wade had never driven the Mustang. God, that crazy woman must've really banged him a good one if he didn't even remember someone driving his car.

"You were certainly in no shape to drive."

"What about your Harley?"

"This isn't the first time I've left my bike with Joe so I know he'll take good care of it, but I didn't think you'd want to leave the Mustang in the parking lot all night. I brought you and the car here."

When she shrugged, the robe slipped off one shoulder. He sucked in a mouthful of air, causing his head to pound harder. Cody seemed quite oblivious that she wasn't helping his condition as she casually pulled the robe back into place.

"I'd better get home," he mumbled. Either that or he'd be sorely tempted to throw her down on the floor and make love to her. When he stood, the room swayed.

Cody jumped up, grabbing him around the waist. He grabbed her shoulders, her body pressed against his. The room stopped moving, but now he had a different problem—his body's reaction to her nearness.

He swallowed hard. Damn, her breasts were crushed against his chest, her hard little nipples poking him. The only thing separating bare chest from bare chest was his thin shirt and her thinner robe.

All thoughts ceased as he surrendered himself to the sensations she stirred inside him. It was doubtful he could've done anything else.

He wrapped his arms tighter around her, pulling her closer. "Have I ever told you how great you smell?" He nuzzled her neck as the room stopped spinning and his equilibrium returned.

"Yeah, you've mentioned it a few times," she said in a breathless whisper.

"Really? I don't remember. You smell like coconut and pineapples. It makes me think about a tropical paradise. You take me on a fantasy every time I get close to you."

His hands slid over her back and down to her bottom. He was right; she wasn't wearing anything beneath the robe. All he had to do was pull the belt and it would fall open.

"Maybe you should sit before you fall down," she said, breaking into his thoughts, but her voice cracked. He knew she felt the same thing.

"This isn't the first time I've been hit over the head. I'll survive that, I'm just not sure I'll survive being this close to you and not doing anything about it." Damn, she was going to be the death of him. "I want to make love to you."

"I offered you my sofa. Nothing more."

He was afraid she'd say something like that. She was running away again.

"You can't blame a guy for asking," he told her.

Before he let her go, he tilted her chin and lowered his mouth to hers. He'd meant the kiss to be short, but as soon as he tasted her lips, her mouth, it deepened into something more. He caressed her tongue, her heat almost burning him.

She broke off the kiss, but didn't move from his arms. "You're a player, Josh."

"Then come play with me. You know you want to."

Silence.

"You're right, I do." She looked up at him. "I swear, if I see a notch on your belt . . ."

"Never."

"I'm a fool, but I want to feel you inside me. I want what we had the last time."

He buried his face in her hair. "No more than I do, sweet lady. Damn, I love the way you smell." He hugged her close to him for a moment, breathing in her heady fragrance.

It still wasn't enough. He stepped back, tugging the belt of her robe loose, letting the ties fall to the side. She sucked in a breath when he ran his hand over the soft material.

His gaze met hers, then lowered as he slipped his fingers beneath the silk, trailing along the underside of one breast. The torture of feeling but not seeing was exquisite.

And one he couldn't stand for long. He pushed the robe off to one side, marveling at the perfection of her breast: dusky areola and tight nipple.

He pushed the other side of the robe off her shoulder. It slid to the floor in a silky puddle and she stood there, gloriously naked.

"I think I could stare at you forever." He brushed his knuckles over her shoulder and down one breast before cupping them in his hands.

She grabbed his shoulders to steady herself.

"I love the way you feel—soft in all the right places." He tweaked her nipples, tugging on them while gently massaging.

"You make my knees weak."

He liked knowing he could do that to her. He sat on the sofa, tugging her onto his lap, but at the last minute she straddled his legs, her hands tugging at his shirt.

"If you think you've seduced me, then think again." She pulled his shirt over his head. "I want you as much as you want me."

"Ah, sweetheart, you can be the seducer."

She tossed his shirt on the floor. "No, we're equal. Nothing more, nothing less. Then when we walk away there'll be no regrets. Agreed?"

He opened his mouth, then closed it. Damn it, why did she have to be so tough all the time? Why did she have to guard her heart? But then, he didn't think he'd find her nearly as exciting if she were any different.

"Equal," he said, rubbing her shoulders. He felt the tension drain away from her.

She smiled, running her hands over his chest, brushing

across his nipples, stoking the flame that already burned deep inside him.

"You're right. This is nice."

Temptation beckoned. He nudged her closer, his mouth covering first one breast, then the other. She moaned from deep in her throat, as if everything inside her had been building since the last time they'd been together.

What was it about this woman that he couldn't get enough of her?

His hand tangled in her hair, pulling her mouth down to his. She tasted like peppermint toothpaste: clean, fresh. He couldn't get enough of kissing her, but she pulled back, nipping at his bottom lip. When he started to reach for her, she took his hand.

"Equal." Her words were raw with hunger.

She raised his hand to her mouth, lightly biting his fingertips before drawing his index finger into her mouth. Her tongue curled against it as she sucked, cupping his finger and sending spasms of pleasure through his body.

He could imagine her mouth somewhere else, drawing him deeper, enclosing him in heat. Her tongue was like a flame, licking and sucking.

She released his finger and leaned forward. "Do you like that?" she whispered close to his ear before she nipped at his earlobe, then tugged on it with her teeth.

Raising up just slightly, she brushed her breasts across his face. When he opened his mouth, she laughed lightly and leaned down to his other ear. He closed his eyes and gritted his teeth.

"Do you like it?" she whispered, dipping her tongue inside.

The blood pounded in his ears. "You know I do." He reached for her again, but she stood, moving just out of his reach.

Was she building him up only to let him down like a stone being dropped from the top of a ten-story building? She must have guessed his thoughts because she turned and gave him a saucy smile.

"I won't be gone long."

Take your time, he thought to himself. *Of course, I'll just be a pile of ashes when you return.*

Closing his eyes, he leaned his head against the back of the sofa, forcing himself to regain control of his body. It wasn't working. All he could think about was Cody, naked and sitting on his lap.

Screw it. He undid his pants and kicked out of them, along with his briefs.

The emptiness of the room surrounded him.

What if she didn't return? Surely she wouldn't be that cruel. He closed his eyes, expelling a deep breath.

Music began to play from hidden speakers. Soothing, like the sound of waves rolling into shore. Some of the tightness left his body. He heard a slight noise and opened his eyes.

She came toward him, her body moving across the room with a hypnotic sway. His gaze swept over her, slowing when he got to the thatch of curls at the juncture of her legs. Damn, he wanted to tangle his fingers in those curls, rub his thumb over her clit before tasting what she had to offer.

When she straddled him, he noticed she had a bottle in her hand. Her gaze moved down him; a smile touched her lips.

"I see you're in a hurry," she commented, eyeing his nakedness.

"And what exactly are you up to?" he asked.

Her smile was wicked. "You said you like the tropical scent I wear. I just . . . warmed up a little for you," she said in a husky voice.

She held the bottle above him and tilted it just slightly until the warm liquid ran onto his chest. "Close your eyes. Let your mind go free." She set the bottle to the side and began massaging the oil into his chest, leaning forward and rubbing her breasts over him.

Cupping her butt, he drew her against his erection and almost lost it when the heat of her body enveloped him in a sensual cocoon. He couldn't stop his groan when she rubbed her breasts against him.

He moved his hands lower, stroking her bottom without really thinking about what he was doing. She'd wrapped him in a haze of pleasure, pressing her sex against him and slowly rotating her hips.

If she didn't stop, he wouldn't be able to hold back, and he hadn't finished with her yet. He snaked a hand between her legs and began to massage.

"Oh, yes," she cried out, jerking her body forward. She closed her eyes, her teeth biting her lower lip.

When she clutched his shoulders, he slipped two fingers inside her. She was hot and wet.

"You're not playing fair again," she moaned, moving against his fingers.

He watched the expression on her face. There was something so fucking sexy about watching a woman in the throes of passion.

Their gazes met and locked. He was on the edge and she didn't look like she'd last much longer, either. He reached for his pants and quickly tore open the foil pack with his teeth. He slid the condom on.

Before he could do much else, she'd straddled him, lowering herself onto his erection. He sucked in a deep breath as her wet heat surrounded him. She moved her body and he slid in deeper.

"Oh, damn," she said. "This feels so fucking good."

Her words sent fire racing through him. He raised his hips; she met his thrusts. When he thought he couldn't hold back another second, she drew in a deep breath and cried out.

It felt as if the world exploded around him. He grabbed her hips, pulling her in tight to his body. She collapsed on top of him, her breasts crushed against his chest.

It took him a few minutes to catch his breath. When he did, realization set in. "Ah, hell," he moaned. "I didn't think it could get any better than the last time. I was wrong."

Cody hadn't thought so, either. This could get really complicated.

Her head rested on Josh's chest. Damned if she didn't like listening to the steady rhythm of his heart and the tropical scent that floated up to her nose.

She liked being enveloped in the quiet of the room.

"You drove my car," he said after a few minutes, breaking the silence.

She chuckled. Boy, Red had hit him a good one with that bottle.

"How the hell can you laugh at a time like this? You drove the Mustang! No one drives the Mustang."

"You're the one who tried to fight my battle. What was I supposed to do? Leave it parked in Joe's parking lot? I couldn't take a chance it would be stripped come morning."

"Besides the fact you've always wanted to get under the wheel. You can't deny it. I've seen that hungry look in your eyes."

She nodded her head toward him. "Touché."

"You're not going to deny it?"

"We both know I'd be lying."

He opened his mouth, then snapped it closed. "I like you this way."

"What way?"

"When you talk about cars . . . your Harley. You're more . . . relaxed. You're always so blasted stiff. Hell, here lately, that's been a chronic complaint of mine. In fact, every time I'm around you."

"Ah, what a shame you've suffered."

"I like it when you laugh."

She snuggled closer to his warmth, even though the room wasn't cold. She just liked being near him. Silence settled over them, and she remembered why she'd gone into the living room in the first place.

"You want to talk about it?" He would know she meant his nightmare. She didn't have to explain.

"Nothing to talk about."

"Sometimes talking helps."

"I don't have them very often. It goes with the territory sometimes."

When she raised her head, her gaze met his. "Yeah, I know what you mean." A brief smile touched her lips before she stood and made her way to the bedroom.

You're getting in over your head, her inner voice warned. *He'll hurt you.*

No, I won't let him.

As Cody struggled to push away the cobwebs that clouded her mind, she tried to think what made this day different from the day before. Nothing came to mind. Maybe she'd had a weird dream and that's why everything seemed strange this morning.

She yawned and stretched.

Something clattered in the other room.

She jerked to a sitting position. Someone was in her apartment. Leaning over, she eased open her nightstand drawer and brought out her gun, pulled the clip back and checked, already knowing it was loaded. Better safe than sorry.

As the doorknob turned, she aimed. The door burst open, banging the wall behind it.

"I thought you might want some coffee." Josh glanced up from the tray he carried. One eyebrow rose. "If you shoot me, the cup will fall and break, the coffee will stain the carpet, and you'll have to get the next cup yourself."

"Funny. Have I mentioned you're a fuckin' comedian?" But the tone of her voice had changed around him. Even she heard the soft timbre. That wasn't good.

When he grinned, those blasted tingles spread right down to her toes.

"A time or two," he told her, then nodded toward her gun. "Mind putting that away before you accidentally pull the trigger?"

"How do you know it would be an accident?" She wished he'd quit looking at her like that. He had a very lethal smile.

"I take it you're feeling better," she said. "I mean, no headache?"

"Never better."

Tucking the sheet more securely under her arms, she replaced her gun. "You know, there is such a thing as knocking before you enter a room, even calling out. I could've blown your head off."

The coffee smelled good, though. After last night, she desperately needed a cup. She needed all her faculties when Josh was around. Hell, just being near him wasn't a good thing.

Her gaze skimmed over him.

Nope, not a good thing at all. He looked like he'd made use of the shower down the hall. His hair was a little damp. He hadn't shaved, though. His scruffy appearance only added to his sexy good looks. No, it wouldn't be such a bad thing waking up next to Josh every morning.

"You going to bring the coffee over here or am I just supposed to inhale it?"

"Are you always this grumpy first thing in the morning?" He ambled over and set the tray on the bedside table.

"You caught me on a good morning. I'm usually worse." She reached for the coffee, added a good portion of creamer and two scoops of sugar. When she looked up, he was staring at her. "What?"

He shrugged. "I don't know. I guess I figured you'd drink it black. Who'd have thought you'd have a sweet tooth?"

She ignored him and brought the cup to her lips. Closing her eyes, she took her first drink of the day. It slid down her throat, leaving a nice warm feeling in its wake. He made a damn good cup of coffee. Not too strong, not too weak.

But when he pulled up a chair and reached for the other cup on the tray, she warily eyed him. It almost felt comfortable having him in the room. She could get used to having him around. This wouldn't do. Not at all. There was something about making love at night that changed in the cold light of day.

"Don't you have someplace to be or somewhere to go?" Like out of her apartment and out of her life?

He took a drink of his coffee and settled deeper into the chair, raising his feet to the ottoman. "Nope."

Her forehead wrinkled.

"Don't make such a production over it. All I'm doing is having a cup of coffee with you. No big deal."

She squared her shoulders, but had to grab the sheet as it slipped, then almost sloshed coffee over the side of her cup. "I'm not making anything out of it." She glared at him. "Did I say anything?"

"Didn't have to. I could see it on your face. You had your way with me and now you're ready for me to go." He looked over the rim of his cup. "Do I make you nervous?"

She opened her mouth, then snapped it closed. "Entertaining men in my bedroom is not something I do." She'd never had a man in her apartment, in fact. She liked to be the one who left.

"Good."

It was too damn early to have a sparring match with Josh. "I didn't say I never have men in my bedroom. After all, you were here last night."

"I wouldn't mind being there tonight, too." His gaze started at her face, caressed her bare shoulders, and lingered on her breasts before moving back to her face.

She swallowed past the lump in her throat. *Don't get too friendly,* the voice inside her head warned.

"I have work to do," she hedged.

"What did you think about the Mustang?" he asked, abruptly changing the subject.

This was a safe enough topic. She exhaled. "It's a nice car."

"Only nice?"

"I like my Harley better." She shrugged. "But yeah, you have a nice car."

She almost laughed at his disgruntled expression. You'd have thought she'd told him that his mother was ugly or something. He raised his eyes, his forehead puckering.

"Just nice? That's all you felt?" A totally dumbfounded look crossed his face. "Just nice?"

Red must've really clobbered Josh good for him not to remember that she'd practically drooled all over the black leather seats. She should probably tell him the truth and put him out of his misery.

"The Mustang is the sweetest car I've ever driven. I thought I'd died and gone to heaven."

He brightened. "Really?"

She nodded. "How long have you had her?"

He sat forward. "Since high school. I bought her from an old man who'd parked the Mustang in his garage. He hadn't started it in years and was glad to get rid of her. I practically stole the car. Then it took all the money from after-school jobs and working during the summer for three years to get her into this condition. Only the best would do."

Josh transformed from the bounty hunter, from the man who changed women more often than he polished the chrome on his Mustang, to that young man he'd once been. She found herself fascinated listening to him talk about the car.

"My dad helped me hoist the rebuilt engine into the cavity beneath the hood. It took us all week and the weekend to get it bolted down and ready to run." He smiled, a faraway look in his eyes. "I think my father was more nervous than I was when I turned the key for the first time. It was the most beautiful sound in the world when it purred to life."

He'd painted a picture so vivid it was almost as if she was there. Then again, she'd been tinkering with engines most of her life so it wasn't hard to imagine Josh working to restore his car.

"So what's your story?" he asked.

His words startled her for a moment. She didn't want to get friendly or anything. Yeah, right, like sitting in the middle of her bed with only a sheet tucked under her arms wasn't getting friendly. The next thing she knew, they'd be making love again. She stifled a moan at the thoughts that conjured.

"With the Harley, I mean," he explained, breaking into her thoughts.

At least this was a much safer topic, and she was proud of the Harley. "It belonged to Joe at one time."

"The owner of The Blue Eagle?"

She nodded.

"I'll be damned." He set his empty cup on the tray and leaned back in his chair. "I never expected Joe to be the motorcycle type."

"He used to run with a gang back in the sixties. He wrecked the bike. That's how he met Sarah. She was a nurse at the hospital. He fell instantly in love. They married a few months later and he never bothered fixing the bike. I was hunting for some tools he said I could have when I lifted a dusty green tarp and there she was. That's when I fell in love."

"You're not going to tell me you restored her all by yourself."

"Don't you think I could have?"

The look on his face told her he was groping around for a nice way to answer. Laughter bubbled out of her. She couldn't stop it even if she'd tried—which she didn't—but it came to a halt when he narrowed his gaze on her. A flush of heat crawled up her face. His look made her more aware just how naked she was beneath the sheet. She tugged the covers firmly under her arms.

"Okay," she admitted. "I had help."

"I knew it."

"I'll have you know, I did most of the work."

"Joe helped, right?"

She put her cup down and brought her legs up, crossing them Indian fashion beneath the sheet. "It wasn't Joe."

"Not Joe?"

She shook her head. Her thoughts wandered back. She could see Rodney as if he stood at the end of the bed. His craggy, lined face, the soft brown eyes that always looked so sad. She'd wanted to remove his pain. She could've been the daughter he'd lost, if he'd only let her, but there had been a part of him that he'd kept locked away, and deep down inside her, she'd known she was only pretending he cared more than he had. Why else would he have left without a word of good-bye?

"You did have someone helping, right?"

For a moment, she'd forgotten Josh was in the room. She looked at him. "His name was Rodney. He lived with my . . . my mother for a while. Rodney knew a lot about different stuff. Motorcycles, for one. We worked on the Harley together. Then when it was finished, he left."

Pain ripped through her. Damn it, she'd been seventeen and he'd been like a father to her for four years. It wasn't supposed to still hurt this much. Damn, damn, damn. He should've said good-bye. Why the hell hadn't he said good-bye?

"I really do need to get down to the office today. I think it's time you left. Your keys are on the table by the front door."

"I'm sorry." He spoke quietly.

She raised an eyebrow. "For what?"

"For the pain he caused you."

She couldn't do this. She couldn't talk about her past. Josh wasn't Dr. Phil, and she didn't want or need his apologies.

"Just go, okay." She clamped her lips together and kept her eyes focused forward. When he closed the bedroom door, her shoulders slumped.

Maybe there was another reason she didn't want Josh around. It was almost as if he could see inside her, that he knew her deepest, darkest secrets. She'd been alone so long now that she was afraid to let anyone get close enough to see what was inside her. What if they found her repulsive? Or what if she grew to like them and they left . . . like her father? Like Rodney? Like the men she'd dated?

It was better to keep to herself and not let anyone in. Have sex, but not let them get near her heart.

She heard the front door close.

It didn't matter. Better to end it here and now before things went any further. Before she began to care too much.

Chapter 7

Josh took the elevator down to the garage, absently turning his car keys over and over in his hand. What had happened? One moment they were having a casual conversation. Cody had actually laughed.

Not that she never laughed, just not like that. Usually it was a sarcastic chuckle or a laugh that followed a snide remark. No, this was different. More like she was actually enjoying herself. That might have been a first, he wryly thought to himself.

But just as quickly as the laughter came, the relaxed moment vanished and Cody shut down. What had soured the mood? Damn it, she'd looked so forlorn sitting on the bed, the sheet pulled close to her body.

As he stepped out of the elevator and walked across the garage to his car, he realized he'd never seen Cody with anyone. A loner.

They were a lot alike.

Hell, even he knew he wasn't that close to the men who were at the bar last night. He only shot pool with them. Superficial friends.

But that wasn't the way his life used to be. His friendship with Wade had been deeper, stronger, but even that had waned. People grew up, drifted away from each other. It happened.

Cody said Rodney had left one day. From her expression, he could tell it still bothered her.

He stopped at his car, letting his gaze slowly sweep over her, noting that the Mustang looked the same as when he'd parked it at The Blue Eagle. As much as Cody worshipped her Harley, he hadn't really thought she'd put a scratch or dent on his baby.

No, she was a woman who appreciated a nice set of wheels. Her eyes always sparkled when she talked about the Harley. Some women had that same light in their eyes when they walked past a jewelry store. Cody's eyes shone when she talked about rebuilding engines.

He grinned. She was definitely one of a kind.

Opening the car door, he climbed inside. The muscles in his shoulders relaxed.

He had to get over her. They'd had great sex a couple of times. It was time he stopped thinking about her so much. His life suited him. He didn't need someone like Cody messing with his head. Hell, he could tell she had problems. What right did he have to try to fix her? None. None whatsoever. Especially when he couldn't fix his own life.

Resting his hands on the steering wheel, he closed his eyes. This was his comfort zone. He breathed in, he breathed out.

His gut clenched.

The scent of coconut and tropical breezes swirled around him. Her scent. It lingered in the car, transporting him to a fantasy of Cody lying naked on the beach, the sun caressing her skin. She'd told him that she'd never been to the ocean, never seen the waves crashing against a concrete jetty. Never felt the salt spray kissing her face.

Maybe someday they would just take off and head down to the coast . . .

Great, how the hell was he supposed to concentrate with her scent lingering and making him fantasize about what it would be like to have sex with her on the beach? Hell, he had a hard enough time when he'd joined her in her bedroom. At the time, he'd thought taking her coffee sounded pretty good. *Admit it,* he told himself. He just couldn't get enough of her.

But nothing had happened this morning. He'd been so damn close to the sexiest woman on earth, and she'd been naked beneath a thin, white cotton sheet, and he hadn't done a damn thing about it. Maybe because he'd sensed it wouldn't be the same this morning. That she needed a little space between them.

Wade would laugh and tell him that he was losing his touch. Wade used to tell him a lot of things, like how he was trying to fix the world . . . trying to save everyone.

That part of himself was behind him now. He'd hung up his white hat. He was in it for the money, and his bank account was starting to look pretty damn healthy. Someday he would have his P.I. agency. Another couple of years, after it was off the ground, he'd be able to sit back and just take it easy—no worries, no problems.

Some people might say he was running away, but he wasn't. Wade was wrong. He was just through trying to save the world.

He started the Mustang and backed out of the space. He'd go home, change clothes, and run down to the agency to see how many files Erik had. At least tracking down a few skips would take his mind off everything.

Namely tropical breezes and a very sexy bounty hunter.

A fresh set of clothes, two cups of strong black coffee and two hours later, he pushed the door open to Erik's bail bond office.

His secretary glanced up, then smiled. Abigail Horton was sweet, if a little absentminded. A grandmother of six, she was forever talking about her grandchildren. Josh didn't really mind, but with Erik's newly married status, the office was more than a little disorganized.

"Josh, hello." She smiled. "Erik's in his office."

He closed the door. "I thought I'd look through some files."

She shook her head. "You work too hard. A nice man like you should settle down and have a few kids."

"But you're already taken. Now, if you'd consider leaving Cid for me I might just take your advice."

She blushed and downed her head. "You're a born flirt, Josh Pierce. I don't have time for this nonsense. Go on with yourself." She nodded toward a box. "The open files are in there."

He went around her desk and picked up the box, carrying it to a desk in the corner. The building was small. One semi-large room, a short hallway with a bathroom on one side and a storage closet on the other. Erik's office was in the back. It served the purpose, and Abby always kept the place smelling like Old English polish and decorated with pictures of her grandchildren and their childish drawings.

The office might look small and insignificant, but Erik had more work than he could handle. One reason why he used three bounty hunters. Actually, Turbo was part-time. Turbo said he'd rather work the recovery network—said there was more competition to keep him in shape.

Josh thought Turbo just liked climbing over other agents so he could get to the top of the heap. The recovery network was a kind of free for all. First one to nab the skip would get the pie.

Josh sat in the chair and kicked back, pulling out the first file. It didn't interest him. He tossed it on the desk and reached for the next one. Calvin Bastrop's file. He glanced through it, thinking he might just take this one on principle.

The cops arrested the little shit for selling drugs to his college friends. That wasn't what caught his interest, though. It was the accusation by a young girl who said she was drugged, then gang-raped.

Maybe she was lying. He didn't know, but just looking at

Calvin's picture, his gut instinct told him she might be telling the truth.

Calvin had the look of a young man who came from money and didn't know when he had it so good: perfect hair, perfect smile, perfect teeth, perfect tan. Smugness oozed from his pores. His eyes said no matter what he did, Daddy would get him off. So smug he'd missed his court date.

First offense—at least that's what his file said. Daddy had probably bailed him out on more than one occasion. First offenders were a bad risk for a bail bondsman. Most of the time, they jumped bail, terrified at the thought of going to jail, but this one wouldn't stray far from home.

He flipped back to the first page. Calvin didn't look the type who would let much of anything scare him at this point in his life. He'd think differently if he ever spent any time in the slammer.

The door opened, drawing his attention. Turbo Manning strolled inside. Six feet tall and with a swagger that got on Josh's last nerve. He was a braggart. Josh came from the school where actions spoke louder than words.

Abigail looked up when the door opened, but downed her head and continued working without a word of greeting.

Turbo didn't seem to care; he grinned and sauntered to the desk where Josh sat. Josh didn't bother moving his feet off the desk's surface, but instead returned his attention to the file he was reading. It didn't stop Turbo from looking over his shoulder.

"Calvin Bastrop, I hauled the rich boy in yesterday. I guess you're too late."

He tossed the file on the desk and picked up another one. Apparently, Turbo wasn't ready to drop the conversation.

"Yeah, you'll have to get up earlier than this if you want to beat me to the punch."

The thought of punching Turbo had entered his mind, but he didn't want to upset Abigail. Instead, he opened another file, scanned the sheet, and flipped the page, casually looking over the next sheet. "Apparently Cody was up before you a couple of weeks ago when she beat you to the skip," he casually pointed out.

Turbo's mouth turned down. "Yeah, well, she just got lucky."

"Not from what I heard."

"You can't believe anything a woman as cold as her says. Hell, I don't think she even likes men. I bet she only does women. She won't let a man even get close to her."

"Maybe you're not her type."

He snorted. "Yeah, and you are? You might as well give up and quit sniffing around her. Ain't no man with balls big enough to get between her legs."

The door opened again and Cody sauntered inside. She nodded toward him, spoke to Abigail, but barely looked in Turbo's direction.

Damn, she looked sweet. Black jeans and a red T-shirt that barely reached the waistband of her jeans. When she moved, a tantalizing glimpse of tanned skin peeked out, tempting him to do more than look.

He really hated when people misjudged others. Especially when it came to Cody. He refused to delve into the reasons why, other than the fact that he didn't really like Turbo.

She abruptly turned around. "Your wallet's at my place. I put it up last night, then forgot to give it to you this morning." She glanced at her watch. "Where are you going to be in a couple of hours?"

"The Corner Café for lunch."

She nodded. "I'll drop it off there. Erik in his office?"

"Yeah."

"See you in a couple of hours."

Her gaze moved to Turbo, but without saying a word, she left the room. Josh watched her walk away. Damn, she had a nice swing in her hips.

When she shut the door, Turbo looked him in the eye. "You gonna tell me you spent the night with Cody?"

Josh went back to the file he was looking at. "I'm not tellin' you shit. Maybe your problem is that you don't have big balls, but I would definitely say Cody is all woman."

"I'll be back later when there's not as many smartasses around." Turbo stomped to the door and slammed out of the office.

Abigail chuckled. "Now that was funny. Have I ever mentioned how much I enjoy having you around?"

He grinned, but was a little embarrassed she'd overheard. Damn, she reminded him of his grandmother.

"I don't know how you managed to spend the night at Cody's apartment, but I'd say you put a glow on that girl's face. About time someone did." She continued shuffling through the papers on her desk.

He opened his mouth, but quickly snapped it closed. What could he say?

"I like that you took Turbo down a few notches. I don't think he's any better than the people he goes after." She looked up then, winked, and went back to arranging the papers on her desk.

He didn't think he'd given Abigail as much credit as she deserved. "I think Cid is a very lucky man."

"Of course he is, and if he forgets, you can bet your last dollar I'll remind him."

Abigail was another one-in-a-million woman. He went back to reading the file. Pete Watson. He glanced at the stats. Thirty-eight, robbery, assault on an elderly woman—stole her purse. He swallowed past the bile that rose in his throat as his gaze slid down the page.

Sometimes his job was personal. There were two things he didn't like: men who beat on women and people who hurt the elderly or kids. He jotted down some notes, but out of the corner of his eye, he watched Cody shut the door to Erik's office.

"Don't work too hard, Abigail," Cody said.

"Oh, honey, I'll never be guilty of that."

Cody sailed out of the office, but in her wake, she left the scent of tropical breezes and fantasies that Josh would rather not think about.

He cleared his head and turned to Abigail. "Anyone on this case?"

"Pete Watson? No, he's all yours. I'll mark it down. Poor Erik's been confusing a lot of files lately."

He didn't think Erik was the only one, but he didn't mention his thoughts on the subject. Instead, he tucked his notes in his pocket, said good-bye, and walked out into the sunshine, inhaling deeply.

Damned if he couldn't smell the tropical breeze out here. For just a moment, he closed his eyes and took another deep breath.

Maybe that was his problem. He never could resist going back for seconds. With Cody around, he'd discovered his appetite for more of her was getting worse rather than better. It was too easy for him to envision her arms wrapped around his neck, her naked body pressed intimately against his. Her breasts crushed against his chest, her tight nipples scraping across his bare skin.

She would probably be the death of him. Oh, but what a glorious way to die.

There was no reason for her to be nervous. *Yeah right,* Cody thought to herself. Then why were her hands damp?
I'm only returning a wallet.
His wallet.

Why did Josh have so much control over her mind, her emotions, her body? The truth this time. No lies, not even to herself. She knew, without a doubt, no man had ever sent a thrill through her like Josh had.

She stopped resisting the memory, letting his touch, the feel of his lips on hers, swirl through her senses. The way his tongue had stroked hers. A deep ache began to throb inside her. One that wouldn't easily go away.

Damn, damn, damn! Why had she let him turn her into a puddle of mush at the mere thought of having sex with the great Josh Pierce?

Uh huh, sure. As if she had any control over her thoughts when the man was around. She had to get over this infatuation with him before he drove her crazy. He didn't know how to be faithful to just one woman. Last month he'd had that brunette bitch hanging all over him. They'd been practically attached at the hip.

No, she wouldn't get involved with him. The people who'd come and gone in her life had taught her well how to guard her heart to keep it from being broken one more time—don't get close enough to get hurt. She could guard her heart against Josh.

Shaking her head, she wiped her palms down the front of her jeans, threw her leg over the Harley, and started the bike. It roared to life. The peace and contentment that usually came when the Harley rumbled beneath her just wasn't there.

She was restless. As if she needed to be somewhere else. Maybe she should take off. Just leave. There was a sudden roaring in her ears, like the crash of waves against the rocks. When she took a deep breath, she could almost smell the salt in the air.

No, getting away wasn't her problem. Her grip on the handlebars tightened.

As she pulled into the flow of traffic, she knew exactly what was wrong. It was as if she stood on the very edge of a precipice, looking down.

She and Josh were dancing, but when he got a little too close to finding out what made her tick, she'd get scared and move back a step, afraid that last step off the edge would send her spiraling downward and the fall might be too much for her to recover from.

She flipped her right blinker, slowed, and turned the corner.

That was the absolute first and last time she ever took a man home with her. Bad mistake.

She pulled into a parking space in the lot at the side of the café, shifted into neutral, and cut the engine. Okay, she could do this. No sweat.

She drew in a deep, shaky breath and swung her leg over the Harley. Reaching into the saddlebag, she brought out Josh's wallet. She'd give it back and wouldn't let him talk her into having lunch with him. She was pretty sure that's why he'd told her he would be at the café. The less time she spent in Josh's company the better off she'd be.

Her gaze skimmed over the cars until it landed on the orange Mustang. A sigh slipped from her lips. He did have a set of the sweetest wheels she'd ever had the pleasure of driving, though.

Shaking off her desire to stroke a fender one last time, she resolutely strode to the door and opened it. Once inside, she let her eyes adjust. It only took her a second to spot him—and know that it hadn't been his intention to invite her to lunch.

Why would he want to have lunch with her when there was already a sexy little blond bitch sitting next to him, staring at him as if he were her knight in shining armor?

Chapter 8

Josh wondered how in the hell he could get rid of Marianne when the bell above the café door jingled. When he started to look up, she grabbed his hand. She was the touchy-feely type. It hadn't taken but one night to feel smothered.

They'd eaten at a nice restaurant, and at first her adoring looks flattered him, but after thirty minutes or so, *the look* began to wear on his nerves. She hadn't been like this when they'd first met, had she?

He'd planned on dropping Marianne off at her apartment and leaving as quickly as possible, but she'd been nervous about going inside by herself. What could he do?

Now he couldn't get rid of her. If he'd known she was in the café, he would have waited for Cody outside, but before he knew what hit him, Marianne had slid a chair close to his and sat down, grabbing his hand—which he now tugged free.

He glanced toward the door.

Great, had his thoughts conjured up Cody? She marched toward them, and she didn't look a bit happy.

So maybe this was for the best. He'd told himself earlier he had to stop thinking about her. They both knew a relationship wouldn't work. Hell, they were too much alike. They'd probably kill each other.

"Your wallet." Cody tossed it on the table.

Marianne looked between them. "Josh, is there something you're not telling me?" Her voice rose an octave with each word.

He closed his eyes and counted to ten. The pounding started at the base of his skull and worked its way around to his forehead. When he opened his eyes, Marianne looked ready to start bawling, and Cody . . . Well, if her eyes could shoot bullets, he'd be dead right now.

He had no idea why she'd be so angry. It wasn't like she would've accepted his lunch invitation.

"Don't worry, honey," Cody grated out. "He's all yours." She turned on her heel and strode back the way she'd come.

"Cody!" He started to stand, but Marianne grabbed his hand. He didn't know whether it was accidental or on purpose that she pressed it against her breasts.

"Let her go. You don't need her when you have me. I'm so much better for you, I promise."

The door slammed behind Cody as she stormed out of the café, the little bell above the door crashing to the floor.

His attention turned back to Marianne. Shit, she had that look on her face. The one that told him she was about to let loose with a major crying jag.

Hadn't she told him she wanted to move to Hollywood and try for an acting career? Well, right now he felt like he'd stepped onto the set of a very bad movie.

"Marianne." He spoke slowly and distinctly. "I spent one night with you. That's all it was. There is no you and me. We're not a couple. I'm sorry, but you need to get a life. One that doesn't include me." He pulled his arm from her grasp.

"You don't . . ." She sucked in a dramatic sob. "You don't love me anymore?"

Josh noticed people were starting to turn and stare. The same people who'd watched Cody leave none too quietly, and it didn't look like their sympathies were with him.

"I've never loved you, Marianne," he said, keeping his

voice down and hoping the crowd didn't go ballistic and form a lynch party.

Damn, tears began streaming down her face. Where the hell were they coming from? She could fill a bucket.

"But what . . . what if I'm pregnant?"

One older woman's mouth dropped open, then snapped closed, her eyes narrowing to slits. He could almost see her swinging a rope from her hand. He'd better think of something else—and damn fast.

Give him a six-foot, brawny-bruiser, fighting mad bond-jumper any day over a crying female.

He drew in a deep breath. "Marianne, we didn't have sex," he softly told her.

She sniffed. "We didn't?"

"No, we didn't." He pulled napkins from the dispenser and handed them to her. "You asked me to your apartment. I'd just come off a two-week case and was so damned tired that I fell asleep on your sofa." He drew in a deep breath. "I left a note on your pillow."

"We didn't have sex?"

He shook his head.

He'd quietly crept into her room, planning on waking her with a kiss and making up for the night before, but as soon as he opened the door, the last thing on his mind was sex.

Marianne's room was wall-to-wall stuffed animals: pink elephants, cutesy puppies in rainbow shades, little kittens with long hair. On one wall, next to a canopy bed billowing with lace, someone had painted a rainbow.

And lying on the bed was Sleeping Beauty, but he couldn't be her Prince Charming. He didn't wear a white hat anymore. She was looking for a fantasy and he certainly wasn't that.

So he'd left what he thought was a sweet note on top of the extra pillow and quietly slipped out of her apartment. Apparently, his note had meant something more to her.

"You are a beautiful woman, Marianne."

Her eyes brightened with hope.

"But I'm not the man you're looking for." He took her hand. It was small and fragile. "I deal with the scum of the earth day in and day out. I see things that would shock someone as sensitive as you. I live fast and hard. You're too good for me. Someday that special man will come into your life. Don't settle for anything less."

"There's not a chance . . ."

"There can't be. Believe me, someday you'll thank me. Now go. Live your life, and never look back." Man, that was thick, even for him. Marianne appeared to be thinking over what he'd said. He didn't let out a breath until she nodded her head.

"You're right." She squeezed his hand. "We're from two different worlds. Mine is pure and untouched. Yours is sullied and tainted. You'll have to go on without me."

Go on without her? Wasn't that what he'd been trying to do since she'd slid uninvited into the chair next to him? If it would get her out of his life, he didn't care what played out in her mind. Damn, she was starting to scare him.

"I'll try." He turned his head away. "Please leave. I don't want you to see me break down." Acting wasn't that hard. Maybe he should've tried out for the stage or something.

"I'll go, but please don't ever forget me. I don't think I could stand it if I knew you never thought about me."

"You'll always hold a piece of my heart. Hurry now, leave before I make a fool of myself."

"Yes, my love." She stood. A moment later, the door opened and closed.

Josh breathed a sigh of relief. The man in the next booth stood, dropped some bills on the table, and glanced in Josh's direction.

"Son, I wouldn't quit your day job if I were you. Your acting stinks. If that girl hadn't been such a twit, you'd still be stuck with her." He ambled toward the door and left.

Okay, so maybe he wouldn't make such a great actor. He followed suit, dropping money on the table at the same time he slipped his wallet into his jeans pocket.

How the hell could a day start out so well, then fizzle so damn fast? He had a feeling Cody was going to be pissed at him for a long time.

It was for the best. His head wasn't big enough for that white hat everyone wanted him to wear. Helping people had only given him a lifetime of miserable memories.

He ran a hand through his hair after he climbed into the Mustang. For a moment, he just sat there, looking at nothing—seeing too much as the memories washed over him full force. For a moment, he let them bathe him in the past. Viv's face swollen and bruised flashed across his mind. Before the past could suck him in further, he drew in a deep breath and shook it off.

No more white hats. He wasn't a hero. Far from it.

Cody knew she shouldn't be upset. Why the hell should she care who was plastered against Josh? How many times had she told herself that he was a player? Hah! Too many to count. So why should she be surprised there was a slutty-looking, blond-haired bitch snuggled up to him and looking at him with such adoration it made her want to puke?

She parked in front of the gym and strode inside. Moji wasn't at the front desk. Good, she didn't feel like talking to anyone.

After signing in, she went to the changing area and opened her locker. Thank goodness most of the women were working out on the treadmills and bikes. She didn't think she could stomach their chatter this afternoon.

In less than five minutes, she was out on the floor with the punching bag in her sights. She made a beeline straight for it. Most of the patrons who used the weight area came at night so she had it all to herself. This was exactly what she needed to get rid of her anger.

But she wasn't stupid. She didn't want cramping muscles in the middle of the night jolting her awake. So she began to stretch, warming them up.

As she loosened up, she kept her attention focused on the punching bag. It became her nemesis. By the time she finished her warm-up routine, the bag was looking a lot like Josh.

Her first kick was low, exactly where she'd aimed. An uppercut followed, then a series of jabs. She began to sweat. Her muscles began to tremble.

Why had she let herself start to like him? Why had she enjoyed the touch of his lips so much? She'd known this would happen. What bothered her most was the fact he knew she was ticked off. Damn, damn, damn. She'd seen that knowing look in his eyes. He better not think it was because another woman had rubbed up against him. It didn't bother her one bit.

Yeah, right.

An ache so big that it made her catch her breath welled inside her. She kicked the bag with all she had. Her foot hurt. It didn't matter. She bounced on the balls of her feet, punching and kicking.

She wouldn't let it happen again. She wouldn't care for another human being—ever. She wouldn't.

Then why the hell did she want to curl up in a tight little ball and cry until there were no more tears left? Hell, she never cried. Not anymore.

Damn Josh Pierce to hell and back.

Her legs were like rubber bands. She grabbed her towel and plopped down on the floor, leaning against the wall and crossing her legs in front of her. God, she was spent. There was nothing left inside her.

She wiped her face. Breathe in, breathe out. Relax the body, relax the mind. Even though her body trembled from exhaustion, she forced herself to unwind.

Josh is nothing to you. He does not have the power to inflict pain unless you let him.

Languidness flowed over her. Peace filled her mind and body.

"Feel better now?" Moji asked.

Startled, she jumped, opening her eyes, then relaxed. "Thanks for aging me ten years. And yes, I *did* feel somewhat better."

Damn it, he could've made some kind of noise. Moji probably enjoyed scaring the hell out of her. He loved the dramatic.

Being five foot seven might've made some men want to become invisible to avoid the inevitable jokes. Not Moji. If anything, it made him more flamboyant.

Moji was one of a kind. He lived his life the way he wanted and to hell with what other people thought. He'd opened a gym, not in the least intimidated by the big, brawny men who worked out.

Being gay and middle-aged, it was probably a smorgasbord of sinewy, sweaty flesh to him. Those same men could ridicule him behind his back, but Moji was an expert in martial arts and they damn sure didn't ridicule him to his face.

And he'd taught her a lot. Where Rodney had shown her how to fight dirty, Moji had refined her technique. Her backstreet style of fighting had a little more finesse now. If she were to call anyone friend, it would probably be Moji.

He sat on the floor beside her. "I was returning from the back, but when I heard all the grunting and groaning coming from the weight area, I thought someone was having wild sex and I certainly didn't want to miss *that*. Then I saw it was just you. I was hoping for two male studs going after it."

"Sorry to disappoint you."

"You didn't. My day has been utterly boring. Besides, I wouldn't want to get shut down if someone was having wild sex in my gym."

He fluttered his hand close to his face.

"I was hoping a shipment of silk material I ordered would arrive to break the monotony of my day, but it hasn't. I'm going to have an absolutely divine kimono made. Blue, to match my eyes."

Laughter bubbled out of her. "You going to wear it around here?"

Tapping a finger on his cheek, he wore a thoughtful expression. "Do you think it would help? I mean, there has to be one young stud I can tempt." He tugged at his cheeks and neck. "Maybe I'm too old?"

She studied him. How could anyone tell? He wore his hair short, the color changing from week to week. Today it was a deep purple with blond tips. To keep up the image that his father was Japanese, he expertly lined his eyes to give them a slight tilt.

Cody knew better.

She'd shown up at the gym late one night, wanting to get in a good workout, and found Moji crying in a back room. Normally, she would've quietly left. Why should she feel obligated to hang around? Guilt had quickly followed on the heels of that thought. She did owe him . . . and she was obligated.

At least enough to make sure he'd be okay when she left. Because of the hours she kept, he'd given her a key so she could use the gym anytime, even after hours. And he'd given her pointers when it came to fighting. For that, she'd make sure he wasn't so upset he'd do something stupid.

Awkwardly, she'd patted him on the back. More than a little tipsy, he began to tell her what had happened. Chet, his partner, had left. Just packed up and left. A short note told him it had been fun, but it was over.

She knew the feeling of being left behind. So she'd listened and he'd talked. Apparently, Moji had been holding a lot back for too many years to count, but that night the dam burst.

She substituted his whiskey for tea and he never realized the difference while he spoke about his family—very upper crust, old money. His father dealt in stocks, adding to the family fortune. His mother not only followed trends, she set them.

He told her all about the older brother and sister who were destined to follow their parents' example.

Then he came along. An unwanted pregnancy. Three children was almost an embarrassment. Heaven forbid anyone would actually think they might enjoy sex. He really tried to conform, but there wasn't enough room for him to squeeze into their cramped little box. Especially when they realized he was gay.

At first, he tried to hide it, but he couldn't hide who he was—not forever.

His father offered him a substantial amount of money to disappear. A few weeks later, it was reported in the papers that their son was killed in a remote country. The stateside funeral was a closed casket. The day they buried him, a new person was born—Moji.

"You nearly killed my punching bag. Who made you so mad?" he asked.

She drew her thoughts back to the present. Heat crept up her face when she thought of Josh. "I don't want to talk about it."

"Ah, a man. It was bound to happen sooner or later."

"No, it wasn't bound to happen sooner or later," she bristled. "I'm not in love."

His eyebrows rose. "Oh, even better. You're in *lust*." He rubbed his hands together. "Who's the lucky man? That big, brawny, tanned Richard? Or maybe Alberto? A little smaller, but I bet not where it counts." He wiggled his eyebrows.

Men from the gym? Not likely. They were already in love with themselves, leaving no room for anyone else. And as to their *size*, that was the least of her worries. "You can be really crude, did you know that?"

"Yes, isn't it a delicious vice? I mean, if I'm going to have one it should be something I can enjoy, and I do love being crude."

"You're so full of it." She chuckled. "You should know by now that you can't shock me."

"I know." The high pitch of his voice disappeared, replaced by a softer tone, and she got a glimpse of the boy he used to be. The alter image was gone in a heartbeat and Moji was back. "But now tell me about this man."

She shook her head. "It doesn't matter who he is. We'll never be a couple. He's a player."

He nodded. "And you caught him playing." He leaned closer. "Give me all the juicy details. Moji wants to know more about his favorite bounty hunter, and the bitch who would dare mess with her man."

Oh, lord, why had she even said anything? Moji wouldn't let the subject drop, either. He was like a Pekinese with a bone. Ornery, stubborn, but still kind of cute. And there was nothing malicious about him.

He nudged her arm.

"Okay, okay. I was returning his wallet. We were supposed to meet at the café, but he was with someone." She clamped her lips together to keep from cursing Josh. She didn't want Moji to make more out of it than was there. If she cursed Josh one more time, he just might.

"And why, pray tell, were you in possession of his wallet?"

"He left it at my place last night." As soon as the words left her mouth, she wanted to call them back.

"The plot thickens. Tell, tell!" He clapped his hands. "It's about time you had hot dirty sex. You've been really cranky lately."

"We had sex, big deal."

His eyes widened. "A hunk. I am presuming he's sexy and super good-looking . . ." He waited for her to confirm.

She finally caved. "He looks good."

"Just good?"

Why had she come to the gym? Oh yeah, to get *rid* of her frustration. "Yes, he's damn good-looking. Now are you satisfied?"

"Not quite, but I'm sure I will be eventually." He drew in a deep breath. "Now let me get this straight. A hunk spent the night with you last night. You were returning his wallet and found him with someone else."

She drew up her legs and rested her chin on her knees. "It doesn't matter. It's not like I have exclusive rights to him." She didn't care. Damn it, she didn't. There was only one thing that remotely interested her about Josh and that was his car.

"So, was the bitch pretty?"

Pretty? She sighed. The girl hanging on Josh's arm wouldn't be easy to forget. "She looked like a porcelain doll. The kind of woman a man likes to protect."

Moji nodded. "A bitch."

The kind of woman she could never be. No one had ever accused her of being a simpering female. And she damn sure wasn't about to change. Why the hell was she even sitting here feeling sorry for herself? Josh was nothing to her. It must be the stifling summer heat getting to her—clogging her brain or something.

She came to her feet. "I need to get going."

He stood, his eyes narrowing as he studied her. What the hell was he up to now? With Moji, it was often hard to tell, and sometimes she didn't want to know what he was thinking, but curiosity got the better of her.

"What?" She stared right back at him. "I just worked out. I know I look like crap."

His brow puckered. "I was looking past the sweat. Although it does look kind of sexy on you. All that shiny skin exposed. Are you sure you wouldn't want to try to convert me?"

She laughed, finally relaxing a little. Moji was one of the few who could make her laugh outright. "No, I don't want to convert you."

"You're right. Why fuck up a perfectly good friendship."

"So, you going to tell me why you were looking at me like I had a big wart on my face?"

"I want to do a makeover on you."

She cocked an eyebrow. "A makeover. Like makeup and stuff? Yeah, right. So I can impress the scum I chase almost on a daily basis? I'm sure that would really impress them."

"No, darling, so you can impress the man you're getting hung up on."

"I am not hung up on him. Jeez, what do I have to do to convince you?"

He shrugged. "Whatever, but do me a favor, next time you know he's going to be at the same place as you, call me up. Believe me, when I get through with you, he won't know what hit him."

"When I get to the point where I feel the need to impress a man, I'll stick my head in a toilet."

When Moji grinned knowingly, she turned on her heel and strode toward the changing room. Men were bad enough. Gay men were even worse. She didn't want or need fixing. She wore makeup—when it suited her.

She snorted. And she damn sure wasn't about to try to impress anyone.

But as she showered and changed, she couldn't help feeling a smidgen of regret. Maybe she and Josh would've been good together—at least for a little while. But how long would it have lasted? Not long. Then he would walk out of her life and another relationship would be over.

The blond could have him, as far as Cody was concerned.

But then, Josh had never been hers in the first place.

Yeah, Josh was certainly making her feel things. Like hurt, pain—and loneliness.

Chapter 9

Josh took his coffee to the table and sat down, idly glancing out the window at the traffic backed up in the street three stories down. People were in a hurry to get home from work.

The pizza place across the street was doing a brisk business. People went in and came back out a few minutes later with cardboard boxes. They were tired. Standing in front of a stove apparently held little appeal after working all day. Hell, he knew the feeling.

He picked up the spoon he'd used to stir his coffee and began tapping it on the table. The people on the street faded. He couldn't say how long he sat there lost in thought.

What the hell was wrong with him? He felt as if there was somewhere else he should be. Something else he needed to do. But what?

He blew on his coffee and took a drink, knowing it would keep him up half the night but not really caring. Maybe he'd stake out Larry the Lizard's apartment complex. He was only a petty thief with a small bail, but he'd skipped out.

He scraped his fingers through his hair, then stared down into the dark coffee. He was so damn bored. A memory tugged at him, and his muscles relaxed.

Cody had liked her coffee, too. He smiled, remembering how she'd added cream and sugar. He really had pictured her as taking it straight up black, nothing to weaken the strong taste. She'd surprised him, but then she did that a lot.

Damn it, he was doing it again.

Why couldn't he stop thinking about her? He set his cup down and rubbed his hand across his eyes. A solid week had passed, but not a day went by that he hadn't thought about her, that something didn't remind him of her.

Maybe that was where his restlessness came from.

Maybe that's why he'd screwed up so many times this week. Things he would never do. Stupid things. He'd let a bail jumper slip right through his fingers and into Turbo's eager hands. Damn, Turbo had to have loved that.

The coffee suddenly tasted bitter. Man, he had to pull himself out of this funk and quit thinking about Cody before she really screwed up his head.

Leaning forward, he grabbed the remote and turned on the TV. The evening news. That should lighten his mood, he thought sarcastically. Car wrecks, shootings, bombings. Yeah, sure, much less depressing.

He listened for a few minutes and was about to switch it off when they flashed a picture across the screen right before the station broke for a commercial: a man in his late forties, brown hair graying at the temples. He had the tanned, leathery face of someone who was in the sun a lot.

The man's face had been splashed across the screen for the last couple of weeks. Hell, how could anyone have missed seeing Adam Sinclair? He had his finger in a lot of pots all over the country, mainly in construction.

Then he'd screwed up. He knocked his partner off. At least he was the prime suspect, and apparently they had enough evidence that they'd arrested and arraigned him. Sinclair wasn't as invincible as he thought.

When the news came back on, he turned the volume up just as the newscaster began to talk.

"Adam Sinclair made his mark in the construction world. The kind of man everyone cheered. The working man's man.

Adam Sinclair was what America is famous for—a country where you can go from rags to riches."

The newsman cocked an eyebrow, pausing for effect. Every listener, unless they were really dumb, knew he was about to drop a bomb.

"He's added another title to his resume. That of bail jumper. The forty-nine-year-old wealthy businessman was scheduled to appear in court late yesterday afternoon on murder charges, but failed to appear."

Josh jumped to his feet, not bothering to listen to the rest. He'd heard all he needed to hear. *Jumped bail.* Dollar figures flashed before his eyes. This had to be the bounty of a lifetime or damned close. This was the case he'd been looking for.

He grabbed a bag of cinnamon drops out of the cabinet and ripped them open. What he wouldn't give for a long draw off a cigarette right now. Instead, he popped the candy into his mouth.

"You shouldn't spend your money on me. I don't need this much food," Pearl said.

If her mother ate, she might not be tempted to turn to the bottle. Cody bit her tongue. Not this time. "I have money. I like spending some of it occasionally."

"You should put it in the bank."

Just take the food. Let me do this, please. Can't you see it's my way of apologizing for the last time?

She set the bags of food on the counter, but before she turned around, Pearl squeezed her arm. Cody closed her eyes. Ah, God, as much as she hated to admit it, she craved her mother's touch.

Pearl moved her hand away, taking the little bit of warmth with her. "Well, thanks. I appreciate it."

Drawing in a shaky breath, Cody turned. Her mother looked away, wringing her hands. Was it that hard to touch her only child?

The truth was staggering as it dawned in on her. Why hadn't she realized it before now?

She looked like her father.

But if Pearl had loved him, then why would she find it so hard to love a daughter who looked like him? Unless there'd been trouble in paradise. She only guessed.

She opened her mouth to ask what the truth really was, but Pearl turned and went to the small living room. "Why don't you dish us up some of that ice cream and we'll catch the news."

Damn it, why wouldn't she talk to her? Pearl was the only one with answers. All Cody's searching had led to dead ends and trails that had turned cold long ago.

It was obvious Pearl didn't want to get too chummy. Maybe she should be thankful for what her mother was willing to give and be done with it, but Cody didn't want to be just thankful.

Coward.

She almost laughed but knew the voice inside her head was right. Her relationship with her mother was tenuous at best. Cody was terrified of breaking the fragile bond they shared. What if her mother stopped loving her altogether? She sucked in a deep breath. There, she'd finally admitted it to herself. A little love was better than none at all.

Just enjoy the moment, she told herself as she dished up a couple of bowls of chocolate fudge ice cream and carried them to the living room, giving one to her mother before sitting on the sofa. Her mother sat in the easy chair.

So she wouldn't have to sit next to her daughter?

Mentally, she shook her head. Now she was being maudlin. Her mother had always liked the easy chair best.

The news was on. She took a bite of ice cream and let her thoughts wander. Trouble was, they wandered straight to Josh. Jeez, out of the pot and right into the fire. Still, she couldn't help wondering if he was with the blond right now. Were they about to go out for dinner? Her hand trembled. Or were they staying in?

Don't go there. Don't feel.

She'd learned to cut her emotions off when she was just a kid. Then Rodney had shown up. Lord, he'd taken the place of the father she never knew. He made her feel again.

And look what it had gotten her.

He'd left. The world continued on as if nothing had happened. No one cared that she'd been hurt. So she sucked it up, moved forward, but she swore nothing and no one would hurt her like that again.

But they had. At least, the first couple of guys she'd dated had, but she wasn't in love with them so she'd gotten over them quick enough and learned to guard her heart—until Josh came along.

She took another bite of ice cream without really tasting it and could almost feel the protective shield sliding into place. Like an elevator door to her heart, it silently slid shut. You could only open it with the right key and she'd make certain she held tight to it this time.

Pearl broke into her thoughts. "There's that man who killed his partner."

"Hmm?" She glanced up. Adam Sinclair. She'd caught some of the story over the past few weeks. "Turn it up."

Pearl increased the volume.

". . . missed his court date. Along with a bounty on his head, the family of the man Adam Sinclair has been accused of killing is offering a reward for the capture . . ."

Excitement skittered down her spine. This was who she was, what she was about. It might not be much, but it was all hers and no one could take that away.

"I've got to go." Cody stood, moving toward the kitchen and depositing her bowl in the sink.

Pearl followed. "You're not going after that man, are you? I mean, they think he murdered his partner."

Cody paused. "It's what I do." She waited for her mother to say something else. What, she wasn't quite sure. Maybe beg her not to go? For a split second, she held her breath.

"You'll be careful?"

She exhaled. "Yeah, I'll be careful."

Pearl watched Cody go to the door, she watched her daughter open it, and she watched her leave. All the time she silently screamed at her not to go.

She slumped into one of the kitchen chairs. "I love you. I love you so much it hurts," she whispered.

But Cody was gone. She couldn't hear the words.

"Why can't I just tell her?" She spoke to the empty room. But what if Cody didn't want to hear them? If she pushed the issue would her daughter stop coming around?

Damn, she needed a drink. No, that was the last thing she needed. Her drinking was what had caused the rift between them, the one that got wider every year.

She looked out the window, saw Cody leave the apartment building and get on her motorcycle.

Her baby. No, that wasn't right. Cody hadn't been her baby in a very long time. Not since James left.

"James." She spoke his name for the first time in years. It sounded strange to her ears.

When he left, she'd begun to drink. It took away her pain and fear of being alone. As long as she didn't venture too far away from her apartment, she was safe in the little world she'd created, never realizing it had become a prison.

Her eyes narrowed. "I hope the bastard rots in hell when he dies."

A shiver swept over her as if talking aloud would unveil the secret she'd carried for so long. No. She shook her head and quickly came to her feet. "Cody will never find out her father lives across town. I won't let him destroy her like he nearly did me. Nope, I won't let that happen." She shuffled toward the bedroom, undressed, and put on her pajamas. She was still trembling when she pulled the covers close around her. Cody couldn't find out about him. She couldn't.

Turbo Manning turned off the TV, a wide smile on his face. Son-of-a-bitch. The bastard jumped bail. He tossed the remote on the couch and rubbed his hands together. This was the brass ring. The bounty of all bounties. Everyone would be after Adam Sinclair. The competition would be unbelievable.

He laughed. God, he loved it. This would bring him the notoriety he craved. He'd be the best of the best.

"Hey, baby." Candy snuggled up close to him, her voluptuous body rubbing against his. "I thought you wanted to fuck, not watch the boob tube. Ain't nothin' on but the news anyway."

"Back off. I'm trying to think."

She sat down, slowly crossing her legs in a fair imitation of Sharon Stone, and Candy wasn't wearing any panties. His dick went hard in less time than it took to blink. Man, she was one hot lady. Not as young as he'd like, but sometimes experience could make up for a few years wear and tear.

Even though the television was off, it drew his attention. There wasn't a whole hell of a lot he could do until morning. He looked once more at Candy. She leaned forward, her breasts practically spilling from her blouse. God, she had a pair of the sweetest tits he'd ever seen on a woman.

When she ran her tongue across her lips, he knew he wouldn't be hunting anyone tonight.

He undid his pants as he walked toward her, reaching inside and pulling his dick out. He groaned when she took him into her mouth. Damn, she was so fucking good at giving head. He looked down, watching her mouth eagerly move over him, licking, kissing, and sucking him back inside.

She looked up and smiled, and for just a second he imagined it was Cody's face looking up at him. He frowned. "Suck it, bitch, suck it."

Someday he'd have the real thing and wouldn't have to settle for a substitute. Once she had a taste of him, nothing else would be good enough for her.

That is, once she realized he was the best.

Chapter 10

Cody stepped out of the powder blue Pontiac she rarely used and walked to the door carrying a box of what she hoped appeared to be business documents.

You are a business associate of the deceased who did in-home secretarial work, she kept repeating as she got into character. She could do this even though she was a two-finger typist at best and her bills were usually shoved into a drawer until the very last day. She loathed paperwork of any kind.

She could only hope the plain tweed skirt and conservative jacket would be convincing. For added measure, she'd put on a pair of heavy, black-rimmed, clear-lens glasses.

Shifting the box and her purse to her hip, she rang the doorbell. A few seconds later, she heard someone approaching. Should she start crying? No, that might be pouring it on a little thick. A sad look should do it.

The door opened. "Yes?"

Mid-fifties, white shirt, and dark brown slacks. Mark Danford, the cousin to Adam Sinclair's now deceased partner, looked quite unassuming. In fact, all he needed was a pen protector in his pocket to pull his nerdy look together.

She'd chosen the perfect disguise—from one nerd to another.

"I'm so sorry to intrude during your time of grief, but I thought you might need these papers. They're not really important, but Mr. Gray paid me in advance so I wanted to return them.

He gave her an assessing look as he took the box.

Oh, no, this wasn't working out like she'd planned. Without a doubt, she knew he was about to dismiss her. Maybe what she'd chosen wasn't right. Nerds apparently weren't attracted to nerds.

"Well, thank you for returning them. Not everyone is quite this honest. I'm sure my cousin appreciated your ethics." He spoke in a nasal pitch that wouldn't take long to become irritating, and started to shut the door.

"He was such a good man." She sniffed—loudly. "Oh my, I do believe I feel a little faint. Could I trouble you for a glass of water?"

She removed her glasses and lightly patted her face.

It wasn't working. He looked at her as if she'd grown another eyeball. Time to introduce him to her femme fatale. She really hated playing this role. She'd rather eat nails than be a simpering female, but if that's what it took, then she'd do it.

"Suddenly, I just feel incredibly warm." She slipped off her jacket and undid the top two buttons of her blouse. Always smart to be prepared. The white blouse was simple, but sexy. It showed the lacy cups of her bra in great detail.

Come on, man, do I have to strip or what? Not that she would ever go that far.

Oh, hell, now he was blushing.

As if he suddenly remembered she felt faint, he opened the door wider. "Yes, of course, come inside."

Once she stepped into the foyer, he set the box on a side table and closed the door.

Her gaze quickly scanned the entrance hall. She stopped herself just short of whistling. Nice digs. Nothing fancy, seeing as the deceased cousin was raking in a sizable income from all accounts, but damned decent.

"The study is in there." He pointed to a room just off the

entrance. "Please, have a seat and I'll get you something cool to drink."

For a second, she'd forgotten about feeling faint. "Oh, thank you ever so much." She fluttered her hands close to the vee of her blouse. He didn't disappoint her when his gaze followed.

He was human. For a while, she'd begun to wonder.

"Yes, okay, I'll be right back." He licked his lips before turning away and hurrying out of the room.

A piece of cake. She'd have all the information she needed in less than five minutes.

She strolled into the study, sitting in the chair across from the desk, and hurriedly arranged herself into the perfect, sexy pose.

No, this wouldn't do. Her skirt demurely covered her knees. She'd already figured this one out. He might not be the type to touch, but he didn't mind looking.

She wiggled her bottom into a different position and inched up the material of her skirt until a little bit of thigh showed, then crossed her legs. There, much better.

"Why don't you just take it off? I bet he'd tell you anything you want to know then," Josh said from behind her.

Her purse clunked to the floor as she jumped to her feet, whirling around to face him.

It *was* him! Standing by the window as pretty as you please and looking as sexy as ever. He stepped out of the shadows and into the light.

"What are you doing here?" she hissed, her heart still pounding inside her chest. Her racing pulse didn't stop her gaze from traveling over him. He wore jeans and a light blue shirt but had dressed the look up a notch with a navy blazer. Looking at him didn't help to slow her pulse.

Damn it, she should have been furious now more than ever, not lusting after him. What was he doing spying on her? "Why are you here?" she repeated.

He straightened and sauntered forward. "I would imagine I'm doing the same as you—going after the big fish that got away."

She should've known. Of course, he wouldn't let a chance like this slip away. What bounty hunter would? Most recovery agents had a competitive streak a mile wide. Always trying to top each other. This case would draw them from far and wide.

She just didn't want to do it at the same time as Josh. Especially since he'd had that blond bimbo practically slobbering all over him.

"Well, go away," she whispered as she sat in the chair once again and tried to pull herself together.

"Why?"

Infuriating man.

"Because I don't want you here." She tugged her skirt back in place when his gaze slid lower—and lingered. A hot flush settled over her skin.

"You didn't return my calls."

"How observant." Eventually, she'd even unplugged her answering machine. His recorded voice on her machine had sensuously stalked her every time he'd called. He probably knew exactly what he was doing to her mind—and body.

Josh was a player—experienced in how to take a woman to the edge of reason. She quickly swallowed past the lump in her throat and squared her shoulders.

"If you're still angry about the other day when you returned my wallet, then . . ."

"Don't flatter yourself," she snorted. The last thing she wanted was pity. "I gave you a place to stay because you saved my ass when Leonard's friend pulled a gun on me, then attempted to again when that jerk from the bar pulled me into his lap. I owed you. I returned your wallet. Don't make any more out of it because it just isn't there."

"And the making love?"

She arched an eyebrow. "You're not the first man I've had

sex with. We had a little fun and released some pent-up emotions. There was nothing more to it than that."

He leaned against the desk. Much too close for comfort.
The other woman was temporarily forgotten as hot and cold
tingles ran up and down her arms. She took a deep, cleansing
breath and inhaled the musky scent of his aftershave and
something else—cinnamon. She ached to stand, to close the
distance between them just so she could feel his lips against
hers.

"She was a girl I took to dinner, then she invited me up to
her apartment. I was exhausted, but she said she was afraid
to go in alone. There'd been burglaries in the area. Nothing
happened. I ended up falling asleep on her sofa."

Yeah, right. "Like you fell asleep on mine? Then ended up
in my bed."

"No, I left the next morning before she woke up. If you're
wondering why, it's because she never tempted me like you
do. There's something about you." His gaze captured hers. "I
can't get my fill of you. Tell me you didn't enjoy making love,
too."

For a brief moment, she pictured them lying in bed naked,
legs and arms entwined. She quickly reined in her thoughts
before they could go any further.

"Don't hold your breath because there won't be a next
time."

"Are you sure?"

"Positive." She squared her shoulders. "Now go away."

He looked up. "Too late."

"I'm terribly sorry. I'd forgotten Mr. Pierce was also in the
study." Mark Danford looked between them. "Do you know
Mr. Pierce? He's one of my cousin's foremen."

One of Josh's eyebrows arched, daring her to blow his
cover. Wouldn't that burst his bubble? But that would make
her fair game, and she had no doubt he'd return the favor.

"I don't believe we've met." She turned back to Mark, dismissing Josh, and pasted a fake smile on her face. She didn't

want to talk about Josh. She was here to get any and all information that might lead her to Adam Sinclair.

Mark sat behind the desk, leaning back in his chair. "It warms my heart that there's been such an outpouring of love toward my cousin. Why, earlier this morning another foreman dropped by." He tapped his chin. "Unusual name. Something to do with . . ." His eyes brightened. "Yes, Turbo. Odd name. I assume it's a nickname. Nice gentleman, though."

Cody's gaze collided with Josh's. She could see the same wheels turning inside his head that were turning inside hers. Turbo had beaten them to the punch. Damn, this wasn't good.

What information had he gleaned? Was he already hot on the trail while they still sniffed around for clues?

"Turbo, yes, I know him," Josh said.

The cousin nodded. "He was very upset over this whole situation. Quite frankly, I had to calm him down before he raced off to Adam's sister's house to see if he was hiding out there." He glanced up. "She's always been such a recluse. His half sister, you know. Not many people are aware she even exists."

"His sister?" they asked in unison.

"I guess I shouldn't say anything. It's certainly not her fault her brother killed my cousin." Mark shook his head. "Allegedly killed. I'm really trying to be fair about the whole thing, but I guess I'm still in a state of shock." He picked up a pencil, running his finger over the smooth surface.

"You poor dear. Were the two of you close?"

And where does the sister live? Cody had to bite her tongue. Rule number one, let them talk and ninety percent of the time, you'll get more information.

"Close? Not really. We spoke on the phone a few times a year. Met for lunch about as often. He was always busy with his construction business." His shoulders slumped and he pushed the pencil away from him. "Now mine, I suppose. I have no idea what to do with it." He looked between them. "I'm a chemist, not a businessman."

"Maybe Adam's sister can be of some help?" Josh asked.

Very good. She cast a quick look in his direction and almost bought the concern on his face. Sure, she was still pissed, but this was business and she could still admire his tactics at obtaining information.

"His sister," Mark scoffed. "I'm sure she'll let me do the work while she continues to live on the allowance her brother gives her. Adam still owns half. No, she's quite content to live her days sequestered behind the walls of her home."

"Surely she has neighbors who visit?"

Mark looked up as if he'd been lost in thought. "Visitors? No, she dislikes people. My cousin told me once she abhors socializing of any kind." He shrugged. "And like I told Mr. Manning, I need her signature on some papers by the end of the week."

He picked up a stack of papers before tossing them back on his desk, then looked up as if realizing they were still in the room.

"Here I am going on about my problems when my cousin has only been in the ground a short time. It's just that I feel so lost in his world. Mine was very simple and uncomplicated until this all took place." He ran a hand through his thinning hair, tears welling in his eyes.

"We should probably go," Josh told him.

Her gaze swiveled in his direction. Go? Was he crazy? She didn't have any more to go on than she had when she got here. It would be stupid to leave now, but he gave her little choice as he took her elbow and pretended to help her to her feet.

She'd kill him, absolutely kill him.

Gritting her teeth, she walked beside Josh. As if she had a choice! His hand on her elbow gave her no chance to escape. Killing him would be too quick. Torture, now that was something that would keep her entertained for hours.

She could see it now. Josh, tied to a chair. No! Dangling from a rafter, his wrists tied with a rope. Boy, would she make him sorry he'd ever messed with her. She'd strip his clothes off and . . . She'd strip his clothes off . . .

Clear your mind! His torture, not hers.

As soon as the door closed behind them and they were beside her car, she jerked away from him. Her pent-up frustration and anger exploded.

"What the hell were you doing? I could've gotten a lot more information."

"I have all we need."

"What exactly do you mean by *we?*" She eyed him with wariness.

"Come in as my partner and I'll tell you."

She opened her mouth then snapped it closed. What the hell did he mean by *partner?* The last thing she wanted to do was partner up with him in any way, form, or fashion.

But damn it, she couldn't stop the shiver of excitement that tickled her spine.

Right on excitement's heels was a good dose of skepticism. If he thought he could put something over on her then he'd better think again. Gullible, she wasn't.

Her eyes narrowed. "What exactly are you getting at?"

"I'll explain everything over lunch."

She eyed him with more than a little trepidation. Was this another scheme just to get her to go out with him?

Yeah, right, like he would want her *that* much. Talk about an overblown ego. "Why not just explain right here?"

"Because I'm hungry," he tossed over his shoulder as he headed around the side of the house where he'd apparently parked.

Drat, she should've scouted the area out a bit more. She'd have seen his car and he wouldn't have surprised her. She was losing her touch. She knew Adam wouldn't be here, though. Mark had posted a sizable reward for Adam's capture.

She hadn't expected to run into Josh, either.

And the sad truth? She was just a little curious about what he had to say.

It would take time to figure out what she needed to do next anyway. Right now, she had nothing to go on. Only dead ends. Josh certainly couldn't tell her anything that would convince her to go into a partnership with him. But damn it, she'd missed being in his company.

Sick, that's what she was, and without a clue where they were going to meet.

"Where?" she called out.

He stopped, and when he looked over his shoulder, he wore a smug expression. Ass. She wanted to wipe the knowing look right off his face.

"I feel like a little heat. You game for Mexican food?" Before she had the chance to answer, he called out the address of a Mexican restaurant in the area.

As if he'd given her a choice. Mexican food. Great, not only would she have to put up with Josh, but with heartburn, too.

Not waiting for him to take the lead, she drove to the restaurant. If he'd thought she would follow him, then he'd better think again.

She was the one with the smug expression on her face when she pulled into the parking lot. *Choke on my dust,* she smirked. He was nowhere in sight. Beating him to the restaurant was a small victory, but a victory nonetheless.

But when she rounded the corner, he was leaning against a post.

"How . . . ?"

"Shortcut." He straightened and opened the door. "After you," he said, and motioned for her to go first.

He'd probably broken every speed record to get here. Not that she cared that much. She stuck her nose in the air.

"Lord, you smell good," he said as she sailed past. "Have I ever told you that?"

She couldn't stop her smile from forming, but was careful not to let him see it. Instead, she said, "Your charm won't work on me, Josh, so give it up."

He chuckled.

Once they were seated and the waitress had taken their order, Cody knew it was time for him to fess up with this grand scheme of his. She only wondered what the hell she had to do with it.

"So, what'd you think of the cousin?" he asked.

"That's it? You only wanted to know what I thought of the cousin?"

"I guess I was curious, but no, that wasn't the only thing I wanted to discuss."

Whatever. She'd humor him for the moment, but he'd better get to the point.

She shrugged. "Kind of nerdy. I didn't think he seemed all that upset over his cousin's murder. I would imagine the money and running a financially stable company would offset his grief, no matter how much he said he was overwhelmed by the responsibility."

"My thoughts exactly."

She leaned against the back of the booth. "Okay, we both thought he was a strange little man. What's that got to do with anything?"

He started to speak but the waitress brought their drinks, along with chips and hot sauce. He waited until she'd left before he said anything.

"I have a proposal to make."

"Oh, now you want to marry me? Sorry, but that won't sweep me off my feet, either."

"Funny. No, I don't want to marry you."

She slapped a hand to her chest. "I'm heartbroken."

Now she'd made him frown. Not that she cared, except he looked pretty darn cute when he frowned. What she wouldn't do to kiss away the tiny lines around his mouth. To smooth away the wrinkles on his forehead.

"If you keep looking at me like that I might not be able to restrain myself from kissing you."

She sat up straight. "I'm not looking at you any differently," she lied, and warned herself to be more careful.

"Yes, you were. We both know there's a sexual attraction. Why deny it? But that's not what I wanted to talk about."

"Then would you mind getting to the point?"

"I think we should become partners."

She cocked an eyebrow. "I thought we'd already had that discussion."

"No, not in that way. I mean combine forces to capture Adam Sinclair."

She laughed.

He didn't.

"You're serious?"

"Yeah, I'm serious."

Partners? With Josh. They'd be spending most of their time together.

Partners?

She folded her napkin, then refolded it.

"So, what do you think?"

Think? Hell, she couldn't think. She opened her mouth but no words came out. Not only couldn't she think, but she couldn't talk, either.

"Say something. I know it sounds crazy, but just listen to me for a minute. As a team, we'd have twice the advantage as other recovery agents. Together we could do it. We could bring Adam in."

"Partners?"

"Yeah." He grinned.

"You and me together?" She shook her head. "It would never work." But he'd made a good point. Twice the resources. They were both damn good bounty hunters.

"Think about it while we eat. You don't have to give me an answer until we finish."

As if she'd ever hook up with him. The man was crazy. She worked alone and she wasn't about to join forces with him or anyone else.

But a little voice inside her head began to whisper.

The capture of Adam Sinclair would be all over the

news. Everyone would see it. How better to reinforce the fact you're doing exactly what you're supposed to be doing?

Respect? Was that what she wanted? Or was it only respect from one person that she craved?

Chapter 11

Josh knew the minute Cody resigned herself to the inevitable. She'd moved a half-eaten enchilada around on her plate for the last ten minutes until, finally, she laid her fork across her plate and looked up.

"Okay, but I have a few things I want to go over with you."

He'd known she would agree. It was the smart thing to do, and she wasn't stupid. He was curious to know what her rules were going to be, and he was sure "going over a few things" meant there would be rules. Every woman he'd ever been in any kind of relationship with had rules. He doubted he was going to like Cody's any more than he had the others.

"Rules?"

She nodded.

"Okay, let's hear them," he said to her as he reached into his pocket for a cinnamon. He offered her one, but she only shook her head.

"Number one: You're not in charge."

"You want to be in charge?" he asked.

His gaze swept over her. She'd fight and argue with him all the way. His blood pounded through his veins at the thought. He could almost feel it coursing through his body, rivers of liquid heat. He hadn't felt like this in a very long time. Not since the night he'd danced with Cody, then tasted what she had to offer.

Now it was as if he couldn't get her out of his head. Spending more time with her should cure him—or kill him, whichever came first.

Once more, he looked at her, but closer this time. She'd pulled her dark hair away from her face. He supposed she'd been trying for a more severe look. She'd failed. Tendrils had escaped to curl around her face, softly caressing her cheeks. He wanted her more than ever.

Teaming up with her had been a crazy idea, but he doubted he'd ever be able to convince himself of that. When all was said and done, he wanted to be around her. Once he discovered she was like every other female, he'd be able to let go.

"Neither of us will be in charge," she told him, drawing his thoughts back to the present.

He could live with that. He wasn't into the "man is greater because he's stronger" mentality. Especially when he'd been witness on more than one occasion to Cody kicking some serious ass.

He straightened. "What else?"

"Number two." She narrowed her eyes. "No sexual advances."

He kept his expression bland. "I don't mind if you cop a feel every so often."

From the frown on her face, he didn't think she appreciated his stab at humor.

"You'll keep your hands to yourself. Understood? When I'm on the job it's all work and no play."

She was damned sexy when she talked business. Why couldn't she see what was going on between them? The attraction was palpable, and he was tired of fighting it, even if she wasn't.

Sure, there'd been other women. More than he cared to count. The urge to be with someone else had never been this strong, though. But then, Cody was the exception to a lot of rules.

The newness would wear off, he had no doubt. She'd be just like all the rest. A couple of weeks and they'd grow tired of each other, then they'd part company without a backward glance, but with one difference. They would walk away feeling sated, ready to move forward, and he would be over this damn infatuation with her.

Then maybe he could get on with his life.

"Agreed?" Her eyes narrowed.

"Sure, I promise not to do anything you don't want me to."

Why not agree? As far as he was concerned, rules were made to be broken. He knew Cody had broken more than her fair share. Damn, they were going to be great together while the relationship lasted.

"You're staring at me."

He loved when she got riled. Her eyes sparkled with an inner fire. "I was thinking. Sorry if you thought I was being rude," he lied.

Cody narrowed her gaze on him. He could've been thinking—or not. Damn, the man turned her inside out and upside down.

She wearily ran her hand through her hair. Sleep hadn't come easy the last few nights.

If she were honest, she'd admit the truth. When Josh had stayed the night in her apartment, their relationship had changed. Now this. She was a fool to go into a partnership with him. He would use her, then throw her away.

When she looked his way, he seemed preoccupied with his iced tea. Maybe she was reading too much into the situation.

"Any more rules?" he asked, breaking into her thoughts.

"No, but that doesn't mean I won't think of some. I'll leave my options open."

"Okay, then we only have one other thing to decide. Your place or mine?"

If he thought this would give him an open invitation into her bed, then he was going to be sorely disappointed. And his expression of innocence didn't fool her for one second. She wasn't born yesterday.

"To go over plans," he continued.

So maybe she *might* have jumped to conclusions.

But his words brought with them a whole new set of problems. She hadn't thought about that part of it. At least, not really thought about it. She didn't like the idea of being on his turf, but knowing where he lived might help her in the future in case she ever had to haul his ass home again.

"Let's work from your place." She slid from the booth and stood. "I'll follow you. That is, if you don't decide to take a shortcut."

"I've never lost a woman who was following me back to my place."

She just bet he hadn't.

The drive to his apartment was short. In fact, he only lived a few blocks from her. Odd that they hadn't run into each other more often.

They parked in the parking garage and took the elevator up to the third floor. Her palms began to sweat as they neared his door. She wiped them on her skirt when he wasn't looking. Her brain screamed that this was a really stupid idea, but her feet hadn't once stopped their forward movement.

But they did hesitate after he opened the door and motioned for her to go in first.

"Not scared, are you?" His glance skimmed over her in a way that made her skin turn from cold to hot.

"Don't be ridiculous." Still, she had to force her feet to move. When the door closed behind her, she wanted to turn around and run as far and as fast as she could. Anywhere that would take her away from Josh.

Hell, it wasn't even Josh who worried her. It was her reaction to his charm, his delicious muscles, the raw sexuality that oozed from him.

She drew in a shaky breath.

On the other hand, she wanted to be the bounty hunter who captured Adam, even if she had to share the money and glory with Josh. She straightened her spine. She would just have to contain her desires, and certainly not let him see how he affected her senses.

One rule Rodney had taught her: Stay strong and don't let the enemy see your weakness, whether facing something as simple as a job interview or capturing a skip. Always show confidence, he'd told her.

And she'd show confidence this time, too.

She sauntered into the living room of his apartment. It looked like most apartments. There was only one difference. A tornado had struck his.

"You don't believe in cleaning? Against your religion?" It wasn't so much dirty as it was littered. Magazines, books— stacks and stacks of them.

He had a couple of pictures framed and sitting on his end tables. An older couple in one. They looked comfortable with each other. His parents? There was a resemblance.

Her gaze moved to the other picture. The younger couple was familiar.

"Friends?" She turned and looked at him. "I mean, you have their picture in your wallet so they must be close to you."

"You snooped?"

Great, this was a good way to start their partnership. *Brazen it out,* she told herself.

"It's my job to learn everything I can about people." She shrugged. "You would've done the same."

"You're right. So maybe you'll be forewarned not to leave your purse out where I can look through it."

"I don't carry pictures."

"No friends?" He smiled.

"No." She didn't bother to enlighten him about her relation-ships. People found out one thing, then they began prying for more information. It was as if they wanted to dissect her and see what made her different from everyone else.

Hell, they should spend some time examining their own lives and stay the hell out of hers. She was perfectly content to go through life without friends. A lot less to deal with.

But she had Moji.

"I have one friend, sort of," she corrected, then wondered why she felt the need to be honest with Josh.

For a moment, she thought he was going to ask questions so she quickly scanned the coffee table for something else to talk about.

Her gaze skidded to a halt. "*Playboy?*"

His face turned a rosy hue.

Interesting.

"You don't strike me as the type who would go for the girlie magazines." When he opened his mouth, she quickly put up her hand. "Don't tell me, you only read the articles."

"It's an autographed copy. I dated Miss April."

Miss April. Okay. Before she could say another word, he started to pull off his jacket. Her eyes widened. If he thought . . .

He paused. "Mind if I get comfortable?"

"As long as you don't strip to your skivvies—and I don't really care if you dated the whole calendar." She didn't care. He could date every bunny and populate the world with little bunnies and it wouldn't bother her in the least.

He grinned as he removed his coat.

Josh really had an ego problem. She *would not* become one of his has-beens. Her feet had traveled that road one too many times.

When he tossed his belt onto the back of a chair, she saw that he'd gone to Mark Danford's house prepared. He wore a belt, and on his belt he'd hooked a telescoping baton, mace, and a handgun.

"Nothing like going equipped," she commented.

"Always." His gaze skimmed over her. "I guess you weren't expecting trouble?"

Did he question that she might not have been ready for anything? If he did, he'd better think again. She raised her skirt; strapped high on her thigh was a nickel-plated 9mm. She unfastened the leather and tossed it to the sofa. "You're right, that feels better." That would show him.

When she looked up, Josh was staring, but not at her face.

"Do you have a problem?"

"No, but you have the sexiest legs I've ever seen on a woman."

Something inside her stomach fluttered. Raising her skirt up to the middle of her thigh hadn't been her most brilliant idea, but she did feel more comfortable without the leather holster strapped to her leg and she had proved she'd been just as prepared as Josh.

Hell, he should know she wasn't the most ladylike person he'd ever met. She'd never be the kind of woman he dated. She was not the type to stare adoringly at anyone. That thought brought a bitter taste to her mouth.

Before she could even open her mouth to tell him that he was barking up the wrong tree if he thought to flatter her, he did an abrupt about-face and went to the other room.

"Back in a minute," he called over his shoulder.

All alone. Well, at least in the living room. Now she could breathe easier. There was something about being alone with Josh that made the room seem like it was closing in around her, not suffocating exactly, but too damn close.

She eyed the magazine. Miss April. Hmm . . . She *had* warned him that she was a habitual snooper.

Casually, she flipped it open to the middle. Miss April unfolded in all her naked glory right before her eyes. Josh had told the truth—it was autographed.

To, Josh and a night spent under the stars, flowing wine, and the best damn orgasm I've ever had!

From experience, she knew Miss April wasn't lying. Kind of slutty-looking, if you asked her. And who would want bazoombas that big? Josh was lucky the cover girl hadn't rolled over and smothered him. Sitting up would probably prove to be hazardous. Besides, it was probably the wine that made her all-night orgy seem so spectacular.

You didn't have any wine, a naughty voice chided, *and sex with Josh had been pretty darn spectacular, too.*

No, she didn't even want to go there. This was a purely business association.

She quickly returned the magazine back to its exalted position on top of the others when she heard a door closing. All she needed was Josh to catch her snooping. As if she really cared what the hell Miss April looked like. The bitch could have three eyes for all she cared.

Josh returned to the living room a few minutes later with an easel, a black marker, and a dry-erase board.

She didn't move, only stared, Miss April completely forgotten. Suddenly, she felt as if it were the first day of school and she didn't know diddly squat about what was to take place. Rather than slip into her seat and try to become invisible, she raised her chin. "I thought we were going to try to catch Adam Sinclair."

"We are." He looked at his supplies, then back at her. "I think better when I'm writing stuff down. I thought we could combine our notes and see what we come up with."

Made sense. Damn, she almost hated that it did.

She had to remember Josh was her partner, not her enemy.

For the next hour, Josh jotted all of their ideas down. The places they knew Adam had lived. They'd already checked those and come up empty. The properties had been sold or were rented out. What information they had wasn't as much as Cody had hoped.

"I think we should watch the half sister's place, see if anyone shows up."

"And I suppose you know where she lives." She stood,

pacing the small confines of the room. The small space was beginning to close in on her. She needed to be outside in the fresh air, even if the thermometer had been steadily climbing all afternoon.

"Her address was on the papers Danford needed signed. Right now, she's all we have to go on."

That's why he hadn't minded leaving. Josh had the information he needed, and if she hadn't decided to go partners with him, he'd probably have left her to flounder on her own. But she had partnered with him, so maybe it was a moot point.

She went to the window and looked at the street below. The pizza place had a steady flow of customers. Her gaze moved to a young couple as they leisurely strolled hand in hand down the street. She was obviously pregnant and they were obviously in love.

Love, a wasted emotion.

"So, where are we off to?"

"Let's just say you might want to pack an overnight bag."

She faced him once again. The look in his eyes should've warned her that she might not like where they were headed.

She crossed her arms in front of her. "Did I mention I don't like games?"

"How do you feel about margaritas?"

A cold, clammy feeling washed over her. "Please, tell me that she doesn't live in Mexico? You and I both know what the Mexican government thinks about bounty hunters crossing into their country uninvited. They're still pissed about that CIA job."

He didn't look like he was joking so she continued.

"I'd rather not share a cell with the other recovery agents who thought they could cross over, grab a fugitive, then scurry back."

"Nope, not quite Mexico. Just damn close."

For a minute he'd worried her. She really didn't want to screw around with a foreign government.

She grabbed her gun, but rather than hiking up her skirt, she dropped it into her purse.

When she looked his way again, she thought she noted a look of disappointment. Partners, yeah, right. All he wanted from her was sex, the kind that got really nasty.

Naked sweaty bodies straining toward climax. Hands caressing, hers sliding over his body, touching . . . tasting.

Her belly tightened as a deep ache grew inside her. Josh was the quintessential bad boy. A man who could bring a woman to her knees with just one look from those sexy blue eyes. She would fight this attraction . . .

Who was she trying to fool? Hell, she wanted the same thing. Maybe they were only fooling each other. Sex between them had been hot enough to set the bed on fire. She only had to decide what was more important: catching a fugitive or making love.

"I'll just throw some stuff in a bag and I'll be ready to go," he said.

She watched him leave. Why deny it? She wanted Josh.

He came back a few minutes later with a small duffel bag. "Ready?"

She nodded, not really trusting herself to speak. He locked his apartment and they left. When he climbed into his junker, she had to admit she was a little disappointed. For a moment, she'd hoped he'd take the Mustang.

The Chevy looked like she was on her last legs. "Will she make it?"

"Yeah. I want to run her on the open road. Blow some of the soot out of her. She's been stuck in the city too long. I'll follow you to your apartment."

She only nodded and walked to her car. It was a damn shame she wouldn't be riding in the Mustang.

True to his word, Josh followed her right up to her apartment, then inside. The hairs on the back of her neck tickled with awareness.

"I'll grab some things and be right out." She hoped he didn't notice the tremble in her voice.

Once inside her room, she closed the door and leaned against it, taking in deep breaths. This wasn't going to work. How could it?

Think about Adam, she told herself. Her tense muscles began to relax. She'd never brought in a bounty this high.

It would probably be enough that she could make a down payment on a place close to the ocean. A new start, that's what she and Pearl needed. To wipe the slate clean and start all over.

Bringing in Adam would prove her worth and tell everyone this was what she was supposed to do.

She pushed away from the door, hating that she felt the need to prove anything to anyone, but she did. Maybe she just needed to prove it to herself so that she'd know being born—her life—wasn't a mistake.

It only took a few minutes to change into jeans and grab a bag that she kept packed and ready to go. She rolled it to the living room.

"Keep your seat," she told Josh. "I have to make a couple of calls."

She dialed her mother's number first. Pearl answered on the third ring.

"Mom, hey, I've got to go out of town for a few days." Her words sounded clipped, unnatural to even her own ears.

"Is something wrong?"

"No," she hedged.

"You're going after that man, aren't you? The one who didn't show up for court?"

Was that a note of fear she heard? No, she had to be mistaken. "I'm going to give you the number of a . . . a friend. If you need anything call and ask for Moji."

"Moji? What kind of name is that?"

"Just call if you need anything, okay? I've got to go." And it would take all day to explain Moji.

"Cody?"

"Yes?"

"You will be careful?" Pearl hurried on. "I don't mean because you pay the rent or anything."

Silence.

She gripped the phone a little tighter. For a few seconds it was hard to swallow. She finally got past the lump in her throat. "Hey, I'm always careful . . . Mom." She took a deep breath and quickly gave Moji's number to her mother before resting the phone back in the cradle, but it was another few seconds before she could regain her composure.

Had Pearl meant what she said? Could she be worried? She quickly tamped down the warmth that was beginning to spread through her.

Damn it, why did her mother have to get all . . . motherly right now?

She squared her shoulders and dialed the gym. When Moji answered, she quickly told him what was going on, then gave him her mother's phone number and hoped like hell the two didn't meet. Her mother would probably have a heart attack. She didn't even want to picture Moji sashaying up to her mother's apartment in a blue kimono and knocking on her door.

When she turned around, Josh had an odd look on his face. "What?"

"Nothing. You ready?"

He started to reach for her suitcase, but she quickly grabbed it. "I can do for myself."

"Fine with me." He straightened and strolled toward the door.

As she followed, she called herself every kind of a fool there was, but she couldn't keep her gaze off his butt or her thoughts out of the damn bedroom.

This is going to be strictly business, she told herself.

Strictly business? His low-slung jeans hugged him in all the right places. Places she'd love to explore with her hands—with her mouth.

Her gaze slowly moved up, landing on broad shoulders, muscled arms. He opened the door, letting her go through first.

"You don't have to act the gentleman," she grated out, more angry at where her thoughts were going than at his politeness.

"You're really sexy when you get angry." He lightly ran the back of his hand over her cheek. "Your eyes dance with a green fire."

For a second, she was mesmerized by the soft tone of his voice, the feel of his hand on her face. She caught herself from leaning closer, tasting his lips.

She straightened her spine. "And you are so full of it, Josh Pierce."

"So I'm told," he said as he waited for her to lock the door.

He'd soon learn she wouldn't be one of his . . . playthings. When she worked, she was all business.

"I can see the wheels furiously turning inside your head." He fingered his car keys as they went toward the elevator.

"Yeah, well, be careful my wheels don't pulverize you."

"That's what I like about you, your sense of humor."

Note to self: don't tell jokes around Josh.

Chapter 12

Josh glanced in Cody's direction. The only real emotion he'd seen during the whole trip down to the border town was when she'd slid into the passenger seat. She'd smoothed her hand over the worn and faded blue vinyl, then sighed with what sounded like regret.

It went downhill from there.

The drive was torture. Not only was she sitting in the passenger seat, but she wore that damned sensual fragrance that wrapped around his senses, transporting him to a beach, the sand, the surf, and Cody going for the all-over tan.

Hell, it was a wonder he didn't have a wreck.

Nine hours of silence didn't help, either. The most she'd said was yes or no answers to his questions.

By the time he pulled into the space in front of their motel rooms, he was ready for a break from her silence. The next clunker he bought would at least have a working radio.

He unlocked his door, went inside, and tossed his duffel bag on the bed. Not the Ritz, but it would suit the purpose—sleep. Unless he could charm his way into Cody's bed. So far, the only thing he could imagine himself snuggling up to was the extra pillow. He had a feeling she was still miffed over Marianne.

His gaze moved around the standard cheap motel room.

Double bed, cigarette burns on the chipped dresser . . . His gaze came to a grinding halt.

A connecting door. Interesting.

He strolled over to it and tested the knob. Not locked. He silently turned the knob and nudged the door open. Cody was in the process of stretching. When she bent at the waist, he unashamedly admired the view. He was suddenly jealous of her faded jeans. What he wouldn't give to cover those sweet cheeks.

She abruptly turned. Her surprise immediately changed to a frown.

"We have connecting rooms. The door wasn't locked," he explained.

She didn't look nearly as thrilled that their rooms connected. At least, not as thrilled as he was. His fantasies, on the other hand, were kicking into high gear. Not only could he visualize her naked on a beach, but naked on her bed.

Until she marched over—and closed the door firmly between the rooms. He heard the distinct click of the lock on her side.

"Now it's locked," she said from the other side.

"What a waste," he grumbled.

For the rest of the night, he tossed and turned, knowing all that separated them was a thin slab of wood. One kick and the door would pop open like a can of soda, and on the other side was Cody, under the covers and as naked as the day she was born.

She'd probably slept like a baby while he'd been in agony all night with sensuous visions filling his dreams: her sheet sliding down around her hips, breasts beckoning for him to come and taste, to suck on her tight nipples, drawing each one slowly into his mouth.

His knock on the shared door in the morning was louder and harder than he'd intended. Almost immediately, he heard it click, then it opened.

"You look like crap, Pierce," she said, her gaze traveling over him. "Kind of like you just came off a weeklong drunk. What's the matter? Lumpy bed?"

"It was hard." He didn't specify what was hard, but it certainly wasn't the damn bed.

Cody looked like she'd had a restful night. She'd pulled her hair back into a ponytail and her face was fresh—and damned beautiful for someone who didn't have on any makeup.

"You okay?"

He struggled to regain his composure. "Fine. Why?"

"I don't know, you look a little tense."

He wasn't about to tell her that she was what bothered him. *Stupid.* He could almost hear her mocking laughter. Man, he needed to get himself under control and think about anything besides how much he wanted to have sex with her.

He spun on his heel, tossing over his shoulder, "I'll meet you at the car." He left his room, locking the door behind him and pocketing his key.

"So where does this sister of Adam's live?" she asked once they were on the road. "We're partners. I need to know as much as you." She turned her wide green eyes in his direction. "You do know where we're going? Please tell me this won't be the typical male thing where you make an estimated guess of the direction we need to go? We can stop and get a map."

At least she was talking. He chose to ignore her smart-ass remark, though.

"She lives on a small country estate about two or three miles out of town." He'd called around after they'd checked in and found exactly where her place was located.

She nodded and went back to looking at the scenery as it rolled past the window.

"You know, this is going to be a really long stakeout if we don't talk."

"Nice weather. Cooler than Fort Worth. Humidity is higher though." She turned and looked at him again. "You think better with a pen and paper. I think better when I'm not talking." She paused for a moment, then continued. "Have you thought about the possibility that we might get inside the sister's home if we work it just right? Maybe walk up to the house, say we have a flat or something. A man and woman together wouldn't be nearly as suspect. If Adam isn't there, maybe we can get information on where he is."

"Yeah, I thought about it. We can probably come up with something—inspectors, telephone company. I think we could manage to worm our way inside, but I thought we'd watch the place for a while. See if anything is going down."

He slowed as they approached a stone fence. As they drove by, he spotted a Spanish-style house sitting in the distance, surrounded by a grove of trees. He couldn't get near enough without screaming to Adam's sister she was about to have visitors.

"That's her place." He nodded toward the house.

Cody sat a little straighter in her seat, her gaze scanning the area.

He continued slowly down the dusty road until he came to a spot where he could pull off and partially conceal the Chevy.

"Are you up for a hike?" he asked.

"After being stuck in the car all day yesterday? Yeah, I'm ready for a little exercise."

"I know what you mean. I'm sure you don't like straddling the Harley for long periods of time, either."

Silence.

Was she thinking what he was thinking? He mentally shook his head. Doubtful. His were the only thoughts that had taken a nosedive into the gutter.

They got out of the car without another word. Their next obstacle was in front of them—the stone wall. They had no choice except to scale it. On the other side were trees, and beyond that the house.

"Nice digs," Cody said as she stood on her toes and peered over the fence. "Adam's sister lives better than his partner."

"Maybe that's why his partner was murdered?"

She stepped down and dusted off her hands.

He continued. "Maybe old Adam was taking more than his fair share and he was caught with his hand in the cookie jar? It certainly wouldn't be the first time something like that has happened."

"Whatever." Her gaze moved down the wall, looking for the best place to get a good footing. "I'm not here to judge. Just bring him to justice."

All work. He really did have to teach her to play. Damn, he'd really like to teach her to play. "You first," he said, and held out his hands for Cody's booted foot.

She cocked an eyebrow. "And then what? Am I supposed to pull you over?"

He loved her dry sarcasm. Almost to the point that he'd like to strangle her. If her lips didn't look so pouty, so kissable, he just might.

"No, I thought I would drag that rock over." He nodded toward a large rock. "You'd still be too short to get enough leverage to go over the wall."

Now what the hell had he said? Her eyes had narrowed. But rather than saying anything, she snapped her mouth closed.

"Fine." She raised her foot and planted it none too gently in the palms of his hands. "You're going to have to give me a little credit. I'm not going to argue with you on this one, though."

"That'll be a first," he mumbled.

"What?"

"Nothing." And she *was* short, at least compared to him. She wasn't much more than five-six. At the most, five-seven. Apparently, she was sensitive about her height.

He boosted her up. She grabbed the ledge and pulled herself the rest of the way. To give her a little more of a lift, he planted his hands on her bottom and pushed.

How the hell was he supposed to know her ass would feel so damn good even wearing jeans? As she swung her leg over, he lost contact with her body and almost stumbled into the stone wall. As he caught his balance and glanced up, he ran into a different stone wall—Cody's angry glare.

"You did that on purpose," she accused.

"No, I swear." He shook his head and held out his hands in supplication, then hoped she couldn't tell his pants were just a little tighter than they had been a few minutes ago.

"Watch it next time."

"Anything you say, baby." He knew his term of endearment would irritate her, but she surprised him by not saying a word. She was a handful when she was pissed, but oh, what a handful. He was beginning to wonder if he'd wanted her as a business partner or so he could spend a little more time in her company. He liked the way she made him feel so alive.

Wade would probably tell him it was the latter. His friend would probably be right.

In the next second, she swung her leg over and dropped to the other side. He made it over the wall and they crept through the trees, as close to the house as they dared, then took cover behind one of the large oak trees. They were able to observe the front as well as the back, but were still far enough away that no one would see them.

He pulled his binoculars out and did a slow survey, scanning the lower floor before moving to the upper windows.

"It doesn't look like anyone is home," Cody whispered, even though no one could hear her from this distance.

"Top floor, second window to the right." He passed her the binoculars.

She took them, then looked toward the second floor. "Okay, I see her now. She's reading." She lowered them as a car approached.

He'd heard it, too, and watched as the familiar red Caddy slowed, then came to a stop. It was an older model car. A 2000, maybe a 2001. Josh even knew where the driver had bought it. Abner's Discount Autos. Discount, his foot. By the time Abner added on all his finance charges, the car cost almost as much as it had when it was new, but then he'd never thought Turbo was the brightest bulb in the package.

"Turbo," Cody groaned. "Damn, I was hoping he wouldn't show."

"Five dollars says he doesn't make it past the front door," Josh said. He squinted. Turbo wore a suit coat and carried a clipboard. Who was he trying to impersonate?

She looked through the binoculars again. "The woman's looking out the window." She chuckled under her breath. "And now she's picking up a phone." She paused. "Now she's reading again. No bet. You think I was born yesterday, Pierce? Turbo doesn't stand a chance. He might have gotten to the house before us, but that doesn't mean he'll charm his way inside. Not that he has an ounce of charm."

"Hey, it was worth a try at an easy five bucks. I won once." He shrugged. "Thought I might be able to do it again."

By the warmth that crawled up her neck, she was remembering the last time, too.

"You got lucky."

"I bet we could find a bar with a pool table. Want to even up?"

"No."

She turned her gaze back to Turbo. Josh smiled, remembering their game and wishing she would've taken him up on the bet. Damn, he liked the way she moved when she shot pool. Sexy as hell.

Someone crossed in front of a window on the first floor. A maid or maybe a personal secretary.

The door opened.

"Oh, lord, you ought to see the smirky smile on Turbo's face. That is one man who is so full of himself," she said, looking through the binoculars again. "And the door shuts in his face. Bye-bye, Turbo."

He stomped back to his car, got inside, slammed the door, and peeled out, leaving rubber in the circular drive that would probably royally piss off the lady of the manor.

"So, any bright ideas how we're going to get inside? Apparently the sister isn't going to be an easy mark."

"I have a couple." He didn't, but he figured Adam would either show or by the end of the day he'd have a plan.

She rested her back against the tree. "And just how do you propose we get inside the house? Breaking and entering? I mean, if he's somewhere inside, he might not leave the house for days. I'd rather not spend any more time out here than necessary watching the house. If you haven't noticed, this ground is pretty damn hard."

Not as hard as she constantly made him. Hell, he was getting used to hard. His condition wasn't relieved when he turned his gaze off the house and back on her. Damn, she was sweet to look at. Her skin so soft. He wanted to brush his fingers across her cheeks, outline her lips, before tasting the sweetness she had to offer.

He drew in a deep breath, but it only made it worse as he inhaled the heady scent she wore.

He couldn't resist. The temptation was too much for one man to bear, especially after having his hands on her ass. No court in the land would convict him.

Leaning forward, he pressed his lips against hers. For a millisecond, her eyes widened and he thought she would push him away. His quick prayer must've reached his guardian angel because she accepted his kiss.

Her lips were hot. She didn't hesitate when he nudged her mouth open. He stroked her tongue with his, reveling in the velvety softness. The earth seemed to move beneath him. Earthquake? Or just her touch? Probably the latter, but if that were the case, he hoped it never stopped.

He moved his hand to her breast. Crap, sometimes he hated

second-chance vests. Right now, hers was effectively cooling his ardor. With more than a little regret, he moved away, trying to regain some measure of his equilibrium.

"You said you wouldn't kiss me." Her voice was thick with barely restrained passion.

For a moment, he thought about pursuing what he'd started. He didn't think she'd resist much—if any. He turned from her, fixing his gaze on the house, and drew in a couple of deep breaths. If he had to look at her, he wouldn't be responsible for what he did next, and starting his own agency meant a lot to him. He had to stop thinking about sex. Yeah, right, like that would ever happen.

"No," he said, once he could catch his breath. "*You* said there wouldn't be any kissing. I don't remember agreeing to any of your rules."

"Then maybe we should end the partnership right now," she quietly told him.

His gut clenched. "Are you saying you didn't like it as much as I did?"

"No. I'm saying it could get us killed."

"When it counts, I won't put either one of us in danger." And he meant what he said. He would never let harm come to her.

She turned her back to him. "I can't concentrate when you kiss me. I don't like not being in control." When he didn't say anything, she faced him. "Do you understand what I'm talking about? If I'm going to do my job, I need to have control over my own body."

Was that what she did when they made love—lose control? A drop of sweat rolled down his spine as he thought about stripping her naked—here, out in the open—and seeing just how much control he could make her lose.

"Josh?"

He brought himself back down to earth. "Yeah, okay. I'll back off." He didn't add *for now.*

Silence. He wondered if she was going to turn around and walk back to the car, continuing the investigation on her own. Loneliness welled inside him. He hadn't realized how solitary his life had become. And he realized he wouldn't like it if she walked out of his life.

She finally broke the silence. "So, what's your plan?"

He breathed a sigh of relief.

Plan? Cody wanted to know if he had a plan. He glanced at her, then at the house. Plan?

When Josh didn't say anything, Cody knew there was no plan. He was playing it all by ear. It figured.

Before her temper could rise, her already short fuse fizzled out. It wasn't as if she had a plan, either, and they were partners. Damn it, he had to quit kissing her. But the thought of never receiving another kiss from him sent cold shivers racing up and down her arms.

"Why don't we watch the house? See if any more surprises develop," he suggested.

His words effectively cleared the warm fuzzy feeling that had swept over her when he'd touched her. They were here to do a job. Nothing more. She drew in a deep breath and concentrated on the job. Forcing thoughts of Josh and sex from her mind.

A few minutes of silence passed.

"You think Adam might show?" she asked. It wouldn't be the first time gut instinct had played a role in capturing a fugitive.

"No, but just in case, I think we should hang around for a while. See what develops."

Okay, so he didn't have any kind of premonition. She looked at the house with dread. This was the hard part of doing a stakeout. Sitting and watching, doing absolutely nothing. It took patience, and right now hers was wearing thin. Usually, she worked crossword puzzles or something equally boring so it wouldn't capture all her attention.

"Have you ever played poker?" he suddenly asked, pulling a deck of cards from his back pocket.

This might be Josh's way of putting some space between them. Playing cards was safe.

"Poker? Sort of." Had she played poker? She bit the insides of her cheeks to keep from smiling.

Fate did have a way of stepping in and evening the score. She sat cross-legged on the ground, keeping her face devoid of all emotion. He stared at her as he sat across from her.

"What?" she asked, keeping her expression innocent.

He let his gaze linger on her face a couple of seconds before he began to shuffle the deck.

"Nothing. Draw poker." He pulled some change from his pocket. "Ante a quarter, one raise, two bumps max. That okay with you?"

"You might have to remind me of the rules, but yeah, I'm game." She reached into her pocket and dropped what change she had in front of her.

"Sure you want to play? I don't want to take your money."

"It beats staring at the house every second. Besides, the harder you stare at something the easier it is to miss the changes."

She might let him take her money and she might not. Fighting wasn't the only thing Rodney had taught her, but she'd keep that to herself. She wouldn't exactly be cheating . . . Okay, so maybe Rodney had taught her to cheat, and she was damn good at it. She could palm cards, deal them so her opponent would think he had an unbeatable hand—except hers would be a little better. At least if nothing happened, the afternoon wouldn't be a total waste. She liked the idea of winning at something.

Maybe she should've suggested strip poker? Damn it, as hard as she tried to be good, Josh still brought out the bad girl in her.

"Cards?" He held the deck, waiting for her to decide.

She looked at the cards she held. A pair of fives. Not

much. She pulled out two and laid them facedown on the ground. "Um, two. No, make that three." She removed another card, then nibbled on her bottom lip to keep from smiling.

Ahh, revenge could be sweet.

Chapter 13

Josh crossed his ankles and leaned against the tree. If he didn't know better, he'd say Cody was cheating at cards. He just hadn't caught her. No one could be this damn lucky.

"I think you've played poker before." He tossed the cards down.

"Beginner's luck." She smiled sweetly.

He almost believed her. Almost. "Yeah, sure. Well, you've taken my change and all my ones. I don't think I want to give you a chance at the bigger bills." He thoughtfully eyed her. "Now, if you want to play a little strip poker . . ."

Her grin widened.

That was too easy. "On second thought, I have a feeling I'd be the only one out in the open, bare-ass naked."

She placed her cards on top of his and leaned back against the trunk of the tree. "Okay, no more poker." She nodded toward the house. "Nothing going on there. I hate stakeouts. They're the most boring part of the job. I think I'll take a nap while you keep watch, then you can catch a few Z's. I have a feeling it's going to be a long day."

When she closed her eyes, he unabashedly stared. Damn, she was so beautiful. The sun glinted off her hair, lending it a blue-black sheen. A tendril had come loose from her ponytail to caress the smoothness of her cheek. He wanted to reach out, see if the strands were as soft as they looked. Instead, his gaze lowered to the fullness of her lips.

If he leaned forward, he would be able to kiss her. Hell, he wanted to do a lot more than just kiss. She opened her eyes. Their gazes met; she shifted hers away, toward the house, before closing them once again, but he knew she wasn't thinking about Adam. She couldn't be, not when he'd caught that brief spark of passion that flamed in her eyes for just a second. A second or a minute, it had still been there.

But apparently she wasn't interested in pursuing her sexual thoughts. He was a gentleman—most of the time. He could respect that even though she was putting them through unnecessary torture.

Minutes ticked by. He had to do something or he was going to pounce. He didn't think she'd like it if he pounced. She might even kick his ass.

"Who's Moji?" he finally asked. Anything to get his mind off sex. As if that would happen in this lifetime.

She opened her eyes, a question forming in those passionate green orbs.

He continued before she had a chance to open her mouth. "You mentioned him at my apartment, then you phoned him from yours." He was more than a little curious. He'd never really seen Cody with anyone.

Something unfamiliar crept over him. Jealousy? No, it couldn't be. He'd known her for a few months now, but he didn't *know* her. At least, not enough to be jealous. Curiosity. That was closer to what he was feeling.

"He owns the gym where I work out."

He frowned when he noted how her expression changed and a kind of softness seemed to descend on her. What the hell was she thinking about? "Moji. Who would name their kid Moji?" Yes, he was being argumentative, and he didn't really give a damn.

"No one that I know. He came up with the name all by himself. It suits him."

"And you became friends."

She bristled. "Yeah, you got a problem with who I choose to like or dislike?"

Now she was mad. He had a habit of pissing her off lately. That wasn't his intent, but damned if he didn't get hard looking at the fire flashing in her eyes.

"No problem," he told her, clearing his throat and glad she couldn't read what he was thinking right now. "I just thought the time would pass quicker by getting to know each other a little better."

"I guess I'm not used to casual conversation." She relaxed against the back of the tree again. "Moji is Moji. He almost defies description."

The guy owned a gym. Most women liked something different from what they were used to, and with that kind of name, he sounded more than a little different. A visual flashed before him. Bulging muscles, tanned skin, Cody and Moji entwined . . .

No, he wasn't even going there. Maybe the guy was really ugly or something. A big bruiser with his nose lying on the side of his face from all his fights.

He could see this was going to bother him for the rest of the day. "Okay, so try."

"Try what?" she asked.

"To describe him."

She shrugged. "Middle-aged, gay . . ."

As far as he was concerned, the rest of what she had to say was lost on him as he inwardly smiled. Gay. He liked Moji already. Well, not exactly *liked*. He was just damn glad the guy didn't have any romantic interest in Cody.

"So, if we're playing twenty questions, tell me about your nightmare." She stared unblinking at him.

For a moment, he'd let his guard down. He had to remember she wasn't like other women. She played hardball. He opened his mouth to tell her that his demons were no concern of hers, but for some strange reason no words came out.

Leaning forward, he picked up a small branch. "I would imagine you have a few demons of your own. No big deal. Sometimes I dream about mine."

He looked past her into the underbrush, and for a moment he was transported to another place, another time. Pain ripped over him. When he looked at Cody, he saw another woman—with darker skin, darker eyes.

"But we're not talking about my demons, we're talking about yours," she gently broke into his thoughts.

He gave a brief smile. "So we are." He drew in a deep breath. "I don't think it was so much one incident," he finally said. "More like a culmination of events, but this one was the one that tipped the scales. I discovered I couldn't save the world because there are some people who just don't want to be saved."

"And the person you tried to save?"

"Didn't want to be saved after all. She was living on a ranch, almost like a compound. I got her out, she went running back."

"And you feel guilty about it," she stated in a matter of fact voice.

The branch in his hand snapped. Surprised, he looked down, then tossed the two pieces away.

"I guess I do. I always wondered if I could've said something different to convince her that she could have a better life."

"What happened to her?"

"He killed her." For just a second, he was back there, running through the underbrush, holding her hand, urging her to go faster.

The cobwebs surrounding his mind cleared and he saw Cody, not the other woman. "We'd found a safe place for her, but she went running back. When we raided the ranch, I found her in the back room. Her neck had been broken."

"But it wasn't your fault. She shouldn't have returned."

He scraped a hand through his hair. "I've told myself that a thousand times. Like I said, it was just one incident in many that made me leave the force. Sometimes they haunt me. I'll live."

Now he'd bared his soul. What was she really thinking? Crap, he hadn't meant to spill his guts. He turned his head away and looked toward the house. Instantly, his confession was forgotten.

"Van," he said, nodding toward the house.

Adam wouldn't just drive up to the house. He'd have to know someone would be watching. There was a slogan on the side of the van, but he couldn't quite make out the words. He grabbed the binoculars. "Pest control," he read the words printed on the side aloud.

"Legit?" she asked, sitting up and leaning forward.

The van stopped and a man climbed out, tugging on the collar of his white overalls. "Steve Byers."

"Another recovery agent?"

"Yeah. Ever heard of him?"

Frowning, she shook her head.

"Steve works mostly out of the Waco area, but I've crossed paths with him a time or two."

"And?"

He shrugged. "Nice enough guy, but he hates losing as much as the next bounty hunter."

Steve glanced from side to side before strolling up to the house. Very casual, unconcerned, but Josh knew better.

He aimed the binoculars toward the second floor and zeroed in on Sinclair's sister. She put her book down and frowned as she looked out the window. A few seconds passed and she picked up the phone. Josh aimed the binoculars at the first floor. The other woman picked up a downstairs phone, listened, then nodded.

"It might be harder than we think to get inside. His sister wasn't born yesterday."

A few minutes later and Steve left, just like Turbo, but leaving behind less rubber.

"Then maybe we should try something different."

"Like what?"

"The truth."

"You want to waltz right up to the front door, ring the bell, and say, 'Hi, we're bounty hunters and we'd like to know if your brother might be hiding under a bed. Do you mind if we check?'" If she thought that would get them inside then she needed her head examined.

"What do we have to lose? We sure as hell won't get past the front door pretending to be something other than who we are, and we haven't seen any sign that Adam might be here. It's obvious we're not going to be able to bluff our way inside."

For a mere second he considered her idea—then tossed it away. It would never work, but unless he came up with something different, she looked hell-bent on trying her scheme. "Let's see what happens today, then go from there."

She glanced toward the house, then back at him. "Okay, we'll do it your way—today." She picked up the cards. "Your deal or mine?"

He could tell by the way she shuffled the cards, stiff-like, that if something didn't happen today, tomorrow she'd make it happen—with or without him.

"Yours."

Cody hated just sitting there. She wanted to march right up to the front door and not wait until tomorrow. Damn it, time was wasting.

Some of the wind left her sails. She knew Josh was right. It was better to watch and learn. Rodney had taught her that little trick, but it didn't mean she had to like it.

She dealt the hand.

Two hours later and they were still playing cards. She'd even gotten tired of cheating. It wasn't as much fun as it had been in the beginning. When she was the only one who knew she was getting away with something it quickly became rather tedious.

Roughing it in the woods wasn't all it was cut out to be, either. The toilet facilities were lacking in amenities—including toilet paper. Leaves just weren't all that absorbent. She had a great deal more respect for pioneer women. She'd washed her hands in a creek that ran close by and that at least had made life a little more bearable.

Until lunch. She'd be the first to admit she could pack away more food than any female she knew. But since neither had brought food, lunch consisted of a box of nonperishables that Josh kept in the trunk of his car for emergencies. Warm soda, chips, and a bag of cookies. *This is the life*, she thought as she dusted the crumbs off her hands. Damned exciting. Yeah.

He broke into her musings. "What are you thinking about?"

"How people depict bounty hunters in books."

"As in?" he prodded.

"Dashing, daring, thrilling. Taking down skips and collecting fat rewards. James Bond stuff."

He leaned back against the tree. "You mean I'm not exciting?" A wicked grin curved his lips.

Josh was back. After he'd told her a little about his nightmare, he'd turned pensive, communicating very little. Sure, they'd played cards, but she could tell his mind wasn't on the game.

That Josh was gone, though. The flirt was back. She liked him better this way. Serious Josh made her nervous. He made her . . . he made her care more than she wanted to admit.

Something had changed. She wasn't sure what it was, but there was definitely something different in the air. But was it a good different or a bad different?

For lack of anything better to do, and maybe because she felt a little nervous, she scooped up the binoculars and scanned the area around the house. All was quiet. Her gut told her

Adam had been here, but he wouldn't be coming back anytime soon.

The rest of the day slipped past until the sun began to set. Splashes of bright yellow and deep orange kissed the horizon good-bye.

A sudden chill washed over her. Goose bumps popped up on her arms. It wasn't that it was cool or anything, she just didn't relish spending the night out here—in the dark. She wasn't that fond of the country.

"Don't they have bobcats or something equally distasteful in these parts?" She slapped at a mosquito almost as big as her thumb. She missed, but she was positive he'd give her another chance to swat at him.

"Ocelot is more common, but they eat small animals. I'd be more worried about rattlesnakes."

"Thanks for making me feel better." Facing down six Leonards in a back alley looked a hell of a lot better than this. Why the hell had she traipsed out here to the middle of nowhere? Oh, yeah, right, to prove she was meant to be a bounty hunter.

She slapped at another mosquito. Probably friends with the last one who'd told all his relatives about the easy pickings.

"You might want to sit out here all night, but I'm going to at least move in for a closer look. See what's going on inside. I'm getting eaten alive sitting here." She stood.

Josh came to his feet. "We'll see if we can spot anything suspicious, and if not, let's call it a night. I don't relish getting eaten alive any more than you do."

She followed him, more than willing that he take the lead. She had no desire to step on a rattlesnake, although she was pretty sure they were supposed to rattle before they struck. Kind of like hearing the bullet before it hit you. Some warning that was.

They crept up to the house and Josh peered into one of the windows. "Someone is coming down the stairs."

"Adam?" she asked in a breathless whisper.

He ducked down, pulling her until she squatted beside him. For a few seconds all she could think about was how the warmth of his touch spread over her. How his hands could cause ripples of pleasure elsewhere on her body.

"Female. Looks more like the woman who's been answering the door," he said, interrupting her thoughts.

It took her a moment to remember she was hunting a criminal. He had a way of making her forget. Not good.

She eased to the window and peered over the sill. He was right. A woman. Mean-looking, too. Damn, she'd hoped it was Adam. As if it could be that easy. Knock down a door, handcuff him, and take him to jail. She should've known better.

She glanced around. "Let's check the outbuildings. Maybe he's holed up in the garage or something."

Except when they got there, the garage was locked up as tight as the toolshed. There was no sign of Adam, either.

"Let's call it a night."

"I'm more than ready. I'm not sure I have any blood left to donate."

They made their way back to the car, but it was slow with only the light of a partial moon to guide them. It would be a fool that turned on a flashlight for the home's inhabitants to spot the beam. But she couldn't help wondering if it was just as foolish not to see where they were stepping.

Something inside her made her want to cling to Josh's arm. Boy, all those carbs for lunch had really gone to her head. She needed something substantial in her gut. Like a big rib eye grilled to perfection.

Thinking of her empty stomach made her forget they were traipsing across unknown territory. Almost.

She breathed a sigh of relief when she slid into the passenger seat. Once they were on the road, headed back to town, all she could think about was a hot meal, an equally hot shower to wash off the layer of grime that seemed to cling to her body, and hot sex.

No, not hot sex. Where the hell had that thought come from? Hot sex should have been the last thing on her mind.

Too bad it wasn't.

Chapter 14

Cody glared at the air conditioner in her motel room. The damn thing had begun to clunk when she'd lowered the thermostat. Clunk, clunk, clunk! It irritated the hell out of her.

She pushed her covers away. It didn't help. She was still hot and miserable. And she could add cranky to her list, too. Hot, miserable, and cranky, not to mention the film of sweat that covered her body.

Another shower might help. The thought of cool water cascading over her body sounded comforting, but she knew after half an hour she'd be sweating again.

Josh could've used a little more discretion when choosing a motel. She didn't care if he'd stayed here before. The place was a dump.

Okay, maybe not a dump. Things also broke down in five-star hotels. She glanced at the clock. Nearly midnight. There was no way in hell it could be repaired before morning. She should ask for another room. If they even had one. An hour ago, a bunch of college guys had registered. She'd glanced out the window and saw the jerseys they wore with the name of their college emblazoned across the back. Noise to go along with the heat. Great. They hadn't quieted down yet.

Her gaze automatically moved to the door that separated her room from Josh's. His room probably wasn't any more soundproof than hers, but she'd bet her last dollar it was nice and cool. And he'd probably be willing to share his bed.

"Damn." She had to stop thinking about Josh . . . and heat . . . and sex. When he was around, all she could think about was sex. Sex with Josh.

She was working. Her thoughts should be centered on capturing Adam Sinclair and bringing him back to stand trial.

She closed her eyes and rolled onto her stomach. What made her so vulnerable to his seduction? And seducing was exactly what he was doing. It was driving her insane with desire.

When she closed her eyes, she could almost feel his hands lightly caressing her body: skimming the surface, brushing across her sensitive nipples, sliding down her stomach, tangling in the curls that covered her sex.

She moaned from somewhere down deep inside.

Why keep fighting it? She couldn't screw up the job when she was off the clock—sort of.

No, no, no.

But it was a good question. When had she ever been this stubborn about anything or anyone? If they had sex, her tension and frustration might be relieved.

She glanced toward his door again, then closed her eyes. What would he do if she strolled right over and opened the damn door? Just stood there as naked as the day she was born?

Her breath hitched in her throat as a deep longing spread over her. She wanted him. Why deny herself any longer?

She reached over and flipped on her bedside light. It was now or never. Standing, she went to the door. Her side was locked—his wasn't. Of course. Taking a deep breath, she opened the door.

A blast of welcome, cool air washed over her. She was right, much better in his room. Her nipples tightened. Cold air? Or expectation? Probably both.

Light from her room spilled into his. His bed was rumpled,

but empty. Her gaze moved around the room. Josh stood in front of the window, looking out, a white towel draping his hips. Deep in thought, he apparently hadn't heard the door open. She stared, wondering how looking at a naked back and bare legs could make her insides quake.

When she cleared her throat, he turned. His expression spoke volumes. Without taking his gaze off her, he closed the blinds, then sauntered toward her. He didn't seem to be in any hurry. His gaze drifted lazily over her bare skin, touching her breasts, grazing her hips, caressing the curls at the juncture between her legs. She drew air into her lungs as her body tensed with anticipation.

He stopped in front of her. "Did you need something?" He reached out, gliding his hand over one breast, tweaking her already sensitive nipple. She arched toward him. Yes, this was what she'd been craving. Not a stranger's touch. No, she needed Josh to bring her body to life.

"I need you," she whispered hoarsely, but he moved his hand away. She couldn't stand it if he rejected her now.

But he didn't disappoint her as he lowered his mouth to hers with a growl. His lips were firm, his tongue searching, stroking. She was just as bold as she tasted him, her hands tangling in his hair, tugging him closer. Warmth spread over her.

She stroked his body, hands testing the muscles of his back. Hard and firm.

When his hands cupped her butt, squeezing and releasing, a rush of heat swept over her. She didn't really give a damn about anything except what he was doing to her body. She bit back her moan as his arousal and the rough texture of the terrycloth towel rubbed against her sex.

When he ended the kiss, they were both breathing hard, her head resting on his chest. She listened to the frantic beat of his heart, his wiry chest hairs tickling her cheek, his breath on her bare skin.

"If we don't slow down," he said, "this will go on record

as the shortest sexual experience in the world and I damn well want to savor the moment." His hand lightly caressed her back. "Twice wasn't enough. My body has ached for you every damned night. I want you lying beside me naked so I can touch you, so that I can have you anytime I want."

"You think I haven't imagined you the same way?" She closed her eyes. Even while she knew it was so damn wrong, she couldn't deny how much she wanted him. "Why the hell couldn't you leave things the way they were? You know there will be complications. I don't need more problems in my life, and I damn sure don't want to care about you."

"I won't hurt you, but we both know we have to find out what there is between us."

Everything suddenly seemed to be happening too fast. She moved from his arms and took a step back. Her gaze roamed over him: broad shoulders, firm chest, a six-pack stomach.

He was right. Why had she been denying herself the pleasure of his body? Even as she wondered, the answer came to her. With each one of her sexual encounters, she'd been the one choosing who to go to bed with. Someone she could walk away from without any regrets. *She* had made the choice. There had been no connection, just sexual release. Not even real gratification.

Sex with strangers was like going to a salad bar, but she knew without a doubt Josh was dessert. He was the chocolate cake, the banana split—all the luscious treats. She hadn't been able to walk away from Josh and that scared the hell out of her.

Trembles of anticipation swept over her. There would be no more denial. She raised her chin. "When I get my fill of you, I'll walk away," she warned.

"Deal."

She wouldn't let him get under her skin. She'd keep the vulnerable part of herself locked away. She wouldn't let herself care about him. It would be only sex, but dear God, she knew it would be the best damn sex she'd ever had.

"No recriminations?" she asked, just to make sure he knew exactly what he was getting himself into.

"None."

She moved closer, taking the lead, and raised her face, lightly trailing her tongue across his lips, enjoying the taste of him while he stood there, letting her explore. She moved back, wondering if he would grab her, maybe throw her on the bed before jumping on top of her.

He didn't.

The man had great control. She'd really expected him to pounce on her. Good. She didn't particularly want to stop exploring his body.

She ran her hands over his hard nipples, then flicked one with her fingernail. He squeezed her shoulders, telling her just how much it cost him to hold back, but she couldn't cease the game she played even if she'd wanted to.

She glided her hand over his chest. "Your skin is firm, hot. Magnificent," she breathed, scraping her fingers lightly through the sprinkling of hair.

Her fingers grazed an old scar she hadn't noticed before. She looked up. "Bullet?"

He nodded.

There was another scar a little lower, but this one was different. "Knife?" She skimmed her fingers across the raised skin.

"Appendix." His grin was a little tight. "Are you through checking out my body?"

She shook her head. "I haven't even gotten started. I didn't take as much time as I wanted when we were last together. I don't want to miss a thing this time."

"We can compare battle wounds another time. I want to feel myself buried deep inside you—thrusting into your hot moist heat. I want to take those delectable nipples and suck them into my mouth one at a time."

He painted a vivid picture. If she closed her eyes, it was almost as if he was already there. She wanted the same thing, but it was still too soon. "In a hurry?" She suddenly smiled, some of her tension eased. It was nice to know a man wanted her this much. No, not just any man. That Josh did.

"What do you think? Do you realize the torture you put me through since the last time we made love? You've avoided me ever since the night I spent at your apartment."

She looked up. Torture? She knew exactly what he was talking about, but it would all end tonight, and for a little while, he would be hers.

"Have pity," he begged.

His eyes were glazed with passion. A surge of power swept over her. So much control and it was all right here at her fingertips. She had no doubt that right at this moment he would do anything she wanted. A heady feeling swept over her.

With that kind of control, she couldn't resist. "Do you like when I touch you?" She pressed her hand to the front of his towel. He jerked toward her.

"You tell me?" He cupped her breasts, scraping his calloused thumbs over her tight and very sensitive nipples. Swirls of pleasure erupted inside her.

"What does my touching do to *you*?" he asked.

"It makes me want more." She hooked her fingers in the towel and jerked. "Just as you knew it would." She glanced down and took in her fill of him. "Nice and hard," she breathed. She lightly brushed the tip of his engorged penis.

He sucked in a breath, his hands tightening on her breasts. She closed her eyes, letting the sensations wrap around her, enclosing her in a sensual cocoon. Josh, tugging on her nipples, massaging her breasts. Her, rubbing his dick, sliding her thumb over the smooth tip, stroking his length.

"I want more of you," he breathed close to her ear. "I want to taste you on my lips."

Tingles of fire rippled over her as visions formed in her mind. Lying on the bed, her legs opening wide. Josh looking at her most private parts right before his mouth covered her. A shudder of need made her tremble.

"Do you even realize what you're doing to me?" she rasped out. She had a feeling he knew exactly what he did. Maybe even relished that he had this much domination over her.

Not that she cared. Not when the heat of his look warmed her all the way to her toes.

He moved one hand lower, stroking between her legs. She nudged closer.

"It feels good, doesn't it? Like tiny earthquakes exploding all over you." His words were husky, rich with his own restraint—his own need. "You're silky and wet. Already hot on the inside, too, I'd bet," his soft words continued.

She moaned, unable to hold it inside.

He brought his finger to his mouth and sucked. "Are you?" Before she could reply, he slipped his wet finger down the fleshy part of her skin before dipping inside.

She dug her fingers into his shoulders, gasping for air. "Yes, oh God, yes." She wiggled herself against him. Almost. Almost there.

Slowly, he removed his finger. She cried out, but her frustration eased when he slid his finger across her clit. He moved it up and down, exploring all of her body as he made it his.

"Do you like that?"

"You know damn well I do." She sucked in a deep breath.

His short laugh tickled her face. Josh liked to be in control. Well, she did, too. She cupped his butt, squeezing. She loved his butt. It was firm, smooth.

Her breasts brushed across the hairs on his chest. She only savored the tingles for a moment before she dropped to her knees in front of him.

For a moment, she could only stare. He was beautiful— and very hard. Her hand circled his penis, sliding the skin down, then back up. He grabbed her shoulders.

"I want to taste you," she told him before looking up at

him. "Can I lick you?" She ran her tongue over her lips. "Taste all of you?"

"Christ, woman, you're killing me."

She inwardly smiled. Enough torture for him—and her. She brought him toward her mouth, lightly kissing the tip of his penis. She swirled her tongue around the head before taking him inside her mouth, gently sucking, then drawing him in deeper.

"Ahhh . . ." He arched toward her, his hands on either side of her head, lightly massaging as he rhythmically moved his hips against her eager mouth.

Closing her eyes, she tasted and sucked, running her tongue over his smooth flesh. She snaked one hand between his legs and cupped his scrotum, letting the weight of his testicles rest in her hand before she began to squeeze and lightly tug on them.

So lost in giving him pleasure, she didn't realize at first that he'd placed his hands beneath her arms and was pulling her up. Reluctantly, she freed him.

He cupped her butt, pulling her even closer, until the lips of her sex snugly fit against his penis. Her juices had already made her wet; when he rubbed against her, flames licked her body.

She closed her eyes and bit her bottom lip. Ah, God, it felt so damn good. The friction was almost unbearable, the tension inside building. But he stopped, moving back a step. She grabbed his shoulders to keep from falling at the same time she moved closer. "Don't stop," she cried, aching with frustration.

"I'm not even near to stopping, baby." He moved her to the bed, laying her back.

His mouth covered one of her breasts, sucking, his teeth scraping across the hard nubs. She pulled his head closer. "More." He didn't disappoint as his hand cupped her other breast, massaging, playing with that nipple as well.

She reached for Josh, wanting to give him as much attention as he gave her, but he moved downward.

"Spread your legs." His voice scraped across her senses. "I want nothing between me and you. I want to know every inch, I want to look at every inch, I want to taste every inch."

His words sent fire racing through her as she opened for him. He spread her lips, seeing all of her, then his mouth covered her. He began sucking, gently pulling on the tender skin. She cried out as the world spun crazily around her.

He slipped his finger inside while his mouth continued to suck on her tender flesh. In and out. In and out. She clutched the bed sheets, tugging on them, her head thrashing back and forth.

"Now," she cried, needing to feel him inside her.

He moved, reaching for his pants, grappling inside the pocket. He pulled out a condom and ripped the foil open with his teeth. Through her haze of desire, she watched the thin latex slide over his rock hard erection, not wanting to miss even this moment.

When he entered her, she raised her hips, meeting him halfway. His length glided inside her slickness. She tightened her inner muscles, contracting herself around him, then raised her hips and sucked him further inside. Opening her eyes, she watched him—saw the pleasure she gave. She raised her hips again, meeting his thrusts.

And she wanted more. She pushed on his shoulders. He rolled to his back and she quickly straddled him.

He slapped her butt. A burst of pleasure mixed with a little bit of pain rushed over her.

"If you wanted to be on top, all you had to do was say so," Josh said.

She lowered her body over him. "And you would have let me?"

He grunted with pleasure. "Probably not. I can't hold back much longer, but I damn sure like the view from this angle."

A smile curved her lips as she rotated her hips in a circular fashion while moving her hands over her breasts, tweaking the nipples. "I'm glad you like what you see." She watched him as he watched her touching herself, kneading her breasts, tugging on her hard nipples.

She raised her hips, then lowered them, as she moved one hand to the vee of her legs, opening her lips and touching herself. She gritted her teeth as her arousal heightened to fever pitch.

"Damn, you're so fucking sexy." His breathing was ragged.

When she would have moved her hand away, he grabbed her. "No, don't stop touching yourself. It's a hell of a turn-on."

She sucked in air when he began touching her body as well, tugging and pulling on the fleshy part of her sex.

He groaned, his hands moving to her hips, grasping them in a firm hold as he met her thrusts, faster and faster. The friction sent spirals of heat twisting and turning throughout her body. His face blurred. She squeezed her eyes shut as spasm after spasm crashed over her.

Oh, damn, it was so good. She gasped for air, struggling to draw it into her lungs. She gripped her thighs, hanging on tight, contracting her inner muscles.

His body jerked, then quivered as his orgasm clutched him. He held on to her as he rode out the wave.

All her energy drained, she collapsed on top of him.

Their ragged breathing intermingled. Slowly, she came back to earth, and when she did, a tear slipped from the corner of her eye and slid down her face. She'd known it would be good with Josh, but damn it, it wasn't supposed to get better each time they had sex. She brushed the tear away before he noticed.

"You okay?"

He sounded a little odd. She wanted to ask if it was better this time for him, as it was for her, but it sounded more than a little clichéd.

"Yeah, I'm okay. You?" she asked.

"Fine . . . fine."

She'd never had a *fine* before. Disappointment flooded

through her before she could stop it. What had she expected? That he would say the earth had moved? That stars had fallen from the sky?

Rolling off him, she turned away. From the corner of her eye, she saw him start to get up, but seconds later he grabbed her up in his arms and nestled her close.

"No, it wasn't *fine*. It was damn good," he growled. "The newness hasn't worn off. Sex with you gets better each time we do it."

"Then why the hell are you pissed?" she angrily tossed back.

"Because it wasn't supposed to be like . . ." He waved an arm, then in a calmer voice continued. "It wasn't supposed to be this earth-shattering, and don't tell me you didn't feel it, too."

She opened her mouth to deny his words, but nothing came out. Instead, she drew in a deep breath. "It was the best sex I've ever had. Even better than the last time," she admitted. "But it doesn't change anything between us."

He didn't look convinced.

"So maybe we're both a little shocked by the intensity of the moment," she hurried on. "It still doesn't change anything. As soon as Adam Sinclair is captured, we'll go our separate ways. No recriminations. We made a deal, remember?"

For a moment, she wondered if he was going to say anything. He finally nodded and she breathed a little easier. The last thing she wanted was to cry over someone else who'd walked out on her. This was just sex—when they were finished, there would be nothing more between them.

He slipped from her arms and stood, going to the bathroom without another word. Loneliness filled her as she watched him leave.

Her gaze moved over his shoulders, his back, his butt, just before he walked out of her line of vision. A ripple of pleasure tripped down her spine. What did it matter? For the moment, he was hers, and lord, the sex had been fantastic.

There was a tightening in her lower region. She mentally shook her head. This wasn't good, not at all. How could she want him again this soon? Had months of celibacy made her sexually starved and now she couldn't get her fill?

She still hadn't moved when he came out of the bathroom a few minutes later and began pulling on his jeans.

Just think about something else, she told herself. As if that was going to be so fucking easy when he was doing a reverse striptease, but having the same effect as if he were removing his clothes. With each inch of skin he covered, she wanted him all the more.

"First thing in the morning we'll go with your plan of telling the truth." Josh walked to the window, opened the blinds, and looked out.

"Are you serious?"

"I haven't come up with a better plan. Yeah, I guess I am."

"It's not because we had sex, is it?"

He suddenly turned, looking at her as he grinned that half smile that made her toes curl. "If I agree with you on everything, can we have sex again?"

"No." The man had an ego problem now more than ever. She shouldn't have given in to the sins of her flesh.

"Then I guess I'll have to charm my way into your bed."

He strode over and took her into his arms, his mouth lowering to hers. She should've pushed him away. She should've told him exactly what she thought of his so-called charm. She should've—but she didn't.

Chapter 15

Josh couldn't get enough of her. What was this spell she'd cast over him?

He tangled his fingers through strands of her hair, marveling at how they felt against his skin. Silken cords curling around his fingers, binding him to her as she lay beside him.

"What have you done to me?" he whispered, not really aware he'd spoken the words aloud.

She stirred. "We had sex. That's all."

When she started to rise, he pushed gently on her shoulder. "Don't go."

She hesitated, and he pulled her closer to him.

"I like having you in bed with me. You smell good."

"I smell like someone who's just had sex." She lifted an eyebrow in his direction.

"No." He leaned closer and smelled her hair. "You smell like tropical breezes. Did you know every time I climb into the Mustang, I can smell this same fragrance. It's been driving me crazy for weeks.

"It's just shampoo and body oil. The same thing I used the other . . . night." She shrugged.

She was running away from him. Maybe not physically, but mentally. She was closing herself off. Blocking him from getting too near. Why was she so scared? She said Rodney had left one day without warning. Had others walked out of her life? Old boyfriends?

"I'd better get back to my room," she mumbled.

Again, he kept her from rising. "Why? Your air conditioner isn't working. The room is probably hot. You'll never be able to fall asleep."

She angled her face until she was looking him in the eye. "How did you know it wasn't working?"

A smile lifted the corners of his mouth. "After the noise died down from those college kids, I could hear it clanking all the way in here. It sounded like a car when it throws a rod. You can't sleep in there without air-conditioning. When you went to the bathroom, I turned it off."

"You think it'll be cooler in here?"

"The temperature of the room will be less hot." He traced his finger between her breasts, then circled one areola before brushing his finger lightly back and forth over her nipple. It immediately tightened. "I can't say much about how cool your body will stay. I know mine is starting to feel a little warm."

He lowered his head, taking her breast into his mouth. He swirled his tongue around the nipple, scraping his teeth across the hard nub, then gently sucking.

Cody arched her back. He inwardly smiled. Damn, she was hot. Hell, so was he. Why he'd pulled his jeans back on was a mystery to him. They both knew making love once tonight would not be enough. Not after waiting so long.

With his free hand, he undid his jeans and kicked them off. He didn't have to take her hand and guide it to him. Her hand was already making the journey. She rolled to her side so she could have better access and grasped him in her hand.

Closing his eyes for a moment, he let the sensations she created wash over him. Slowly her hand moved, sliding his foreskin up, then down again. Slow and easy, she let the passion build inside him.

"Do you like that," she whispered close to his ear. Her tongue flicked his lobe before delving inside.

The heat from her mouth nearly consumed him. He might have started this sensual game, but she'd taken control. He could only mumble something unintelligible as he sank into a cloud of pleasure.

She moved her mouth to his nipple, licking and lightly biting.

"And this? Do you like my mouth on you?"

Before he could say anything, she slid farther down in the bed and lightly placed kisses on the head of his erection, flicking her tongue back and forth over the tip. He jerked toward her mouth, heard her laughter, but couldn't do a damn thing about it. He was locked in a world of delight so erotic he couldn't do much of anything.

"Do you want me to stop . . . or take all of you inside my mouth? I like kissing and licking you. Sucking you deep inside my mouth is even better, though. I like the way you feel against my tongue."

He arched closer to her mouth. "Take me," he moaned.

She didn't disappoint, but licked the full length of his erection, then sucked him inside—one slow inch at a time.

Ahh, damn, it felt so good. The wet heat of her mouth enclosed him in a tight cocoon. He let the sensual sensations swirl around him in hazy deep blues and reds, but he knew that he had to stop her. He didn't want to be the only one receiving pleasure.

He pulled her body up, urging her on top of him after he slipped on the condom he grabbed off the nightstand. She sank her body over his, impaling herself. He stilled her movements with his hands on her hips.

"Just stay like this for a minute," he grated out, barely in control of his body. He took a few seconds to catch his breath, then sat up, locking his hands around her back so she didn't lose her balance.

She grasped him around his neck, her legs automatically wrapping around his waist and bringing her closer to his body. Their noses were almost touching.

"Nice," she murmured, wiggling her bottom on top of his thighs.

"I'll make it even better. Hang on." He stood and sank further inside her, grunting with pleasure.

He gritted his teeth as he fought the incredible feeling of being this damn deep inside a woman. When she tightened her inner muscles, squeezing and releasing, he thought he'd lose it right then. It took a conscious effort to breathe in and breathe out.

"More," she begged, nipping at his ear, then swirling her tongue inside.

Locking his hands beneath her, he raised her, then lowered her back down on him at the same time he moved his hips forward. He watched the expression on her face. She caught her bottom lip with her teeth and moaned from low and deep in her throat.

He thrust inside her again and again, until his legs grew weak and he had to sit on the side of the bed, but he immediately rolled her onto her back and continued the momentum, thrusting deeper and deeper. She cried out, caught in the throes of her orgasm. He was afraid his body would disintegrate any second now if he held back much longer. He let go, let the fire of Cody's body engulf him in wave after wave of pleasure.

Damn, it was incredible. His orgasm wrapped around him, spreading outward to each nerve ending before it exploded again and again.

He finally drew in a deep, shuddering breath, burying his head in Cody's hair.

The French called an orgasm the little death. Maybe they were right because he felt like he'd died and gone to heaven. He rolled his weight off her, but kept her close to him, not wanting to lose contact just yet, needing the connection of her body as well as her mind. Hell, he didn't think he ever wanted to lose contact with this woman.

He brushed the hair out of her face. "What are you thinking about?"

"About how sore I'm going to be in the morning."

As sarcastic as she tried to be, she still sounded like a woman who'd been completely and utterly satisfied. "Ah, but wasn't it worth it?"

She was quiet for a moment and he wondered if she would answer him.

"Yeah, it was worth it."

Chapter 16

Morning came too soon. It seemed to Josh that they'd just fallen asleep when light filtered in through the window blinds. He could've spent another couple of days with her arms wrapped around him, but with daylight came the realization that they were here to do a job. Odd how he seemed to keep forgetting.

He stepped out of the shower and grabbed a towel. After he dried off, he pulled on clean clothes. His thoughts were in the next room, though, with Cody, knowing she'd just stepped out of the shower because he'd heard the water stop.

She'd insisted on going back to her room to shower and get dressed. He'd known there was more to it than the fact that her clothes were there. She needed time alone to absorb everything that had happened between them, and something had happened. He couldn't exactly say what it was—a subtle difference from the other times, or maybe it had been there all along and they were both beginning to notice it.

Hell, he couldn't blame her for needing time alone to digest everything. He was still trying to figure it out.

But it certainly didn't help what his body was going through at this very moment.

Knowing what she looked like naked, what she felt like, what she tasted like—his imagination was driving him crazy as he thought about her stepping from the shower. It was as if he had X-ray vision and he could see through the walls.

He closed his eyes and let his thoughts take flight.

Slowly, she'd run the white towel over her damp body. Caressing her breasts, the nipples tightening, begging for more attention. Then she would slide the towel over her abdomen, down to the juncture between her legs.

Would she get off remembering how he'd touched her there? How his mouth had sucked and licked?

He drew in a ragged breath, wondering if he had time for another shower, but this time he'd use straight cold water. Not that he thought it would really help. All he could think about was sinking into her hot, moist body.

Shit, what was his life coming to? No woman had ever consumed his thoughts like Cody was doing right now. He'd figured spending time with her would help, but he was afraid he'd only accomplished the exact opposite.

Wouldn't Wade have a field day with this? He'd probably tell him something crazy, like how he was falling for Cody. Now that was a ridiculous notion. Cody could be so prickly-tempered, she'd make a porcupine run in the opposite direction.

A knock on the door from Cody's room drew his attention. She must be ready to go to Sinclair's sister's home. At least that would give him something more to think about than sex.

He opened the door—and thoughts of sex were firmly back in place. How could one woman look so damn tempting in a pair of jeans and a T-shirt? She'd left off her vest, her shape clearly defined beneath the cotton material. He wanted to unhook her bra, slip it off . . .

"You ready?" she asked, breaking into his thoughts.

"Yeah." But not for what she was thinking. One look from her deep green eyes and he was more than ready. Maybe because she hadn't just glanced at him. No, it had been a lot more than a glance. Her gaze had caressed him . . . slowly, sensuously. She tried to hide how she felt behind a tough veneer, but he knew better.

When she swept past him, it was all he could do not to grab her in his arms and feel her body melt against his, prove just how much she'd enjoyed having sex with him.

That wouldn't put Adam behind bars, though.

She opened the door and stepped into the bright sunshine. She'd only walked a couple of feet before stopping so suddenly that he almost ran into her.

"You have a flat," she said.

His gaze moved to his back tire. "Son-of-a-bitch." He'd just bought those tires. He strode the rest of the way and knelt down, running his hand over the rubber. He hadn't picked up a nail. More like a knife had slashed across and down the rubber.

"I hate to tell you this, but the other back tire is flat, too," she said as she walked to the other side. She squatted and felt along the tire. "Knife," she said.

"This side, too." He stood, their gazes meeting across the car before he made a sweep of the parking lot.

"The college guys?" she asked. "Maybe they thought they were being funny."

"Maybe, but we aren't the only bounty hunters on Adam's trail." He wouldn't put it past Turbo to have discovered where they were staying. If he had, then Turbo also knew about him and Cody joining forces. That would really piss him off, especially when she'd scorned his advances.

They spent the rest of the morning and well into the afternoon getting new tires. It seemed every gas station in town was on a tight schedule. When they were finally on their way, Josh had time to think about something besides slashed tires and if Turbo or someone else was responsible.

What came to mind was Cody.

She was quiet on the drive to Adam's sister's house. Hell, she'd been quiet all morning. Was she thinking about the way they'd spent last night? He hoped she was. He hoped it was plaguing her as much as it was him. He hoped she wanted a repeat performance.

If not, he was a doomed man.

As he turned up the drive, it struck him again what an idiotic scheme this was. Just walk right up to the front door and explain they were bounty hunters looking for Adam. It would never work. How the hell had he let her talk him into doing this? It was crazy.

That was it. The more he was around her, the more he was losing his mind.

He cast a look in her direction. She'd tempt a saint.

"Are you having second thoughts?" she asked, apparently noticing the sideways glances he was giving her.

"Yeah."

"Do you want to change your mind?"

"No." He looked at her and grinned. "Who's to say a little boldness might not work on Sinclair's sister? Maybe she doesn't like deception. This will be the first time I've been this honest on a case, though. It'll be interesting to see what happens."

He pulled to a stop and killed the engine. It was tempting to look up at the second-floor window. He could feel the woman's gaze on them as they walked toward the front door. Now or never. He rang the doorbell.

The sound of heels across a hardwood floor was a distant tap-tapping that drew nearer before the door opened.

The same woman who'd been walking down the stairs last night stood before them. She was taller up close. Maybe five-eleven, and she wore her gray hair in a severe bun at the base of her neck, pulled so tight her wrinkles were more like slash marks. Everything about her was stiff, cold, unyielding. This didn't bode well.

"Yes," she said, dragging that one word out. Her eyebrows rose almost to her hairline and she actually sniffed, as if in disdain of her mistress's unwelcome visitors.

Beside him, Cody stiffened her spine and squared her shoulders. He didn't know who he felt more sorry for, the woman looking down her very narrow nose at them, or Cody. She might have guessed wrong about using honesty as her strategy.

This was Cody's ballgame, though. He'd let her throw the first pitch.

"We're here to speak with Bertrice Sinclair."

The woman's lip curled. "Do you have an appointment?"

Cody raised her chin. "You know damn well we don't."

"Then what is your purpose in seeing Ms. Sinclair?"

Josh had to give her credit. The old battle-ax didn't blink an eye. He didn't have long to wait to see what Cody would say next.

"We're recovery agents. Adam Sinclair skipped bail. We can bring him in, or someone else can. Our way will be a hell of a lot easier on her brother than some of the goons out there who call themselves recovery agents."

The woman opened her mouth to deliver what Josh was almost certain would be a stinging retort, but the phone beside the door gave a shrill ring. Her mouth snapped shut as she turned to answer it.

"Yes, Ms. Sinclair." She looked over her shoulder. "Are you sure? They say they're recovery agents. Yes, ma'am." She replaced the phone in the cradle.

When she turned back to face them she didn't look a bit happy.

She opened the door wider. "Ms. Sinclair will see you."

As soon as they were inside, she shut the door behind them, none too gently. Josh looked at Cody as they followed the woman up a winding staircase. Cody didn't have to say *I told you so*. Her smug expression said it all. Well, they hadn't gotten any information yet, but he'd like to know what was going through her mind. Like how she knew Sinclair's sister would let them inside the house.

Cody could feel Josh's gaze on her. She didn't even try to stop the self-satisfied smile from turning up the corners of her mouth. At least she didn't stick her tongue out at him. He should be grateful for that.

Her gut instinct had been right this time. Adam and his sister cared for each other. That was evident in the way she lived. They were very nice digs. This must've set Adam back a pretty penny.

A heavy, ornate iron chandelier cast a warm light over the downstairs entry. Paintings of landscapes lined the wall where one would normally see family portraits. She knew Adam had come from humble beginnings. Was this his way of taking care of his sister? Is that why he'd killed his partner?

At the top of the stairs, Tight Ass went to the first door and opened it. Her glare warned them she would be close by if Bertrice needed her. Cody glared right back, letting her know she wasn't in the least intimidated, and waltzed inside the room.

Some of her bravado diminished when she noted the stern, unyielding look on the face of the woman sitting in a high-backed chair by the window. She was unable to meet her look for long.

She glanced away and noted the cane that leaned against her chair and the brace on one of her legs. Cody looked past it, her gaze taking in the rest of the room.

A four-poster bed in rich, dark wood. A gold comforter. The dresser matched the bed. Everything neat, no-nonsense. Just like the woman in the chair.

"Sit," she told them in a strong voice that belied the fragility of her body. "I don't want to strain my neck in order to see who I'm talking with."

Tight Ass quietly closed the door as she left.

"We're sorry to disturb you," Josh said, pulling two chairs forward.

"No, you're not. You're probably laughing, thinking you got past the front door where the others hadn't." She shrugged slender shoulders. "I would, too, if the truth be known."

"We didn't lie," Cody said. "If we're the ones who bring your brother in, then it will go easier for him. You have our promise on that."

The older woman cocked an eyebrow. "And who's to say you're not lying?"

She was toying with them. Was she bored? Was that why she'd asked them to come upstairs? Adam's sister had dangled the carrot, but would she let them get close enough to grab it?

"You'll just have to take our word for it, but one thing we both know is that time is wasting. Another bounty hunter could be close on your brother's heels. I know some of them. They won't be nice," Cody warned.

"Adam is my half brother. Same father, different mother."

"Not having the same mother never mattered, did it?" Josh asked.

The spark of defiance in Bertrice's eyes died and some of her strength seemed to melt away. "Did it matter?" She smoothed her white dress over her lap, straightening imaginary wrinkles. "No, it never bothered us that we had different mothers."

She sighed.

"I was just as excited about the new baby as everyone else, even though I don't know how Dad and Annie expected to feed another mouth when they couldn't put enough food on the table as it was. I was young enough that I didn't really care that we were poor."

Cody glanced toward Josh, wondering where Bertrice was going with all the family history. There was an almost imperceptible lift of his eyebrows, as if to say he was wondering the same thing, but at least Adam's sister hadn't kicked them out yet.

Bertrice took a drink from the glass of water that was on the small table beside her chair, then patted her lips with a linen napkin trimmed in lace.

"Adam's mother died when he was two," she continued.

"She caught the flu and it turned into pneumonia. Our father was inconsolable. It was left to me to raise Adam even though I was only twelve. Again, I didn't care. Where other little girls had dolls, I had the real thing."

She closed her eyes for a moment and Cody wondered if Bertrice had dozed off, but a few seconds later, she opened her eyes and began to speak again.

"I dropped out of school when I was a sophomore. Not that it mattered. I didn't like school anyway, but Adam did. I knew he'd want to go to college someday. He'd need money, so no one would laugh at his mended clothes." She smiled. "He did well for himself, but he never forgot about me."

"Do you know where he is?" Josh asked.

She ignored his question and continued. "He didn't do it, you know. Adam respects life. Even with all my help, he still had to work hard to get where he is. It was always honest work, too. He would never kill another human being. It's just not in him."

"Maybe it was an accident?" Cody supplied.

She shook her head. "He told me he didn't, and I believe him."

Cody wished for Bertrice's sake that was true, but from experience, the opposite was the norm. Maybe this time would be different.

"Until Adam has his day in court, he can't prove his innocence," Cody told her.

Bertrice stared long and hard at them before sighing deeply. "I don't need all this." She waved her arm over the room. "I only wanted Adam's happiness. He'll never have that as long as he's on the run, always looking over his shoulder. He deserves better."

"Where is he?" Josh prodded.

"Yesterday there were men here. I didn't like the looks of one of them. He made me afraid for Adam." She leaned forward, her eyes narrowing to slits. "Do you swear that he'll come to no harm?"

"We'll do our best." Josh took her hand in his. "I give you my word that I'll treat him with as much respect as you do."

Bounty hunters knew how to lie, but Cody had a feeling Josh was telling the truth. One look at Bertrice and Cody knew that Adam's sister believed Josh would do his best to uphold his end of the bargain.

Her hand slipped from his. "Adam has a vacation home in Mexico. Just a small place. You'll find him there." She reached for her notebook and pen, then began to write. When she finished, she handed Josh the paper. "This is where you can find him. Now go, I'm tired." She turned her head away, effectively dismissing them.

They left the room. True to her word, Tight Ass was right outside the door and had probably heard every word. She didn't say anything as they followed her down the stairs. When she opened the front door to let them out, she gave them a warning.

"Ms. Bertrice might look like she has one foot in the grave, but fair warning, harm one hair on Adam's head and she'll make sure you pay." Without another word, she shut the door behind them.

"Bitch," Cody mumbled before trotting down the steps toward the car.

But hey, it'd been worth putting up with Tight Ass's attitude to get Adam's whereabouts. She just hadn't expected to care about this case. Before meeting Bertrice, her only concern had been proving she was damn good at what she did. She certainly hadn't wanted to care about Adam's sister.

A niggling of guilt pricked her. It had been obvious Bertrice loved her little brother. Damn it, if he was innocent, then why had he run?

After they were inside the car, Josh turned to her. "So, what do you make of the sister? You think she's turned a blind eye to little brother's business activities?"

She clasped her hands in front of her and stared straight ahead. "Who knows? Sometimes you only think you know a person, then you realize they're not at all like you thought they were. People are always surprising the hell out of me."

There'd been too many surprises in her life. In a flash, she knew Josh had been one of them. She hadn't expected the sex to be so damn satisfying every time. Just thinking about how they'd spent the night made her want him again.

Without a doubt, she knew he was going to hurt her. Hell, maybe she was the one who would cause herself the most pain.

He broke into her thoughts. "We might as well eat and go back to the motel. I don't like the idea of crossing the border this late."

"I don't like crossing into Mexico at all," she grumbled. "The Mexican police would love to throw two more bounty hunters in the slammer and keep them there forever and ever."

He grinned as he started the car. "Yeah, but they won't know we're bounty hunters. As far as they're concerned, we're just two tourists out to see the sights. I told you it'd pay if we became partners."

She leaned back against the seat and eyed him. "You don't think we'll be a little conspicuous? Vests, mace, a couple of guns, knives . . . ?"

"I have a special compartment beneath the car where we can store everything. No one would even think of looking there. We'll cross over as typical tourists." He turned slightly in his seat and faced her. "Not nervous, are you?"

"Are you crazy? Of course I'm nervous. I'd be a fool if I weren't. Don't worry, though. I won't blow our cover."

"Good. Then I only have one question."

"And what would that be."

"Where do you want to eat?"

"As long as it doesn't include beans and rice, I'm game for just about anything."

*   *   *

Cody swirled the cheese around her finger, then stuck out her tongue and licked, but left most of the cheese. When she caught him staring, she laughed and opened her mouth, taking her finger inside and sucking it clean.

"I love pizza. Good choice," she said.

"Almost as much as I love watching you eat it." Damn, she was killing him. Everything she did had a sexual nuance. She probably didn't mean for her actions to come across as sexy, but they were, and it was tormenting the hell out of him.

"You're not eating," she pointed out. "If we're going to get an early start, then we'd better get to bed at a decent hour."

Cody, bed, and decent. Which word didn't belong? He finished off the last bite of the pizza, then washed it down with a beer.

Why had he wanted to partner up with her? Oh, yeah, so he could get her out of his system. Smart move. He needed to have his head examined.

"You ready?" He couldn't eat another bite if his life depended on it. All he could think about was getting back to his room and putting a little space between them. Either that or he was going to have sex with her again.

Which wasn't such a bad idea, come to think about it, except for the fact that they needed to concentrate on bringing Adam back to the States. Crossing the border could get dangerous and they'd need to keep their wits about them.

Not that they could do a damn thing about it until morning. Oh, hell, who was he fooling? They both knew what they'd be doing when they were behind closed doors.

She stood and he followed suit, dropping money on the table. When she reached into her pocket, he said, "I've got it." She visibly stiffened. Before she could go into another spiel about paying her way, he added, "You can get the next one."

She hesitated only briefly. "Okay."

They were both silent on the way back to the motel. He wondered if they were thinking the same thing. They hadn't really spoken about last night. What the hell could they say?

He parked the car in front of the rooms. She went to hers and he went to his.

A good night's sleep, his ass. How could he sleep when all he could think about was Cody lying naked beside him? And it was too damn hot in his room. What was it about the air conditioners in this motel? He fiddled with the thermostat, but the air was still only slightly cooler than it had been a minute ago.

Finally, he gave up, knowing it would do no good to call maintenance. It was a cheap motel. They wouldn't really care. He wondered briefly if they'd fixed Cody's.

He stripped and grabbed a towel. A cool shower might bring relief in more ways than one. A knock on the door dividing the rooms made his heart catch. Just as quickly, hope died. It was probably nothing. Maybe she wanted to borrow something.

He started to open the door, remembered he was bare-ass naked, and wrapped the towel around him, tucking it in at the waist, then opened the door.

All the air left his body. Cody casually leaned against the door, stark naked.

"I needed a towel," she said. "Mind if I borrow yours?" She slipped her hand in at the waist and tugged it off. Just as casually, she turned and strolled back into her room.

"I never said I'd loan it to you." He trailed after her, liking the way her hips swayed and the sexy little bounce her butt cheeks made with each step she took.

She cast an innocent look over her shoulder. "So take it away from me. That is, if you can."

He always had loved a challenge.

Chapter 17

Cody laughed when Josh barreled after her. She feinted to the right, then at the last minute moved in the opposite direction, leaving him with an armful of empty space.

"Oh, you can do better than that, can't you? I mean, you are a big, bad bounty hunter." She waved the towel as if it were a red flag.

He didn't disappoint her, and lunged again. She whirled at the last minute, moving just out of his reach, but keeping her eye on him. She loved watching the way he moved. It showed off his body to perfection. He really did have a nice body.

Firm and hard. Very hard.

And if this was all the time they had together, then she'd decided to make damn good use of it.

"So, you like to play games," he said.

She'd never had the inclination before now, but yes, her very naughty thoughts amazed even her. She had a feeling playing games with Josh would be a lot of fun.

"Maybe I do. Does it bother you?" she asked.

He slowly shook his head. "We're consenting adults. We can do whatever we want as long as it isn't illegal. I know lots of games."

She caught her breath, her imagination running wild. Before she realized what he was doing, he'd eased up close, then lunged, pulling her into his embrace.

"You cheated," she accused him.

He grinned. "Yeah. That's the only thing about playing games. I always cheat."

Not that she really cared when his mouth lowered to hers. What was it about Josh that could send her over the edge of reason? She wanted to explore every sexual fantasy she'd ever imagined, but only with him.

She pressed her body closer to his, enjoying the feel of raw strength that she encountered. She splayed her hands across his back, moving them lower until she cupped his butt. Moaning, she pressed closer, rubbing her sex against his erection.

His hands roamed the length of her back, cupping her bottom. He squeezed and massaged, bringing her even tighter against him.

She could feel herself getting close to an orgasm. It was too soon. She wanted tonight to be even better than last night, but damn, the friction of his erection against her sex felt really good.

Through the thin walls came a haunting melody as someone played a CD. The gentle chords wrapped around her. "Let's dance," she said forcing herself to move away. Her body undulated to the beat of the music, swaying back and forth, the hypnotic sounds taking control.

He lay back on the bed, pulled the pillows beneath his head and stared. "You dance . . . for me."

She didn't need any more encouragement. She'd always liked music and how it could invade her senses. Having Josh watch her made her feel very sexy, very wanton.

Raising her hands, she threaded her fingers through her hair, bringing the strands up, then letting them tumble back down.

"I want you," he said, his hand lightly skimming the length of his penis.

Her movements wobbled as she watched him stroking

himself. She licked her lips, wanting to taste, wanting to take all of him in her mouth.

"Keep dancing," he murmured. "I like watching the way you move. I like when you touch yourself."

She raised her chin as a burst of defiance swept over her. Why should he be the one dictating what she did? She would do whatever damn well gave her pleasure. Why should he be the one in charge?

"When you massage your breasts, tugging on your nipples, it drives me insane. Do you realize how much power you wield?"

Her flare of rebelliousness dissolved as quickly as it had sprung up. It was a heady feeling knowing she could drive Josh over the edge.

She picked up the oil she'd used that morning and left on her nightstand. Their gazes locked as she slowly removed the lid, squeezing a large amount of the tropical fragrance on her palm before setting the oil back down. She began to move her hips to the music, slowly sliding her hands to her breasts and cupping them in her palms, smearing the liquid over them. She tweaked her nipples, letting her head drop back as sensations of pleasure wrapped her in a snug cocoon.

Her hands glided over her body, slick from the lotion and heightening her sense of pleasure.

"Touch your sex," he rasped out. "Open yourself for me."

She raised her head and stared as he continued to slowly stroke himself. His gaze moved with her as she splayed her hands and slid them down her body. He sucked in a breath when she spread her lips and began to massage her clit.

She moaned. Ah, damn, it felt so good. The building of tension was extraordinary. She'd never felt this hot in any of her sexual experiences.

"Talk to me. Tell me what you feel."

She stared at him through a fog of building passion. "It's incredible. I'm wet and so damn hot."

"Do you want more?"

"Yes," she breathed, meeting his gaze unflinching. "I want to feel you inside me. I want you to fuck me. Damn it, I can't stand any more." Her body was at such a fever pitch that she didn't know why she hadn't collapsed.

Apparently he sensed how close to the edge she was, because he was there beside her before she was even aware he'd moved. He scooped her up and carried her to the bed, laying her gently on the mattress. His body covered her like a warm blanket on a cold day.

But it wasn't cold. Far from it. Her body was on fire for him and it seemed to take too long for him to put on a condom, but when he entered her, it was so worth the wait. She wrapped her legs around him and pulled him in deeper.

"Raise your hips," he told her, pulling out.

Mindlessly, she obeyed, wanting him back inside. He stuffed a pillow beneath her bottom. When he entered the next time, he sank deeper, filled her more. She couldn't stop the moan that escaped past her lips.

He paused. "I'm not hurting you, am I?"

She laughed. It bubbled right out of her. "Only if you stop. Then I would be in a hell of a lot of pain."

He grinned. God, she loved the way he smiled. She loved the way their bodies seemed to automatically fit together. She loved the way it felt to have him deep inside her.

"More," she said.

"Greedy, aren't you."

"Damn right."

He didn't deny either one of them any longer as he began to move above her. The heat inside her intensified until she thought she would explode into a fiery blaze of passion. The first wave of her orgasm swept over her and her body began to shudder in ecstasy.

"I love to watch you in the throes of an orgasm," he said just before he groaned and became lost in his own release.

No more than she enjoyed watching him. When he rolled

off her, he took her with him. "I think I like playing games with you." And why shouldn't she? Never in her life had she felt this satisfied.

But I won't care about him, she told herself. It was still only sex. Very adventurous, very fun sex. Who was to say she wouldn't find the same thing with another man?

He lightly caressed her back, then pulled her close. "Me, too," he said so low that at first she wondered if he'd said anything at all.

She yawned and snuggled close to his side. She'd never slept all night with any other man. She liked the sound of Josh's heartbeat this close to her ear. It was a comforting sound. Something she could easily get used to.

Josh cast a sideways glance in Cody's direction. Both hands were gripping the seat and her skin was a little pale. Damn, she wasn't kidding when she said she was nervous. He wasn't even sure if she was breathing.

"You can stop holding your breath, we've crossed the border," he told her. He never thought he'd see the day she was scared of anything.

"Was I that obvious?" She glanced in the rearview mirror.

He chuckled. "Only to me. Don't worry, we'll be in and out before you can name all the capitals of the states."

She frowned. "I don't know all the capitals."

"Then we might be in trouble," he said with a straight face.

She slanted an eyebrow. "You're a regular fucking comedian."

"Thank you."

"Just don't give up your day job."

He turned serious. "I know as well as you the dangers of crossing into Mexico. Juarez isn't one of my favorite places to visit and I damn sure don't plan on spending the rest of my life in a Mexican jail."

"In and out."

He nodded.

"So, how far do we have to go before we reach Adam's place?"

"About ten miles."

"Do you think his sister might have been feeding us a line of crap? Throwing us off the scent?"

"Who knows, but we have to check it out."

He drove slowly through the border town. It was seedier than some of the more popular crossings, but it still catered to the tourist industry. Vendors hawked their wares, trying to pick up a few pesos in the hopes of putting something more substantial on the dinner table than beans and tortillas.

A person could buy anything in Mexico. The object was not to get caught if it was illegal. Jail time in Mexico might not be as long, but when the rundown state of the prisons was factored in, it could seem like an eternity, even if one had the money to purchase one of the better cells. It just wasn't worth it.

"They're awfully young," Cody said under her breath, looking at the raggedly dressed group of kids playing with sticks and a rusty tin can on one of the corners, some begging for money from people passing by.

"You grow up fast here. It's the only way to survive. About forty percent of the population of Mexico is at poverty level. Life is hard."

The town didn't look that threatening in the daylight. The locals would want to keep their tourist business. Night would be a different story.

"You ever been to Mexico?" Odd that they'd had sex and he still knew so little about her. Suddenly, he wanted to know more.

"I've stuck pretty close to home. I always figured we had enough criminals in Fort Worth to keep me busy."

"But you've always wanted to go to the coast."

"I'm surprised you remembered."

When she looked at him and smiled, something in his gut

clenched. "There's very little that I forget." He relaxed in the seat, laying one arm across the steering wheel. "There's nothing like seeing the ocean for the first time. On a calm day, it looks like a plate of blue glass. If it's cloudy, then it takes on a gray-green color. There's nothing better than watching it during a storm when the waves crash against the rocks and spew foam straight up like a geyser."

"Someday I'll go."

At least talking about the ocean had relaxed her. He had a feeling it was going to be a temporary condition.

He glanced in the rearview mirror again. A car had been following him for the last couple of blocks or so. The white Oldsmobile had seen better days: dented hood streaked with rust, one headlight missing, and if he were on the street watching it pass, he'd probably hear a sound worse than his air conditioner clanking last night. The car looked like a refugee from a war-torn country as it limped behind them. The only thing that made it stand out from other vehicles was the strobe lights on top.

How the hell had the cops picked up their scent this damn fast? Unless someone had informed them there would be two bounty hunters crossing the border.

Turbo. Nah, even he wouldn't stoop that low.

Cody jerked upright in her seat. She'd apparently glanced out the side mirror and spotted the car, too. What the hell had he gotten her into? Nothing that he couldn't get them out of. He hoped. For the first time in a hell of a long time, he felt a moment of fear and uncertainty.

"Cop," she breathed.

"It might be nothing. Just checking out the strange car in town."

"Or not," she said as the cop flipped his overheads on. "How's your Spanish?"

"Rusty at best. You?" He pulled to the curb.

"I skipped class a lot in high school. I think I can cuss him out for you."

"That might not be a good idea." He sent a quick prayer upward as he watched a big bruiser hoist his bulk out of the car and lumber toward them. Just before he got to the door, he spat a stream of brown tobacco juice on the street.

Now Josh didn't have to wonder about the stains on the front of the cop's yellow shirt.

Josh rolled down the window. The cop rattled some Spanish off. He shook his head. "No *comprende*."

"*Policía*." The cop hoisted his pants.

"No, shit," he muttered.

"*Gringo*." His accent was thick, but Josh caught the scorn he apparently felt for Americans.

Before he could answer, the cop glanced past Josh and looked at Cody. Josh's gut tightened when the man stared a little too long.

"We're Americans. Did we do something wrong?" Josh asked, drawing the man's attention back to him. Too many people went missing in Mexico. He damn sure didn't want them to be the next statistic.

"Follow," the cop said. Without another word, he went back to his car.

"Damn!" Cody sat forward in her seat. "What the hell did we do?"

"Nothing," Josh said between gritted teeth.

He'd been to Mexico before. In and out without ever causing a hint of suspicion with the local authorities. So what was different this time?

"Where the hell are we going?" she asked.

"They don't have anything on us. Just stay calm. Remember, we're tourists."

He followed the cop all the way to the police station. Each block they went, the acid built inside him until he thought he'd choke on it.

"Maybe we can make a run for it. It's not like we're that far from the border."

He shook his head. "We'd never make it. Stay cool.

There's not a damn thing they can do. They might ask us a few questions, but they'll have to let us go."

"This is Mexico. They can do anything they want."

Yeah, they could, but he didn't tell her that. Someway, somehow, he'd get her out of this. Suddenly, bringing Adam in, starting his own agency, all that didn't mean as much to him as it once had. It seemed a hell of a lot more important that he keep Cody safe.

He pulled into the parking space next to the cop and they got out. The cop didn't speak, just went to the door and opened it. Apparently, he expected them to follow. What the hell else could they do?

He reached out and took Cody's hand, squeezing it. He wanted to tell her again that everything would be okay. She looked at him, then smiled, as if to tell him they weren't beat yet. Some of her bravado was back. Good. He hadn't thought anything would get her down for long. She was a fighter.

They went inside. A ceiling fan whirred above their heads giving little relief from the rising temperatures inside the stale, dusty office.

The cop walked straight through to the door at the back. Josh put a hand out to stop Cody. She latched onto it, her grip cutting off the circulation in his fingers. The cop turned at the door.

"It eez a minor problem. You will wait in here *uno momento, si?*" He smiled, showing a chipped front tooth.

A smile that wasn't a bit friendly.

Fuck, what the hell was going on? The police couldn't know why they were here. When another cop stepped behind them, they had little choice except to walk to the back and into the cramped jail cell. The door slammed behind them with a loud bang. Cody visibly jumped.

"They know," Cody whispered after the officers left. She began to pace the dark, musty cell.

"They don't know," he told her. "How could they?"

"I'm thinking it wasn't college kids who slashed the tires."

He ran a hand through his hair. "I thought the same thing," he admitted. "It had to be Turbo who informed them we'd be crossing the line. He'd like nothing more than for us to rot in jail."

"Well, I don't plan on sticking around any longer than necessary." She stopped pacing, pressed her hands against the crumbling rock of the jail cell. "With a little effort, I think we could push the wall down."

"Yeah, right on top of our heads."

She whirled around to face him. "They don't have the death penalty or anything here, do they?"

He gathered her in his arms. "It'll be okay." He was starting to sound like a broken record. "And no, they don't have the death penalty."

"You better be telling the truth, Josh Pierce. I'd hate like hell to kick your ass."

With one finger, he tilted her chin and lowered his mouth to hers. Damn, even in a stinking Mexican jail she tasted pretty sweet. Now was not the time to get horny. He ended the kiss, but when she would've pulled away, he snuggled her closer to him. He wasn't ready to break the connection between them.

"Welcome to Mexico! I am Hector Gonzales, *el capitan.*" The man who spoke was around their age, probably no more than thirty-five. He stopped at their cell. His smile was wide and friendly, but Josh could see the hard edge glittering in his eyes.

"Is this the way you greet all your tourists?" he asked as Cody stepped from his arms and glared at their visitor.

"No, of course not." The smile left his face. "Only the bounty hunters who would bother our good citizens. Especially those who contribute very nicely to our economy."

Josh had no doubts left. Turbo had notified the Mexican police that they were crossing. He hadn't believed even Turbo would stoop that low. Damn it, Josh knew he wasn't completely blameless, either. If he hadn't been so caught up with

Cody, he would've paid more attention. There was only one way they were going to get out of this—their original cover of being tourists. He hoped the man believed him.

"What? Bounty hunters can't go on vacation?"

"Certainly." The man beamed. "But we were informed you would be searching for Adam Sinclair. Is that not so?" He raised his eyebrows.

"No, it isn't." Think! Why did people cross the border? Other than bargain-hunting, there was only one other thing he could think of. Lord help him for what he was about to do.

Josh took a deep breath. "We're here to get married. You can still get married in one day, right?" He pulled Cody into his arms and hugged her close. He didn't dare look at her face. He hoped she went along with his scheme. And he hoped the jackal in front of him believed his lies.

Chapter 18

Married? Married! Was Josh crazy? Never mind, Cody had a feeling she already knew the answer to her question. He squeezed her waist in silent warning. Did he think she would blow their new cover? Tell the chief of police that no, they weren't here to get married, and he was right about them crossing the border to hunt for Adam?

Hell, she'd say she was going to marry Turbo if it kept her out of a Mexican prison.

"You mean we're not going to get married today?" Her bottom lip trembled.

Hector had the grace to blush. "But we had a call saying you were here to take Adam Sinclair back to justice."

"A jealous boyfriend." Josh shook his head. "But you saw us kissing. Didn't it look like love to you?"

Hector took a minute to digest everything. "But Adam Sinclair has crossed the border, no? And you admitted you are bounty hunters."

Cody batted her eyes at the young chief of police. "But we had no reason to lie. I've never heard of Adam Sinclair." She downed her head. "We've had other things on our minds."

She covertly watched the changing expressions on his face. Was he going to buy their story? *Come on, you jerk.*

Suddenly, Hector squared his shoulders; anger mottled his

skin. "*Stupido!*" he bellowed. Two officers came running from the front.

He rattled something off in Spanish. One of the men fumbled with a set of keys at his waist, but finally got them loose and handed them to Hector.

As Hector unlocked the cell, he said, "My apologies, I will make, how you say, amends."

"That's not necessary," Josh began, only to be interrupted.

"I insist." He beamed. "I am newlywed, also. My Maria would be very angry if I let you get married in a flea-infested office. No, you will be married in my home!"

Cody stumbled. It was one thing to say you were going to marry someone, another to actually do it. Her gaze flew to Josh. Her eyes dared him to get them out of this one. Married! She didn't want to get married.

"Actually," she began. "We thought we'd find a priest and get married in a little country church." They were called priests, right?

"*Sí, sí.*" He nodded. "I have a place in the country. It would be my pleasure if you would allow me to offer my humble home for your wedding."

Before she could politely turn down his offer, Josh spoke up.

"We'd be more than honored."

She squeezed his hand as hard as she could while keeping a smile pasted on her face. She'd kill him—as soon as they were back in the good old U.S.A.

Marry him? Not likely.

Surely he could've come up with some other reason for them being here.

They went back into the front office. Before they had done more than step inside, Josh nuzzled her neck. "You're not acting like a woman who wants to get married," he whispered. "Don't worry, I know enough that it won't be legal unless we have blood tests and there isn't enough time."

She'd like to be the one who drew first blood. She turned her head, but some of her anger faded when her lips brushed against his. She had to clear her throat before she could speak. "I probably don't act like I want to get married because I don't want to marry you."

"We'll only be going through the motions," Josh said under his breath.

When he nuzzled her neck, it wasn't thoughts of what would be legal that were crossing her mind. For a moment, she forgot that she was standing in a police station in a foreign country.

"See!" Hector roared. "*Stupido*! Can you not tell when two people are in love? Do they *look* like they are here to capture Señor Sinclair?"

The two cops lowered their heads and shuffled their feet. One had the nerve to speak up. "But the caller said they were here to take Señor Sinclair back across the border." He looked at his cohort. "Eez right?"

"I don't hear nothin'."

Hector threw his arms into the air. "A jealous lover!" He shook his head and muttered something in Spanish before turning back to them. "Please." His voice had softened and he smiled. "You will leave your car here and come with me. I will take you to my home and we will have everything arranged for a *magnífico* wedding, no?"

No was right. How the hell had she ended up in Mexico about to marry Josh? Oh, yeah, because he'd told her that she'd do a lot better as his partner than on her own. She snorted. This was real fucking good.

Okay, she had to think. Surely there was a way she could get out of this. A plan. Yeah, that's what she needed. A plan to get them out of this fix. She could do it. There were a number of things she could think of that would stop the marriage and still keep them from going to prison.

She just couldn't think of one right now.

Deep breath.

Surely they could hatch some kind of plot before they had to get married. As if sensing her growing panic, Josh squeezed her hand while they walked toward the car.

El capitan's blue Buick was a little newer than the patrol car, but then he was the man in charge. He wasn't bad looking. Briefly, she wondered if he might be swayed by a woman's wiles.

Just as quickly as the thought crossed her mind, she discarded it. He'd already said he was recently married. She doubted he would stray this soon after getting hitched.

She and Josh could have a fight. That might be an option, but would Hector then start to wonder if Turbo had been telling the truth? She envisioned herself all alone in a dark cell, the rustle of hungry rats scurrying in the corner as they waited for her to fall asleep.

A shiver of revulsion ran down her spine.

"My Maria will be so happy I am bringing guests home. She comes from a big family and is, how you say, home-aching for her mama. Planning a wedding will make her much pleased."

They got in the backseat while Hector moved to the driver's side. This wasn't good. Not at all. He started the car and backed out. Each building they passed, each block they crossed, she felt as if control of her life was slipping from between her fingers. She'd always had control. The one thing no one had ever taken away from her was her right to choose what she did.

Josh rested his hand on her knee, stopping the frantic tap-tapping rhythm she'd been beating out on the floorboard. She hadn't realized her nervousness was getting the better of her.

She took a deep breath and slowly exhaled. Then another. Calm wove its way around her. What was the worst thing that could happen? That she might actually end up married to Josh? He was right. It wouldn't be legal without the necessary blood tests.

She swallowed past the lump in her throat.

No problem. Okay, she felt better. Sort of.

"This eez my humble home." Hector waved his hand toward a Spanish-style mansion.

Whatever she'd expected, it wasn't this. Modest, that's what she'd envisioned. A modest two-bedroom house. Talk about a man's home being his castle. This was an estate. Apparently, Adam had greased Hector's palm very well. No wonder he wanted to protect him. Heaven forbid his source of income might dry up.

They drove up the circular drive and he stopped in front of the sprawling house: stucco bleached a creamy white from an unrelenting sun and a red-tiled roof. Native plants flanked an inset doorway, softening the front entrance.

"You have a very nice home," Josh commented.

Hector beamed. "It has been in my family many generations. Someday I will pass it down to my oldest son."

She might have been wrong about Hector taking bribes. Still, she couldn't resist asking, "And if you have a daughter first?"

Josh squeezed her hand a little too tightly. She didn't care. Sometimes she had to step on that soapbox.

"I apologize . . ." Josh began.

Hector waved his hand. "Eez okay. I understand Americans do not think as we do sometimes. If I am blessed with sons and daughters, I will make sure they are taken care of properly." He bowed slightly in her direction.

For some odd reason, she felt as if she'd been put in her place. Before she had time to dwell on it, the front door opened and a slender woman stepped out. Cody could only stare. She was beautiful, with dark hair that had been pulled back in a loose bun, tendrils caressing her face, giving her an almost angelic look.

"Hector." Her voice was soft, throaty, and the way she looked at her husband, Cody had no doubt that if they weren't there, Hector's wife would've gone straight into his arms and kissed him quite soundly.

Hector didn't appear immune to her charms. He even took a step toward his wife, but apparently remembered he'd brought guests home and stopped at the last minute.

"Maria, these are my friends, Josh and Cody." He beamed with pride. "And this is my wife, Maria."

"My husband's friends are most welcome."

"They are going to be married. I could not let them do so in a dingy office."

Maria looked at them with wide eyes. "Married? In town? No, no." She shook her head. "We will plan a wedding here." She clapped her hands, then hurried forward, taking Cody's hands into hers. "It will be such fun, no?"

"No," she muttered before she could stop herself.

Maria turned quizzical eyes on her. Cody had a sudden vision of a dark cell and a rat running across her feet. "I mean, yes, it will be grand." She only hoped Maria believed her. Cody didn't relax until Hector's wife smiled.

"Come." Hector waved toward the house. "Let us go inside where it eez a little cooler."

"*Si*," Maria voiced before turning toward the house and hurrying up the steps. "Louisa, drinks for our guests." She clapped her hands and a maid came to the door. "Drinks, drinks, *por favor*."

Cody finally got up enough nerve to look at Josh. His lips had thinned to a straight line after their host and hostess turned to lead the way inside. All this time, she'd been thinking of what was happening to her, but she never once thought about how Josh felt. Looking at him now, she could see he wasn't at all enthused with the turn of events. Not that she blamed him, but she couldn't stop the niggle of regret. Would marrying her be that much of an inconvenience? For some strange reason that bothered her.

They went inside. The difference between the exterior and

interior was like night and day. The heat outside was already beginning to grow uncomfortably warm, but once inside the foyer the adobe walls and terra-cotta floor dropped the temperature by at least ten degrees.

"Welcome," Maria said as she waved her arm in front of her, beckoning them inside her living room.

Heavy, deep brown leather furniture dominated the room. All of it looked handcrafted, some possibly handed down from one generation to the next. Rustic, but with a beauty only age could give it.

She wondered how it would feel to know so much about your ancestors. Her mother never spoke of her parents. They were dead. That's all Cody knew. A sudden longing to have all the answers, to know more about her father, filled her.

Lord, now wasn't that hysterical. A forced marriage and all of a sudden she wanted to plant a damned family tree, with branches reaching far and wide. Hell, her poor family tree was stunted, and she seriously doubted there would ever be any branches.

Louisa brought a tray of drinks, thankfully interrupting her thoughts. She didn't need to get maudlin now. If Turbo had been the one to inform the police they were crossing the border in search of a bail jumper, then he'd be on Adam's trail. The idea they might lose Adam to Turbo left a bitter taste in her mouth. The sooner they were married and on their way, the sooner they could get back to their original plan.

"To new friends," Hector said, raising his glass.

It wouldn't do any good to tell him that she didn't have nor want friends. No, that wasn't true. She had Moji. And now Josh. She closed her eyes. No, lovers weren't the same thing as friends—were they? She opened her eyes and drank half the iced tea in her glass, but it did little to make her feel refreshed.

"Come, we go upstairs. Leave the men to their talk," Maria said, grabbing Cody's hands and pulling her along with her. "We have much to talk about for the wedding. So many plans to make."

Cody glanced toward Josh, silently begging him to rescue her, but he only shrugged. What else could he do? His hands were tied as tightly as hers. This wasn't good. She was so out of her element.

As gently as she could, Cody disentangled her hand from Maria's. The woman acted as if they were best friends.

"Come, come," Maria said. "There's much to do."

Okay, fine, but she damn well didn't have to like it. Why the hell had Josh suggested getting married in the first place? No, she wouldn't rehash it all again. What good would it do?

She trailed reluctantly behind Maria as she led the way up a wide staircase. Cody didn't even take time to admire the oak banister, or the way it gleamed from hours of polishing.

At the top of the stairs, Maria swept down the hallway to the last room on the right.

"This will be your room." She opened the door. "If you do not like, then I will show you another."

Not like? Walls painted a deep, warm rose made her want to kick off her shoes and sit for a while. Her gaze moved slowly around the beautiful room. A four-poster bed graced one wall. It wasn't frilly, but it was very feminine, with detailed scrollwork. A plush bright yellow comforter draped the bed in luxury. Cody almost couldn't resist the urge to flop across it and cuddle one of the many pillows that layered the bed. It just looked too damn inviting. A matching vanity, armoire, and a small sitting area completed the decor.

"No," Cody said with a slight shake of her head. "This will do fine. I mean, better than fine. Wow, it's beautiful."

Maria's smile widened. "This is my favorite room. Sometimes I come here and read. It brings me peace. I hope it will do the same for you."

She grabbed Cody's hand and pulled her over to the small sitting area. What was all this touchy stuff? The inside of a jail wasn't looking quite as bad as it once had.

They sat in the chairs. More like sank into the plush cushions. It was a chair so deep and cozy, with an ottoman for her feet, that she could probably spend the night in it and wake up the next morning feeling refreshed.

"Where did you meet my Hector?" Maria asked, leaning back in her chair with a look of expectation on her face.

She paused only briefly. "In jail. We were prisoners." Now she'd see how long it would take Maria to throw them out of her lovely home and she and Josh could continue with why they were really in Mexico. This should get them out of their fix.

Maria opened her mouth, then snapped it closed. A bubble of laughter erupted. "Oh, that eez very funny." Realizing what she'd said, she put a hand over her mouth, but the laughter continued. "I apologize most humble."

"Before or after you stop laughing?" she asked.

That brought more laughter from Maria. "Truly, I am not laughing at you. Hector has a way of . . ." She frowned. "Flubbing up. Yes, that is what he does. Flub up. He's very sweet, but he flubs up a lot."

"You aren't concerned we were in jail?"

"If I were, then I would not speak to most of my family. They are very fierce. Sometimes bad *banditos*." She looked thoughtful. "But still good. Hector, his family eez on the other side of the law. He eez a great *capitan*. But I did not mean you were a *bandito*. Hector has made a boo-boo, no? You do not look like you are bad person."

It was nice to know she didn't look like a criminal. But she still couldn't tell Maria the truth. She might inadvertently let something slip.

"Hector thought we were here to capture a fugitive."

Maria's eyes widened. Apparently, she didn't think they looked like they were on the right side of the law, either.

"We're bounty hunters," she explained. "We bring bail jumpers back to stand trial. But that isn't why we're here now. We just wanted to . . ." *You can do this.* "We just wanted to get married. We're very much in . . . in love." Briefly, she wondered how many liars were in hell.

"*Si*, he has much love for you." Maria smiled warmly.

A flutter of excitement rushed through her.

They were only words. Only words! He didn't love her. She didn't even want her thoughts to head in that direction. It was this damn marriage. A marriage that wasn't remotely real. One that would end as soon as they got back to the States.

"So you couldn't wait to be married and ran off to Mexico." She hugged her middle. "It is like a fairy tale."

No, more like a fucking nightmare, and she'd do whatever it took to get them out of this mess.

"Young lovers running away. It was the same with Hector and myself." She jumped from the chair. "We must make your day *perfecto*," she declared. "You have a dress?"

Oh, no. This is where it might get tricky. "Not exactly." A sudden idea came to her. "I wanted to buy one of those long, sweeping skirts. They're so romantic. You know, barefoot and all that."

"No, you must be beautiful. I have the perfect dress. Come, come."

They went back down the hall. Why did she have a feeling she was the proverbial calf being led to slaughter? Man, was Josh ever going to pay for this.

They went inside another bedroom and Maria opened a closet. Reaching high onto the top shelf, she carefully brought down a large white box and set it on the bed.

"This is what you shall wear," Maria said reverently.

She untied the blue ribbon and lifted off the lid. When she folded back the tissue paper, Cody gasped. White silk and beads. Maria's wedding dress. It couldn't be anything else.

"I can't wear that," she whispered. "It was your wedding dress."

"*Si*, but it is good luck to my marriage if you wear it for your wedding."

If she wore that, Hector and Maria would be getting a divorce before the end of the year. Her marriage to Josh was a farce. All she would bring was bad luck. She damn sure didn't want that on her conscience.

"No, I couldn't. I really appreciate the offer, but I couldn't."

As if Maria didn't hear a word she'd just uttered, she instead removed the dress and shook it out.

Good lord, Cody had never seen anything so beautiful. The gown wasn't frilly. It didn't have a lot of bows or ruffles. Just pure, straight lines.

Tentatively, she reached out and touched the silk. *This must be what heaven feels like,* she thought.

She drew in a deep breath and took a step back, shaking her head. "No, I can't. This is your dress. It should be passed down to your daughters."

"But think how Josh would feel if he saw you in this. He would not be able to resist."

She smiled and Cody saw something a little mischievous twinkling in her eyes. Maybe there were more layers to Maria than she'd first imagined.

"Think about what he would see coming down the stairs if you were wearing this dress."

Maria laid it on the bed. Gently, she placed her hands on Cody's shoulders and turned her toward the full-length mirror. Before she knew what was happening, Maria had picked up the dress once more and put it in front of Cody.

"Think what expression would be on your man's face."

Slowly, her gaze moved over her reflection. It didn't look like her, but she knew it was. Sure, she'd worn skirts before and knew she looked damned sexy.

But this was different. She looked like fuckin' Cinderella.

Her breath caught in her throat. This wasn't her. She didn't have the fairy tale life and never would. But for just a second, it was nice to pretend.

"What would Josh say if he could see you like this?"

Maria would make a damn good salesperson. For just a

second, Cody bought her sales pitch. She pictured her hair
swept up and away from her face. She saw herself walking
down the wide staircase. And when she looked into Josh's
eyes, she saw admiration and . . . and . . . and what? Love?

That was the joke of the century.

But she did want to wear the dress. It was an exquisite cre-
ation. She would probably never have the chance to wear
something so beautiful again. So what if this wasn't a real
marriage. Did it really matter? She might as well look the
part.

She drew in a deep breath and turned toward Maria.
"Okay, I'll wear it."

Maria clapped her hands. "Your man will not . . ." She
nibbled her bottom lip, then looked back up, excitement
twinkling in her eyes. "He will not know what slapped him."

Oh, she was sure of that.

Chapter 19

Josh wondered what Cody and Maria could be doing upstairs for so damn long. He didn't think she'd blow their cover by telling Maria they hadn't actually wanted to get married. She was too smart for that.

But she'd been really pissed. So pissed that he'd thought for a while she'd like nothing more than to spend the next few years in a rat-infested jail rather than marry him.

That shouldn't have bothered him. What guy wouldn't want a brief affair with no strings attached? Sex on a silver platter. But it bothered him enough that he didn't want to dwell on the reasons behind why he felt that way.

He'd also known the minute she accepted that there was no way around their situation. The marriage wouldn't even be legal. It wasn't that big of a deal.

His stomach clenched.

Would it be so bad being married to her? Hell, he could probably do a lot worse. They were in the same line of work. He wouldn't have to worry about her asking him to give up his job. They could even work as partners. So far they'd done okay.

Except for getting thrown in jail. But he'd gotten them out. If they hadn't been together, it might not have been so easy. Yeah, they made a pretty good team.

Especially in bed.

He closed his eyes for a moment, remembering how it had felt to have Cody's arms wrapped around him. The way she'd pressed her naked body closer to his.

Something clattered in the other room, bringing him back to earth.

What the hell was he thinking? Married to Cody? She was the most sarcastic, ill-tempered woman he'd ever had the misfortune to meet.

"I have called the priest. He will be here tomorrow. This is good." Hector strode in from the other room.

It took a few minutes for his words to sink in. Tomorrow? No, that wasn't good. In that time, another bounty hunter would get to Adam. They would lose whatever advantage they had.

"I don't think it will be possible," he said.

Hector raised his eyebrows. "You would rather marry the woman you love in a dirty office?" He shook his head. "That eez not wise, my friend. I know women. My Maria would not let me ever forget the embarrassment of something so cold. No, you will marry here and have a much happier bride."

He opened his mouth, but snapped it shut. What could he say without making Hector wonder if they'd been lying to him?

"You are right, of course. I'd hate to upset Cody." Maybe he could talk Hector into telling her? She wasn't going to like this new development.

"Come, I will show you to your room. Then we will eat."

"Yeah, sure."

He had no choice but to follow. A few minutes later, he wondered exactly where Hector was taking him. They left the house and went around the side, stopping at a small building.

"This is where the unattached men stay. We follow the old

customs of our ancestors. Few people do." He shook his head. "Sometimes the old ones are smarter than we think, eh?"

Hector cast a knowing look in his direction, as if he guessed that he and Cody were already sleeping together.

"My Maria, she likes to follow the old ways. We will humor her, then our women will be happy, and it is such a small thing to ask."

"This will be fine."

Hector had a way of manipulating the situation to his advantage. He'd make a great diplomat. Josh felt as if he'd been outmaneuvered. Check, but not checkmate. By putting him in the cottage away from the house, it would be easy to slip away undetected. He was almost certain Cody could do the same. By this time tomorrow, they'd be crossing the border, with Adam in tow.

Josh grinned. He could be just as crafty.

But when Cody came downstairs for dinner, he knew something was up. He didn't have to wait long to find out what had pissed her off this time.

"Josh, I'd like you to meet Adoncia," Cody said between clenched teeth.

Maria glided forward. "Adoncia was my chaperone, and then my maid. Now she will see to Cody. It is an old custom in our country that an unmarried girl be chaperoned. This will be such a grand wedding. I am so happy you have brought your new friends home so we can celebrate the occasion as it should be celebrated."

Hector beamed.

Josh coughed to cover his chuckle, but he didn't think he was very successful. Not if the glare Cody cast in his direction was anything to go by.

Then he glanced at the chaperone. The hairs on the back of his neck tingled. For a moment, he wondered if he might be turning to stone, or a pillar of salt. He forced his gaze from her beady black eyes and looked at Cody. One of her eyebrows rose, as if to say, *I told you that you wouldn't like her any more than I do, but you're not the one who has to put up with her.*

Great, there went his idea of sneaking away from the hacienda.

"And my mama will arrive tomorrow, and a few relatives." Maria beamed.

This was supposed to be a simple wedding. He took a deep breath. A few relatives, that's all. They'd only be guests of Hector and Maria a few more days. If it kept them out of jail, they could manage.

Dinner went smoothly, if he discounted the fierce glare of the chaperone every time he so much as looked at Cody. Hector and Maria carried the conversation. He couldn't have said what they talked about, or even what he ate. The only thing going through his mind was how ill at ease Cody seemed. He had a feeling she wasn't comfortable doing family gatherings.

"And your mama and papa will be here for the wedding, too?" Maria sat forward in her chair.

"No!" Cody blurted, coming halfway out of her seat. Realizing she might have been a little too verbal, she quickly sat back down and picked up her napkin. "Josh and I are orphans." She dabbed at the corner of her eyes.

"Yes," he quickly interjected. "We were raised in the same orphanage. There was little food—and it was cold."

"Oh." Maria's breath caught in her throat. "No mama? No papa? An orphanage?"

She looked between them, and for just a moment he felt lower than the lowest scum on earth. Hell, he hadn't meant to make her cry. He only wanted to embellish a little so the story would become more real.

Cody bit her bottom lip, apparently feeling pretty badly herself.

"Please, it's okay. You don't miss what you never had." Cody motioned toward him.

For a moment, he couldn't talk. She spoke the words as if she had firsthand experience. It made him wonder again about her relationship with her mother.

"Yeah," he added. "But we had each other."

"A fairy tale. A very beautiful fairy tale. Eez okay. *Mia familia* is your *familia*. *Si*, Hector?"

Hector sniffed. "*Si, mi amor*." He took Maria's hand across the table and squeezed it,

Great, now he felt even lower, and he hadn't thought that would be possible. Even Adoncia had tears in her eyes.

When he went to his room later that night, guilt went with him every step of the way.

Cody glanced at Adoncia. A white cotton nightgown completely covered the woman. A cot had been moved into the room for her. Maria had said that it was tradition. Cody had had just about all the tradition she could stand for one day.

All forms of torture came to mind, but not for her chaperone. No, she wanted Josh to suffer for this one.

Feeling stifled by the other woman's presence, she went to the double doors that opened onto the balcony. Maybe some fresh air would help her to chill out. Once outside, she did start to feel a little more relaxed. She took a deep, cleansing breath, leaning against the iron rail.

It was beautiful here. A sort of peacefulness she'd never experienced before. So maybe it wouldn't be so bad staying a day or two.

The thought of losing Adam's bounty didn't sit well with her, but there would be other bounties. She was good at her job. She didn't have to prove a damn thing to anyone. Especially . . .

Especially who? Her mother?

Ridiculous. Maybe their relationship wasn't so hot. She'd learned to adjust. That's all love really was—learning to adjust. There was no big bang or flashing lights. No all-consuming need to feel someone's arms wrapping around you. Hugging was a really stupid custom. One she could do well without.

Her gaze absently moved toward Josh's quarters. She could see his balcony from where she stood, and the dark shape of him when he moved. There was no light spilling from his room as there was from hers, but she knew he'd been watching her.

What did he think of all this? Was he angry Adam might slip between their fingers? Surely he had to be upset. It didn't show. If he was ticked off, he hid it well.

She went back inside and turned off her light. Adoncia was already on her cot. For a brief moment, she thought about seeing if she could sneak out the door. She and Josh would be long gone before anyone awakened in the morning. She took a step in that direction.

"*Sueno*. Sleep." Adoncia turned on her cot and faced the wall.

How the hell had the woman known what was going through her mind? The old battle-ax. She flounced to the bed, stripped out of her clothes, and without bothering to put on the gown Maria had left for her, climbed between the sheets.

At least she had the bed all to herself. Josh liked to hog the covers. He also had a habit of laying his arm over her and pulling her close. She, on the other hand, liked to stretch out.

She flopped to her other side, punched her pillow, and lay back down. What was it about the bed that made it suddenly uncomfortable? She should have been luxuriating in the plush mattress. She rolled to her stomach. It didn't help. With a sigh, she gave up and snuggled the extra pillow close to her. She could have almost believed it was Josh.

Night drifted away, and the sun crept up above the horizon, an orange glow casting her approval on the earth. As it rose, so did the sound of voices.

Cody opened one eye, staring at the white eyelet lace that

trimmed her pillow. It took only a moment to acclimate herself to her surroundings.

But where was all the noise coming from? It almost sounded as if they'd been invaded by a herd of cattle.

She jerked up in bed. Oh, lord, *were* they being invaded? Maybe someone wanted to oust *el capitan*. Put in a new *capitan*. Would they all be shot? She jumped from the bed and reached for her clothes. They were gone. Where the hell were her clothes?

She turned toward Adoncia's cot, but the old woman was gone, too. Lying on the cot was a full skirt and a white blouse. Hell, she'd wear anything right now. She damn sure didn't want to go to her grave the same way she came into this world.

Beneath the skirt and top were underclothes. They certainly didn't look like they would fit Adoncia's ample girth. She quickly dressed, running her hands through her hair.

Okay, she needed to assess the situation. She crept to the door leading to the balcony. Easing the door open, she slipped out. There were people everywhere, but she didn't see any guns or a firing squad. Actually, it all looked quite festive.

"Codeeee! Are you awakened yet?" Maria opened the door and stepped into the room. "Cody?"

"Who are all those people?" she asked as she stepped back inside the room.

"Oh, you *are* awakened. Is good, no? They are my *familia*. Your *familia*, too." She beamed. "*Mamacita*! Come meet your new daughter."

A slender woman pushed open the door and hurried inside. She was an older version of Maria. Just as beautiful, but with a maturity that only came with age.

Maria's mother rattled off a string of Spanish and hurried forward, enfolding Cody in her warm embrace. She wanted to jerk away from the woman, but instead she closed her eyes and let the woman's warmth penetrate her shield.

Damn, she needed a pot of coffee if a hug from a stranger could make her feel like this.

"*Niña.*" She kissed both Cody's cheeks before stepping away and again rattling off a string of Spanish.

"My mother says her new daughter will make a very beautiful bride and you are to call her mama."

"I thought this was going to be a small wedding," Cody said while still trying to maintain her smile. This was way too much. She suddenly felt as if she were suffocating.

"*Si.* Small." Maria nodded.

"It sounds like half of Mexico is in your house and outside on the patio."

"My *familia.* It is custom when there is a wedding that all the family is invited."

"*Si, familia.*" Maria's mother nodded.

"But how did you get the wedding invitations . . . ?"

Maria interrupted with her own string of Spanish. She and her mama laughed.

"We do not send invitations," Maria explained. "All family members are invited to the wedding. It is our custom."

Great. And was Maria related to everyone in Mexico? From the noise downstairs, it was a distinct possibility.

"We will party today." Maria clapped her hands. "There will be much food and wine and dancing. You will get to know your new *familia* so when you marry the day will be most special."

Special, yeah, right. And not even close to being legal. Okay, no biggie. Then why did it feel as if bees buzzed inside her stomach?

And why did it feel so damn real?

This wasn't how it was supposed to be. She didn't believe in the fairy tale wedding. No one stayed with someone forever. They always went away. Then the one left behind had to put the pieces of their life back together again.

Except in her mother's case. She was certain Pearl had never really gotten over her husband having left her. If they had been actually married, and Cody had her doubts. Not that it mattered to her. But something inside her said this wedding was wrong. She just didn't know how to extricate herself from the mess they had made.

"Come, we eat and then we plan the wedding."

"Coffee," Cody mumbled. "And lots of it."

Once downstairs, she saw it was worse than she could have ever imagined. Men were moving the furniture and women were bringing in fresh cut flowers and arranging them in crystal vases. When Cody made her entrance, everyone immediately stopped to stare.

She brushed a strand of hair behind her ear and looked around for a hole she might crawl into. Before she could run anywhere, Josh stepped forward. Like Moses when he parted the Red Sea, the crowd of people separated.

Her gaze drifted over him, drinking in every inch. Someone had replaced his jeans with black slacks and his T-shirt with a white silk shirt that was unbuttoned halfway down. Her mouth began to water. She couldn't seem to take her eyes off him.

"My love," he said when he drew closer and took her hand.

His lips brushed her palm, sending tingles of pleasure all the way down to her toes. The crowd seemed to disappear and it was just the two of them. She took a step toward him. Their gazes locked and she saw something flicker in his eyes. Almost as if he were seeing her for the very first time—and he liked what he saw.

But this was crazy. Of course, it was all pretend. Before she could dwell on what she saw or didn't see, Mama and Maria grabbed her hands and pulled her away from Josh.

"There will be plenty of time to spend with each other after you are married," Maria called over her shoulder as they hustled her away to the kitchen.

Josh smiled. What was he thinking? Something about all this wasn't right, but she couldn't put her finger on what it was. Not exactly. Before she could even try to figure any of it out, someone pulled out a chair and gently pushed her into it.

A cup of coffee was set in front of her and she didn't care about trying to figure out what the hell was going on as the rich aroma of the strong black coffee wafted to her nose. Everything else might be chaos, but this was heaven.

She added a liberal amount of cream and sugar, stirred, and brought the cup to her mouth. That first taste. Delightful.

"This is my sister, Delores." Maria pulled a shy young girl of fourteen in front of her.

The girl curtseyed, giggled, and hurried to the back of the room. Apparently, this was when all the introductions would be made. One by one. Not that Cody really cared as long as someone kept refilling her cup.

But people just kept coming out of the woodwork. Maria didn't stop at first cousins—no, there were third and fourth cousins—but they all acted as if they were just as close as Maria's brothers and sisters.

And now they were treating her as if she were a part of the family. She should've felt warm and fuzzy, like when Maria's mother hugged her. She didn't. Terror was closer to what she felt. Everyone wanted to touch her or hug her. The room was beginning to close in on her.

Maria's mother spoke in Spanish.

"Okay, you can meet our Cody later," Maria said. "She eez not so used to a big family like we are. Shoo." She waved her arms and the rest of the greeters hurried away, laughing and giggling.

Thank God. She didn't think she could handle meeting another person. Were they trying to populate the world or what?

"I am so sorry. I did not realize this would be so much for someone who has never known a *familia*. Please forgive?"

Maria lowered her head, clasping her arms in front of her. Cody shifted in her chair. She'd never really had someone care about her feelings like this.

"I think I have something in my eye," she muttered, and brought the linen napkin up, dabbing at the moisture. What the hell was wrong with her? Damned if she wasn't getting sentimental.

"*Hola!*" A balding, rotund man spoke.

Another relative? She blinked past the tears in her eyes. Maybe, maybe not.

The man smiled. "I am Dr. Hernandez. I will take a little blood." His smile widened. "We want everything to be legal, no?"

No, she didn't. Josh. Where was Josh? If he drew blood, the marriage would be legal. Oh, lord, she was going to be sick. "Actually, I'm allergic to needles."

He laughed as he took her wrist, turning her arm up. "Americans. I love how they make the jokes." He reached into his black bag and brought out a cotton ball soaked in alcohol. Before she could think of anything else to say, he'd swabbed her arm and inserted a needle.

Her stomach churned when she saw her blood filling the syringe. She could take seeing someone else's blood, but looking at her own always made her queasy. She was so going to kill Josh.

The doctor removed the needle, put cotton over the puncture site, and brought her arm up to stop the bleeding. Maria fanned her face. When her gaze met the other woman's, Maria smiled.

"The fainting feeling will be over *uno momento*. I do not like when the doctor takes my blood, either. Crackers, they will help."

She said something in Spanish, and almost immediately there was a bowl of crackers set in front of Cody. She would eat one just to make Maria happy.

Strangely, after only one, the queasiness began to go away. She was still going to kill Josh, though. Not legal, her ass.

"Better?"

Cody nodded.

"Good, now we make you more beautiful. Josh will be fighting off the men. My cousins can be very amorous when it comes to a beautiful woman. We will hope there are no fights, eh?"

She hated to tell Maria, but she really doubted Josh would fight over her. Unless she was the one who threw the first punch. Then he would probably step in and help her out. Maybe this time he wouldn't get clobbered. She smiled, remembering the last time he'd assisted her.

"You have a memory?"

"A what?"

"A memory. You smiled as if you were having pleasant thoughts. Like a memory."

"*Si*," Cody said. "I had a nice memory." Odd, but the more she was around Josh, the more nice memories she had.

Life was getting complicated. Especially hers. She'd always worked alone. Didn't want or need anyone. She liked it that way.

Now Josh had shoved his way past her defenses. Maria and her family were close on his heels. The sooner she left Mexico, the better.

Mariachis were playing in the courtyard, the music drifting into the main room of the house. People laughed and partied. The sweet scent of flowers filled the room, along with an air of gaiety.

But Josh didn't see Cody. He hadn't seen her all afternoon. Now he was getting worried.

Had she managed to sneak away while everyone was busy preparing for the wedding that would take place tomorrow? No, she wouldn't leave him holding the bag, just because he'd been the one who blurted out that they were here to get married. Would she take into account that it had kept them out of jail? Or would she conclude that she'd be better off going it alone?

Damn it, maybe she had. Cody had been really pissed. He

could just imagine how she'd felt when the doctor had taken her blood. He cringed at the thought. Their marriage would be legal.

Odd, but it didn't seem to bother him. It should have, but it didn't.

He remembered how she'd looked coming down the stairs this morning. It was all he could do to swallow past the lump in his throat. She was breathtaking, and she'd easily managed to steal his breath away.

Damn, wouldn't she have a field day if she knew he was really falling for her? His hand tightened on his glass. He and Cody? Not in this lifetime. What the hell was he thinking? It must be the moonlight, and the spicy food he'd eaten today. All these people milling around didn't help any.

The sooner they were married and out of here, the better. Unless of course Cody *had* slipped away undetected. If so, Hector would probably lock him up and throw away the key. Then Maria would kill Hector.

"You look like a man anxiously awaiting his bride-to-be," a voice spoke from behind him. A very American voice, and so out of place here.

He turned, ready to greet the man, but his words caught in his throat.

"Hello," the man continued. "I'm Adam. Adam Sinclair."

"Josh . . . Josh Pierce."

Josh noted the watchful gleam in Adam's eyes. The man was playing him—seeing what he was up to. He didn't have long to wait for his next move.

"The bounty hunter." Adam casually took a long pull from his beer.

"Yes, Cody and I are both bounty hunters." Had Adam spoken with his sister? Probably. Was he here to turn himself in? Or was he playing cat and mouse with them? Seeing if they would admit they had crossed the border after him?

"I spoke with my sister. She said a man and a woman

wanted to take me in. Funny thing is, they never showed. Just some jerk who goes by the name of Turbo." He snorted. "He's not nearly as tough as he thinks he is. A few months in a Mexican jail should have him begging for mercy."

Josh was tired of playing games. "Did you kill your partner?"

"What do you think?"

"Your sister doesn't think so."

"So, you were the ones. I suspected as much. My sister described both of you."

He looked at Adam. Really looked at him. His face was lined from years of working under a harsh sun right alongside his crews.

Who really knew another human being? There was something about him, though. Call it gut instinct, but Adam Sinclair didn't strike him as being a murderer.

Years working undercover had trained him well. He'd learned to watch for certain signs to see if a person was lying or telling the truth. He watched for those signs now.

"Did you kill your partner?" he asked again.

"No, I didn't. Dan Gray was a good man."

Adam hadn't hesitated, but looked him right in the eye when he answered. He also seemed genuinely saddened by the death of his partner.

"Then why did you run?"

Adam's gaze dropped to his hands. "I was scared." He raised his head. "That's a hard thing for me to admit, but it's the plain and simple truth."

"It's not for me to judge if you killed your partner or not."

"But you have an opinion."

"You don't look like a killer." He didn't add, *but neither had Ted Bundy or a whole bunch of other murderers.*

"So why are you getting married?"

Adam already knew the truth, but it still wouldn't hurt to lie, and it might actually keep them out of jail. "We were combining business with pleasure—getting married and bringing you in. Your friend Hector wouldn't hesitate to lock us up and throw away the key. We decided business didn't mix."

Adam was silent for a moment, as if he pondered the situation. "It'll be interesting to see if you follow through. You could do worse. She's very beautiful." He nodded toward the stairs.

Cody and Maria were walking down the staircase, Maria in a plum-colored dress, Cody in a deep blue one. Two princesses going to the ball. He straightened, unable to take his gaze off her. Damn, she was something to behold.

Her hair had been swept away from her face, tendrils curling softly on each cheek. Her makeup was different, not that she ever wore much. Her eyelids were smoky brown and her lips deep red, bringing out the fullness.

It was all he could do not to rush forward and pull her into his arms, covering her mouth with his. How long had it been since he'd kissed her? It seemed like forever.

"I think you used getting married as a ruse to keep out of jail, but maybe it wasn't so much of a scam. You have the look of a man in love with a woman. Maybe fate has stepped in."

Josh dragged his gaze away from Cody. Adam was way off the mark. He admired Cody, but as soon as they returned to the States, they'd quietly end their brief marriage. He wouldn't mention that to Adam right now, though.

"You going back? To the States?" he asked.

"I haven't decided yet. I have enough money in a bank here that I would never want for anything. My sister will see that my partner's cousin won't cheat on the books. I could stay and not worry about a trial or jail time."

"You could, but I don't think you will."

"We'll see. Now go to her. Tell her how beautiful she is. Bring her over and introduce us before the night is over. I want to see if she hides her excitement as well as you."

Josh hesitated. He'd never just walked away from a bounty.

"Don't worry. I won't run. At least not until after the wedding. It would be an insult to Maria and Hector if I left now."

This was a test. It had to be. Adam was the bait. They wanted to see if either he or Cody would try to get him across the border.

Damn it, he didn't know what to think anymore.

Josh had no reason to believe Adam when he said he wouldn't leave, but he did. If he was wrong, they'd be passing up a sizable chunk of money.

His gaze returned to Cody. As he walked toward her, his heart began to beat faster. Damn, she stirred his blood like no other woman ever had.

This marriage is a farce, he told himself.

Then why the hell did it feel so real?

Chapter 20

As Cody took the last step, she looked up, her gaze locking with Josh's. What was he thinking? Did he like the way Maria's cousin had trimmed her hair, then pulled it up on top of her head, letting wisps of hair curl around her face? Did he notice the sultry shades of brown and mauve that Maria had brushed on her lids? Or the long blue dress she wore? Did he notice the changes?

And what did he think?

She and Maria stopped in front of him, and apprehension filled her.

"Maria." He nodded, then turned toward Cody.

He took her hand, stroking his thumb lightly back and forth across her palm. She ached for more than this small caress. Her hand began to tremble.

"You look more beautiful every time I see you," he told her.

They were only words, she reminded herself. Words meant to convey the message they were madly in love. He meant none of what he said. He enjoyed making love to her as much as she'd enjoyed making love with him, but they weren't *in* love. Big difference.

She could play the game, too. Hell, she'd invented games a long time ago just to survive. She was damn good at playing them.

"And you look very handsome, my love." Her voice was throaty. She lowered her lashes, but covertly watched his reaction. His pupils dilated, and he leaned closer. He was a damn fine actor. For a second, she could almost believe he wasn't unaffected by her appearance.

"There eez Hector." With a knowing wink, Maria hurried to join her husband.

Adoncia stayed a few steps back. The other woman didn't say much. She didn't have to. One look from her narrowed eyes and Cody knew whatever she was doing wasn't allowed.

Like sleeping nude. When she'd gone to her room earlier, a white cotton nightgown was draped on the bed. Hint, hint? Well, she certainly didn't want to cause old eagle-eye to have a coronary, so maybe she'd wear it tonight.

Josh, on the other hand, was quite a different story, and she wasn't thrilled with the new developments. She smiled sweetly. "They drew my fucking blood this morning," she said between clenched teeth.

He glanced around, then guided her to the courtyard where some of the couples were dancing a slow waltz.

"They drew mine, too," he said, pulling her into his arms. His fingers ran lightly over her bare back.

Just a simple caress, but it made her legs weak. She wanted to lay her head against his shoulder, to touch his smooth cheek. She wanted to feel the warmth of his lips on hers.

Instead, she drew in a shaky breath and kept her back straight. Keeping a considerable amount of space between them was a good idea.

"That will make the wedding legal," she told him.

Her smile was frozen in place as she nodded at a cousin who danced past. She had no idea what the woman's name was, but she was certain it was a second cousin. Maybe. There were so many cousins, if she threw a stick, she'd hit at least three or four.

"We can get it annulled when we get back to Texas."

"You've got that right," she said.

"Unless we consummate the marriage."

His grip tightened when she stumbled.

Consummate? Her mouth went dry just thinking about slow, sensuous sex with Josh. Visions filled her head of their naked, sweaty bodies entwined, straining toward the ultimate release.

Oh, lord, she could almost feel his hands cupping her breasts, his thumbs tweaking her hard nipples.

Take a nice, slow breath. Don't hyperventilate.

She opened her mouth, then snapped it closed. She could deny that their lovemaking wouldn't happen, but she damn well couldn't stop the flood of heat that spread through her like a forest fire.

Besides, whatever she said would be a lie, and they'd both know it. Making love again was inevitable. It was the *when* that was driving her nuts.

"Then we'll get a divorce," she informed him.

"That costs more, and they can get really messy. I mean, what if you decide you want my autographed *Playboy*? We didn't sign a pre-nup or anything."

She met his gaze. The man was seriously deranged.

But his eyes twinkled in a way that made her feel like they were sharing a joke. She bit her lip to keep from smiling. It didn't do any good. A bubble of laughter escaped, drawing knowing smiles from people close enough to have heard.

"Now that's the way an about to be married woman should look and sound."

Pain ripped through her. That was his game? She apparently hadn't looked in love enough? Damn it, for just a moment she'd felt—oh, hell, what did it matter. This wasn't real.

"By the way, we have a very special guest," he said, breaking into her thoughts.

"Did more relatives arrive? Wow, that would be a big surprise. As if I'm not tripping over them now."

"Not a relative."

She eyed him with more than a little suspicion. What was he trying to pull now?

"Who?"

"Adam Sinclair."

She stumbled again. He caught her to him. She wasn't sure what affected her more—Josh's body pressed intimately to hers, or the fact that Adam was here. Unless she'd misunderstood him.

"Could you repeat that?" Her glance swept the room.

"Adam Sinclair is here. He's a friend of Hector's. A nice guy."

Adam Sinclair. Here? No, she wasn't falling for his attempt at humor. She met his gaze. He looked sincere, but she'd discovered with him it was hard to tell.

"He's here, and you've spoken with him." She still didn't believe him.

"I swear."

Oh, lord, he was telling the truth. "Does he know we're bounty hunters?" She scanned the room once more, but more slowly.

"Yes, to your question."

Her gaze swept past a man in a gray suit, then jerked back. He smiled and saluted her with his beer.

"That's Adam Sinclair," she whispered. "But . . . but . . ."

She caught Maria's eye as they danced by. Hector's wife smiled. She smiled back, hoping it didn't come off as sickly as she felt.

Trust had never been her strong suit. It hadn't improved in the last day or so. "It's some kind of trap. They want to see if we're on the up and up. If we make a grab for Adam, we'll spend the next thirty years in some rat-infested cell."

"That's what I thought, but now I'm not so sure. Remember, Hector said Adam contributed a lot to the community. It would stand to reason they'd be friends. I told Adam our plan had been to combine business with pleasure, but we decided to forget about the business side and just get married."

"He bought it?"

"Doubtful, but his hands are tied as long as we keep up the pretense."

Damn, so near yet so far. Adam had a hefty bounty on his head. Her palms began to itch. "How the hell can he look so blasted casual when he's a fugitive? He must know there are at least a dozen or more recovery agents after him."

Josh laughed. "You going to handcuff him?"

She glanced around the room. Josh had a point. They wouldn't make it out the front door. No wonder Adam didn't show any sign of being worried.

"And that would be minus one bounty hunter."

"Hmm?"

"You said there were at least a dozen bounty hunters after him. Minus one. Turbo is sitting in a cell as we speak."

"I can't say as I'm broken up by that bit of news. I never have liked him. He has a real ego problem." She arched an eyebrow. "So, are you going to introduce me?"

"Will you be good?"

His words sent a rush of heat over her. Adam, everyone at Maria and Hector's estate, might as well have not been there. There was only the two of them. Just her and Josh. A slow smile curved her lips. "I'm always good," she said with a husky drawl.

He drew in a deep breath. "And when you're bad, you're even better." He massaged her earlobe. She closed her eyes, letting his touch consume her. An ache began to build inside her. How could his touch set her on fire so quickly?

"Have you ever had sex in the middle of a dance floor, surrounded by strangers?" she asked.

"That would be a new one for me."

Even though she wasn't looking at him, she could still hear the smile in his voice.

"You're about to find out if you don't stop what you're doing," she warned.

He sighed with regret, but before he moved away, he kissed the top of her head.

"Come on," he said, taking her arm. "I'll introduce you to the bane of our existence."

As they neared Adam, he glanced up.

"When Hector told me how he'd arrested you," Adam began. "I told him you were lying about coming to Mexico to get married. But watching you on the dance floor . . ." He shrugged. "Now, I'm not so sure." He ran his thumb over the rim of his beer bottle. "If you hadn't spoken with my sister, I might believe you were in love."

Man, was he wrong. Love only caused pain. They were good at acting. It came with the job. Still, Cody couldn't stop her pulse from speeding up when she looked at Josh. And why not? He was a sexy, virile man. What woman wouldn't have a fantasy or two about him? And so much worse for her because she'd already experienced more than the fantasy. But if Adam wanted to believe they were in love, that was okay with her.

"We were mixing business with pleasure," she said, going along with what Josh had told her. "I'm sure you've done that once or twice." She shrugged. "It didn't work out, so we decided to take business out of the equation. No harm, no foul."

As if he were reinforcing her words, Josh lightly caressed her bare arm. At least, she thought he was trying to prove they were really in love. She didn't really care. His touch sent tingles of delight up and down her arm. It was something she could get used to.

She bit back a groan. No, she couldn't get used to having him around. He'd leave. Like all the others. She squared her shoulders, promising herself she wouldn't care about him— or his touch—vowing she wouldn't let him hurt her.

Adam set his beer bottle on the tray of a passing waiter. When he turned back to her, he smiled. "You have a very good outlook on life. You'll find it easier to get by if you accept the triumphs with a grain of salt, and the failures with a shrug. There's always tomorrow."

For a moment, she wondered if he'd read her mind, but no, he wasn't talking about her relationship with Josh. He couldn't know they'd end the marriage as soon as they returned to the States. He'd only meant life in general and the fact that they'd lost the chance to take him back to face trial.

She raised her chin. "I would think you might be a little worried. They won't give up. Someone will always be looking for you. After all, you are accused of murdering your partner."

"Touché." He grabbed a beer from another waiter and downed half of it. "Excuse me, but I think I'll find a bed somewhere. You know, when I was younger life was much less complicated. I knew what I wanted. I thought if I could just get my company off the ground, I'd have it made. Now this."

Cody studied his face. There were tired lines around his eyes and he looked much older than he had on television. More haggard. She almost felt sorry for him as she watched him walk away.

"Don't get emotionally involved," Josh told her. "Adam is a fugitive. If we don't bring him in, someone else will."

"Of course I don't care about him. I was only thinking about what a great story this would make. Think about it, someday you can tell your kids you spent your first honeymoon chasing a fugitive."

"Do *you* want to have kids someday?" he countered.

Kids? She'd never really thought about it. For a moment, she envisioned herself cuddling a baby in her arms. Josh's baby. Butterflies tickled her belly as an unfamiliar warmth swirled inside her.

She glanced up, her gaze meeting his. "No. Why the hell would I want a kid?"

"No motherly instinct? No need to reproduce?"

"Not at all." But that didn't stop this new sensation from enveloping her in a cocoon of soft fuzzies.

Good, lord. Where had these thoughts come from?

Her, a mother? Hell, she wouldn't know how. Damn it, why did Josh have to open up this subject? Make her start feeling things she didn't want to feel.

"And you?" she asked, wanting to redirect the conversation away from her. "Do you want kids? Isn't that supposed to be the measure of a man? Being fruitful and multiplying or some such crap?"

"Maybe someday."

Josh, a father. She could actually picture him bouncing a kid on his knee. A little Josh.

"I don't want to chase criminals all my life," he said.

"What do you want to do?" Strangely, she wanted to know what the future held for Josh Pierce.

"I want to open my own P.I. agency. Go into business for myself."

"You mentioned that before, but aren't you doing that already? I mean, technically, we don't have a boss. We answer to ourselves. If we work, we make money. We don't bring anyone in, then the bills don't get paid. It's as simple as that, but it's still our decision."

"Yeah, right, living out of the back of a car ninety percent of the time. I wouldn't call that my own business." He ran a hand through his hair. "I'd like something a little more stable than this."

"You two look very serious," Hector said as he came up beside them. "Are you excited about the wedding tomorrow?"

"Very," Josh said, then smiled.

"*Si*, much better than a cold, dirty office. You will have much luck in your marriage because you are starting off right."

"We are very grateful," Josh said.

He spoke with a sincerity that made her believe he might be telling the truth. No wonder he'd been one of the best at undercover work. The man was a consummate liar. She'd have to remember that in the future.

"If you'll excuse me, I think I'd like to dance with my fiancée," he said.

"Ah, yes, believe me, I do understand." Hector nodded toward Adoncia. "It was the only time I was able to hold Maria in my arms with her chaperone hovering so close."

Good move on Josh's part. The less they had to talk to their hosts, the better off they'd be. If Hector suspected the marriage was a farce, she had a feeling he'd be really ticked off. She could see them languishing in a cell for a very long time.

Josh led her to the dance floor and swept her into his arms, their steps matching the slow seductive strains of the mariachi band. Odd how they fit so well together.

"Did I tell you that you look beautiful tonight?"

Now what was he trying to pull? They didn't have an audience so why was he pouring on the charm?

"Do you question every compliment?" He stared into her eyes. "What the hell kind of upbringing did you have?"

She looked away, unable to meet his penetrating gaze. "The same as any kid, and I didn't say a damn word."

"You didn't have to," he mumbled. His eyes softened. "I wish I could take away your pain."

"Why? We're nothing to each other."

"I thought we were at least friends. Was I wrong?"

A guilty flush swept over her. They were more than strangers. They'd been lovers. Hell, tomorrow he would be her husband. Not that any of it would be real, and that was certainly fine with her. But strangers, they weren't.

Friends had a nice ring to it. She could probably manage that. As long as he didn't want to get too chummy after their partnership ended. "Yeah, we're friends."

One corner of his mouth tilted up. His smile reached all the way to his eyes. God, she loved the way he smiled at her. As if she were the only woman in the room, as if she really meant something more to him than just a friend.

He's going to break your heart.

Yes, I know.

A weight lifted from her shoulders. She'd finally admitted it to herself. Josh would more than likely break her heart.

He laughed suddenly as the music picked up tempo, then whirled her around and around the room. She met his gaze, and laughed right along with him, and for the first time in her life, she did feel free.

He'll break your heart. Just like all the others.

Yes, I know.

Chapter 21

There had been something different about Cody last night, but Josh couldn't quite figure out what it was. The change happened when they were dancing. For a little while, he'd seen the real woman behind the mask of indifference she always wore.

He looked at his reflection in the mirror above the sink. This wasn't good.

How could the temptation of a woman bring him to this? That's all it had been. The partnership had been a ruse to get her into his bed—and maybe out of his mind. They'd have a torrid but brief affair, collect Adam and return him to the States, and he'd kill two birds with one stone.

Marriage hadn't been part of the equation—or that he would care more about Cody than he had before she agreed to the partnership.

Damn it, he tossed the tie down and was reaching for the top button of his white shirt when his hand stilled.

What the hell was he doing? Risking spending the next few years in a Mexican jail? That's what would happen if he called off the wedding.

Crap.

He picked up his tie, took a deep breath, and quickly tied it into some semblance of what it should look like, then slipped on the heavily embroidered jacket. Hector had made sure he would look the part of a well-to-do groom and had a local seamstress alter a suit that once belonged to Hector's father.

Josh stared at his reflection. He wasn't a titled land baron, but he looked like he could be. Talk about feeling like a fraud.

How would Cody view him? As if he didn't already know the answer to that. She was furious with him for getting her into this mess. The only reason she hadn't blown the whole thing sky high was because her aversion to spending time in a Mexican jail was as strong as his.

He had a feeling she'd tell him again how pissed off she was when she had him alone.

There was a sharp rap on the door before it opened. "Ah, you are ready, *amigo*." Hector studied him for a moment before nodding his approval. "Cody will not be able to resist you." He smiled.

Josh only hoped that was the case. If she found him irresistible, then maybe she wouldn't want to kill him.

Hector handed him a white velvet bag that jingled. Curiosity got the better of him. He poured the contents on the bed and gold coins tumbled out. Thirteen, to be exact.

"For you to give your bride. The priest will bless them. Then you give them to Cody to show her that you intend to support her."

Yeah, she'd really like the idea of him supporting her. That would definitely make her happy—right after she shoved them down his throat.

Thirteen. He hoped Cody wasn't superstitious.

Why was she so damn nervous?

Cody tugged at the bodice of the satin gown. Maria was just a bit smaller in the bust. If she sneezed, she'd pop out for sure.

And she was slowly being suffocated by the crowded room. There were at least ten women jammed into the tiny bedroom. Ten chattering women. Since they were all speaking Spanish, Cody couldn't understand a blasted word they said. Giggling, chattering women. If she ran from the room screaming, would they lock her away in an asylum for the insane?

Sweat rolled between her breasts.

She had to get some air. It was too damn hot in here. She closed her eyes and swallowed back the scream that threatened to erupt from her mouth at any second.

"Our bride needs air," Maria said before switching to Spanish and shooing everyone out of the room.

When Maria closed the door, Cody sighed with relief.

"I was the same way before I married Hector. I almost called off the wedding." She walked back across the room and opened the balcony door.

A light breeze drifted into the room like a whisper, but it was enough to begin to ease the tension inside her.

"You will feel much better in a few minutes." She smiled with such warmth that another wave of guilt washed over Cody. If Maria knew the truth, she'd be so hurt.

Oh, no, she had started to like the other woman. That wasn't good. Crap, what the hell was happening in her life? She was stuck here, about to become Mrs. Josh Pierce. Her stomach rumbled and there was a sudden tightness in her chest.

She waited for the uncomfortable feeling to go away. That wasn't the worst of it, though. She didn't want to hurt Maria.

You're a bounty hunter. Trained to fight. Emotions aren't a part of your life.

Then why did she feel as if emotions were consuming her?

"You are feeling better?"

She glanced up. A worried frown marred Maria's features.

"Much better," she lied. "Pre-wedding jitters, I guess."

"*Si, si.* It is okay to be nervous. You have *mucho hombre.*" She raised her eyebrows and a saucy grin appeared on her face. "You will have many wonderful nights together."

If this marriage were real, she had no doubt Maria would

be right. She walked to the window, drawing in a deep breath. The honeysuckle-scented breeze was soothing to her frayed nerves.

"Josh loves you very much."

She glanced over her shoulder. What was Maria basing her observations on? The fact that they were getting married? Cody wouldn't burst her bubble and tell her love didn't even enter into their relationship.

"You doubt me. I can see it in your eyes, but it is true. I see the way he looks at you." She brought a large round box from the closet and put it on the bed. "His gaze follows you around the room like you are the only woman there."

Lust, not love. She couldn't fault him for that. Hell, she wanted to experience what they'd had in the motel room again, too. It seemed all she could think about lately. Making sweet love all night long.

No, not love. It would only be sex. But damn good sex, and it wouldn't matter that love wasn't a part of what they shared.

So maybe they would share their bodies with each other once more. She closed her eyes and leaned her head against the doorframe. Visions swirled behind her tightly closed lids. She watched the erotic pictures like a movie being played out.

Her hands clenched and unclenched as she envisioned Josh slowly unzipping her dress and pushing it off her shoulders, exposing her breasts to his hungry gaze. His mouth would lower, her back would arch . . .

"This was my grandmother's veil," Maria said, breaking into her thoughts.

She bit back a groan and quickly brought herself back under control before she turned around. White silk, lace, and a jewel-encrusted veil made her catch her breath.

"It's beautiful," she whispered, walking closer. "Are you sure you want me to wear it?"

"Of course, we are sisters, remember? Besides, you will do it honor to be worn by someone so beautiful."

"Passable. Nice-looking." She shrugged. "I'm not so sure about beautiful."

"Now you are making jokes." Maria smiled, then placed the veil on top of Cody's head, adjusting it before pinning it in place with white combs. "There. You are like the princess in the fairy tale." She waved toward the full-length mirror.

She turned, and for a moment could only stare at her reflection. Maria was right, she did look like a fairy tale princess. Too bad her Prince Charming was a cardboard cutout and tomorrow she'd go back to doing what she did best—capturing bad guys.

But nothing in the world could make her ruin Maria's moment.

"Thank you," she said.

Maria beamed. "It will be a wonderful day for you both." Music started playing. "It is time." She pulled the lacy material over Cody's face, partially concealing it.

Oh, lord, it wasn't butterflies fluttering in her stomach. No, it was more like a beehive had busted open and the nasty little creatures were buzzing all over the place. She expected to feel their sting any second now.

Deep breath. She could do this—as long as she kept telling herself it wasn't real.

After pasting a smile on her face, which she was sure came off sickly, she followed Maria. Thank goodness for the veil.

The music changed when she reached the top of the stairs and the small band began playing the bridal march. She swallowed past the lump in her throat and raised her chin before she moved down the stairs, all the time praying she wouldn't trip. Odd, the things that were going through her mind.

The room was almost bursting at the seams with Maria and Hector's relatives, but they'd left a wide path for her to walk down, and at the end of it were Josh, the priest, and Hector.

She almost did trip then. God, Josh was handsome as he

stood in front of a white arch that had been decorated with a garland and flowers. Hector had apparently loaned him a suit.

Stepping back in time. That's what all this felt like. Josh might have been a *hacendado*. The owner of a magnificent estate as he stood there wearing an intricately embroidered black suit that must have taken hours to sew.

And for just a little while, she'd be calling him husband.

Her breath caught in her throat and for a brief second she wished . . . Hell, she didn't know what she wished. Marriage with Josh? Not likely. He was a player. A one-night stand. Their one-night stand was lasting a little longer than either had planned, but that's exactly what it was nonetheless.

How in the hell had they fucked everything up so badly?

Josh reached for her hand. His was warm and strong, hers cold as ice. When he smiled down on her, she knew everything would be okay. Together, they would make it right.

Then she looked at the priest. Oh, lord, how many guilt trips would she go on in this lifetime?

He smiled the kindest smile she'd ever seen.

Apparently, she'd be taking a hell of a lot.

Maria and Hector stepped toward them, looping a white ribbon over her and Josh. This was it. They hadn't fallen for their alibi after all and they were tying them up.

"A tradition." Maria smiled. "A lasso. It represents your joining."

As long as no one got kinky or anything, what did it matter? They were going to hell for sure now. No one took something symbolic and sacred and stomped all over it. She wasn't that religious, but she did have beliefs and God was one of them.

He *would* have His revenge.

When Josh reached into his pocket, she wondered what he was up to now. He pulled out a white velvet bag. The priest said something over it and Josh gave it to her.

What the hell was she supposed to do with it? Obviously, there were coins inside. At least that's what it felt like. She met Josh's gaze.

"The bag holds thirteen gold coins. It represents my commitment to support you."

Even looking through the lacy veil, she saw his eyes twinkle. If this were a real marriage, she'd toss the money at his feet. Support, her ass. She would never need anyone to support her. She'd made it this far without a man's help and she certainly didn't need help now.

Smiling, she lowered her lids demurely. "*Gracias.*"

The priest began to speak so she turned her attention back to him. She had no idea what he was saying, but she could guess. After a few lengthy minutes passed, he held a cross toward her.

"You will kiss the cross to show your faithfulness," Maria whispered.

Oh, yeah, they were definitely going to hell. She kissed the cold metal. Josh did the same. How could he seem so calm? And so devilishly handsome?

The next thing she knew, Josh raised her veil. His lips met hers in what she thought would be a brief kiss, but as soon as she felt the heat, his arms pulling her closer, she forgot the crowd of relatives and let herself be caught up in the passion of his touch.

The clapping of hands and the cheering jerked her back to earth. The priest removed the white ribbon and handed it to her and they were led outside, where tables ringed the patio.

Champagne toasts followed. People that Cody had met came up to congratulate them. She cast sideways glances at Josh, who seemed quite comfortable playing his role of new husband. He laughed and shook hands while she felt as if she were having an out-of-body experience. Not a good feeling.

Her wedding. What a joke. Oh, lord, would anyone think badly of her if she just up-chucked everywhere? No, then she would ruin Maria's beautiful gown.

The guests joined hands and formed a heart shape.

Now what?

"I believe the first dance is ours," Josh said, holding out his hand. "Our first dance as man and wife."

She had no quick retort as she went into his arms. Why the hell did it feel so right having him hold her? They should've made a better attempt at escaping—before they were married.

"What are you thinking," he whispered close to her ear.

"That we're going to hell. That God will have His revenge because we took something holy and tarnished it."

"What happened to the woman who lived to bring the next criminal to justice? You showed no fear. What's changed?"

He was right. She was different, but did she like the new Cody? Was she getting soft? Crap, she was. But how did she go back to being that hard-assed person? Did she remember the way?

Did she even want to? She wasn't sure anymore.

She met Josh's penetrating gaze as he waltzed her around the patio. He lightly caressed her arm with his thumb, sending tingles of pleasure over her. His gaze was like blue fire, heating her body with awareness.

Ah, yes, they would definitely share their bodies again. Her nipples were tight with anticipation of his hands stroking, fondling.

So maybe she would go to hell. Josh would be there right alongside her. Right now, the only hell she could foresee was not ever making love with him again. That would be pure torture, a self-made hell.

"I want you," she told him, vowing to take one day at a time.

He sucked in a deep breath. "You think they'd throw us in jail if we dropped to the floor and had a go of it?"

She laughed, but when the song stopped, her laughter died as he pulled her against him and lowered his mouth. His tongue stroked and teased. She tangled her hands in his hair and brought him closer.

God, she wanted this man again and again and again.

He'll break your heart.

I don't care.

"How soon can we leave?" she asked.

Maybe asking the question aloud jinxed her. Two hours later and she was still wondering the same thing. What was worse, Josh had been spirited away by a bunch of the men.

This was supposed to be her wedding day, damn it. The groom wasn't supposed to desert her.

But then, she wasn't a bride. At least, not a real one. The *marriage* was real, though. She could pretend, at least for a little while, that Josh wouldn't be like all the rest. He wouldn't leave her. Not tonight. He would be all hers.

Chapter 22

Maria and three of her giggling sisters led Cody to the guesthouse where Josh had stayed the night before. Now what were they up to, she wondered.

As soon as they were inside, she instinctively knew the room didn't look like this when Josh stayed there. Rose petals covered the gauze-draped bed and were scattered on the floor. A bottle of champagne chilled in a bucket of ice and there was a gold plate filled with succulent strawberries and fat purple grapes.

Candles were on the fireplace mantle, waiting to be lit, but the vanilla-scented wax already mingled with the scent of the roses.

"A woman's wedding night should be one that she will never forget," Maria said softly. "Come." She pulled her the rest of the way into the room. Behind a silk panel was a claw-foot tub filled with water and a layer of rose petals. Cody inhaled the heady scent. Her tense muscles were already beginning to relax.

Maria's sisters removed her veil, and after her gown was unbuttoned, they took that, too, and, except for Maria, slipped from the room. Maria removed the rest of her clothes, and as Cody stepped into the tub, she was instantly surrounded by warmth.

Maria tipped a small glass bottle, letting a few drops of the liquid spill into the water.

"For energy. I think you will need it this night." She laughed lightly before tipping another bottle and letting the oil spill into the water. "This formula eez passed down from mother to daughter. It will bind you and your husband together forever with a love that no one will be able to separate."

As the oil spread across the top of the water, goose bumps spread over Cody's arms and the hairs on the back of her neck stood up.

Yeah, right, she silently scoffed. As soon as they were back in Texas, they'd get divorced. No love potion could bind them together.

But it smelled good.

"Just relax. Let the waters soothe your troubled soul."

Had she heard her right? No, probably not. Maria put a glass of wine on the table beside the tub and went around the screen to give her privacy.

She could really get used to this kind of life. A deep sigh escaped. She sipped the wine as the room filled with the soft sounds of music from a CD. The wine was good. It had a slight undertaste that she couldn't quite put her finger on. Not that she really cared. She would enjoy the moment, and for once let all her problems slip away.

Closing her eyes, she let the world pass her by, the warmth of the water enveloping her in a cocoon.

The next thing she knew, Maria was helping her to stand, wrapping a fluffy white towel around her before she stepped out of the tub.

"I feel strange." And not so out of it that she didn't suspect there had been more in the wine than squished grapes. "What did I drink?"

"My great-grandmother was a gypsy." Maria tilted her head and looked at Cody. "Did I not mention that?"

"No." The background music seemed to take on form as

colors swirled around her. Deep sensuous blues, hot reds—
she could almost reach out and touch them.

"*Si*, she was an important person in *mi familia*. She had
many potions."

Maria casually picked up a towel and began to pat Cody's
damp skin. Her light touch was almost sensuous. What was
happening? More importantly, what had been in the wine?

Maria guided her from around the silk screen. Two of her
sisters had returned. Cody liked them. They were really nice,
even if they didn't speak much English.

"Come, lie on the bed. We will put oil on your skin. Josh
will not be able to resist."

Lie down? Yes, that sounded like a good idea. A nap
would be nice.

Maria's sisters removed the towel. They pulled the cover
back before she lay on the bed. The silk sheets brushed her
skin, and her nipples tightened.

They began to massage the warm oil into her skin with
light, circular strokes. The musky scent drifted to her nose.

"This magical blend of oils has been passed down from
one generation to the next. Each touch from your husband
will be enhanced. His breath will heat your skin like no other
man. You will remember this night forever. He will be your
love, as you will be his."

Her words continued, soft and melodic, switching from
English to Spanish.

Cody didn't want to think, just feel the sensations that
took her to another realm. But the next thing she knew,
Maria urged her to her knees and slipped a white diaphanous
gown over her head. The hem billowed around her like a
cloud as she sat in the middle of the bed.

Then she was alone. She knew it wouldn't be for long.
Josh would come to her.

She looked around the room. The music still played in the
background, the candles flickering. She felt as if she were tee-

tering on the edge of a cliff, a breeze drifting over her. Just that light touch sent her pulse racing.

The door opened. She looked up. Josh stood there for a moment before he closed it behind him. Her gaze drank in the sight before her. He wore the black pants and knee-high boots, but the jacket was gone and his white shirt was open almost to his waist, showing an expanse of sinewy muscles and tanned skin.

She sucked in a deep breath, her body aching for his touch. It seemed like forever since she'd felt it, and she needed to feel it now. Maybe the oils and the wine had a lot to do with it; she didn't know or care. This would be their night. Maybe their last one. Who could know for sure, but she damn well wanted it to be one she would remember for the rest of her life.

"You're beautiful," he said as he sauntered forward. He removed his shirt, tossing it to the floor. Stopping at the open bottle of champagne, he poured them each a glass.

She watched his movements as if in a dream. When he sat on the side of the bed, he handed her one of the glasses, twining his arm around hers.

"To my bride." He took a drink.

She did the same. The wine quenched her parched throat. One drop fell, landing on her gown. Josh's gaze went to the fallen drop. He leaned forward and licked the spot with his tongue, scraping across her sensitive nipple. She gasped, her hand trembling, threatening to spill the rest of her drink.

Josh took her glass and set it on the bedside table with his, then turned back. He noticed his own hand trembled almost as much as Cody's had. Who could blame him? Maybe it was that glass of wine Maria had given him. It had tasted a little odd.

Or maybe it was the fact that Cody sat on her knees in the middle of the bed, surrounded by rose petals, wearing a gown that hid nothing from his view. The thin material only cast tempting shadows, and he planned to explore each and every one of them.

He faced her once again. Was there ever a woman more sensual, more sexy than this one? He didn't think so. At least, none that he'd ever crossed paths with.

"Do you know how much I want you?" he asked.

Surprise widened her eyes, then suddenly he saw a flash of pain. "It's only sex. Maybe we are going to consummate our marriage, but none of this is real." She reached a hand out and caressed the side of his face.

He grabbed it in his, kissing her palm. "We could make it real," he said into her hand. The realization of his words hit him like a blast of cold water. He wanted their marriage to be real.

How long had he loved her? But he knew the answer. He'd loved Cody from the very beginning. From the first moment he'd laid eyes on her. He liked the brassy, bold lady she was, but he'd always sensed the pain she'd hidden away from the rest of the world.

He looked at her. She hadn't heard him. Or if she had, she didn't acknowledge his words. Did it matter right now? He would have the rest of his life to convince her they were meant to be together.

He pulled her close, until she was sitting on his lap. Her eyes were such a deep green as she stared at him, her lips full, pouty, crying out to be kissed.

Ah, sweet temptation. He lowered his mouth to hers, running his tongue across the fullness of her lips before dipping inside, stealing her sweetness, her soul. He wanted her so bad he ached.

He cushioned her back with one arm while his free hand cupped her breast. She moaned when he teased her nipple, plucking at the tender nub.

She pressed her body closer, rubbing her bottom against him, and he almost lost it. He quickly set her from him and moved off the bed.

"Please." She reached for him.

"I'm not leaving your bed, sexy lady. I'm just getting more

comfortable. You've caused the material of these blasted pants to . . . shrink."

She grinned and lay back amidst the pillows, her hair fanning out beneath her. A seductress, teasing him with her body. Looking innocent and seductive all at the same time. One knee came up, shielding the thatch of dark curls from his view.

It had been forever since he'd seen her like this. He wouldn't allow any shields between them now. He wanted to see all of her. He put a hand on her knee, massaging lightly, watching her expression. She didn't disappoint. She closed her eyes, biting her bottom lip. He brought her knee down and out, exposing her, except for the thin gown. Even that was hiding too much.

Taking the hem, he slowly pulled it up to her hips, gazing down at her curls, the fleshy part that peeked out between the folds. "I love looking at you," he said, his words husky with restrained passion. He spoke the truth—he would never get tired of looking at her.

Lightly, he scraped his fingers through her curls. She gasped and arched toward his hand. He rubbed his finger down her sex. She cried out, opening her arms to him.

How he wanted this woman.

He took a step back and slipped the button of his pants through the buttonhole. Her gaze moved downward as she watched him slowly tug on the zipper. Her hands knotted in her gown, drawing it upwards. When the material brushed across her nipples, she gasped. His dick quivered. There was something erotic about a woman who could pleasure herself and not be ashamed or embarrassed by her actions.

She met his gaze. Something must have shown on his—desire, hunger? He wasn't sure, but her lips curved upwards just slightly. Did she think she was in control?

She wet her finger, sucking on it for what seemed like an eternity. His dick began to burn and ache as he watched her move her finger in and out of her mouth, then circled her tongue around it.

Hell, why would he ever have the mistaken notion he might be in control?

She moved her finger from her mouth, slowly sliding her hands over her breasts, tweaking the nipples and moaning as her body arched.

Swallowing took supreme effort as he watched the sensual show she performed for him. Was this how the goddess of love enticed men to her? Making them fall in love with her before she tossed them away? If so, he could understand the exquisite pain and pleasure they went through before going crazy.

Cody slid her hands over her stomach and down her thighs. "I want you so badly I can almost feel you inside me," she said.

He snapped out of the daze he was in and shoved his pants down. It didn't take but a few seconds for him to be completely naked and climbing between her legs. He stopped when his face was inches away from her pubic hair.

"Damn, you're so beautiful." He blew against her curls, watching them spring back into place. "Open yourself for me," he whispered.

She moved her hands to the folds that hid her from his view and opened herself.

"Perfect," he breathed. Lowering his head, he took her inside his mouth and began to suck. She tasted sweet and musky— all woman. A woman he couldn't seem to get enough of.

The first spasms trembled over her body. He felt each one of them as she came. He didn't stop the motions of his mouth until she cried out and her body stiffened.

"Ah, damn," she cried, a tear slipping from the corner of her eye. Her breathing was ragged.

There was a certain amount of pride that he could give her an orgasm this powerful using only his mouth. But damn, his need was so intense that he could barely move. All he could think about was entering her hot body, letting her sex flood his with heat.

Just thinking about it didn't help his condition. He scooted up in the bed until he could cradle her in his arms. The softness of her body, her curves, melted against him. He rolled them onto their sides, gently nudging her legs open, pulling one over his hip as he eased inside her.

She was so fucking wet. Hot and wet. He caught his breath as the ache inside him grew fierce. She clenched her inner muscles, tightening herself around him.

"Ahh," he moaned before rolling her onto her back and sliding deeper inside her body. For a moment he rested, catching his breath.

Then he began to move, slowly at first. He looked into her face, capturing her gaze as he moved faster. She bit her bottom lip when he slid almost all the way out, then she sucked him back. Deeper and harder he sank inside her. Faster and faster. The world spun out of control. His body clenched, jerked. He might have groaned; he wasn't sure as spasms of pure pleasure wrapped around him and reeled him into a vortex of lights and sounds he'd never heard or seen before. As the world stopped spinning, he sank into Cody's softness.

Not for the first time did he wonder if the wine Maria had given him might have been drugged. Hell, he didn't care. This was the best sex he'd ever had.

He rolled his weight off her, stared into eyes filled with confusion, maybe a little bit of fear, and knew she'd felt the same thing he had.

But would she embrace it—or run away?

Sometime during the night, he rolled over and reached for Cody, and she wasn't there. He moved his hand over her spot and patted her pillow. Cold washed over him even though the room had been warm earlier.

He opened his eyes. It took a minute for them to adjust to the dim moonlight cascading through the window. She'd pulled back the drapes and opened the window. Just the hint of a breeze tickled his skin. He had a perfect side view of her luscious bare body.

She raised her head, as if giving homage to the gods. Her body was clearly outlined in the light streaming in. Her breasts were like succulent fruit, the nipples hardened by the breeze that kissed them. Her slim waist curved to her nicely rounded hips and the thatch of dark hair.

He wanted her again. Damn, how he wanted her. He pushed back the covers, but stopped when he heard the small cry she made. His gut clenched and his heart caught in his throat. He wanted to tell her he wouldn't hurt her, but words wouldn't prove anything. She'd have to learn to trust that he wouldn't leave her like everyone else had.

The only problem was, he wasn't sure she ever would. Pain ripped through him. He'd finally found the woman he wanted to spend the rest of his life with, but she might not feel the same about him, the player. The man who didn't stay in a relationship longer than a month.

How fucking ironic was that?

Chapter 23

"I wish you would stay." Maria turned pleading eyes toward her husband.

Hector shook his head and pulled his wife close. "You still have all these guests. They will keep you entertained for a few more days. This is Josh and Cody's time to be alone," he gently chided.

"Then you will promise to come back, *si*?" She wiped at the tears on her face.

Cody took a deep breath—and lied. "Of course we'll return." How could she tell her they would be divorced within a few days? Damn, how sappy was she going to get before she got back to her old self?

Maria threw her arms around Cody and hugged her tight. For a moment, she just stood there, unable to move. Slowly, her arms came up and she hugged Maria. Strange new emotions wrapped around her. Tears welled in her eyes.

"You will always be my sister," Maria whispered before she let her go.

Cody didn't tell her that always was a long time and bonds were easily broken. Bonds that you once thought were there forever, but were only a figment of your imagination. But she didn't tell her that. Why burst her bubble?

Instead, she smiled, then climbed into Josh's car. Hector

had it driven to the house that morning knowing they needed to get back to Texas.

She looked out the window as they drove away, not prepared to share with anyone how much she'd enjoyed being around Maria and her boisterous family. Besides, she didn't want Josh to see the tears in her eyes.

Damn, she'd forgotten to ask Maria what had been in the wine. Aphrodisiac? Possibly. Whatever the hell it was, she didn't want to drink any more of it. She had gotten up in the middle of the night, careful not to awaken Josh, and stood by the window. Her emotions were all out of whack. Not only had she had the best sex of her life, but there was more—almost as if she were falling for him.

Boy, those thoughts would really get her into trouble! Her and Josh together—forever. Yeah, like that would happen in her lifetime.

She sat up when she saw they were going toward the border. "What about Adam?" She turned and looked at Josh.

"He's either long gone or still at the ranch somewhere. Either way, we might as well give up on ever bringing him to justice. Unless you'd like to end up like Turbo?"

She shuddered at the thought. Until they were safely across the border the threat of spending time in a Mexican jail still hung like an axe over their heads.

"Maybe we should just chalk Adam up to the one who got away."

"My thoughts exactly," he said.

She didn't relax until they were on the other side. Texas. She breathed a sigh of relief, forcing herself not to ask Josh to pull over so she could get out and kiss the ground.

Apparently, stopping wasn't on his list of things to do. Except for grabbing a bite to eat, Josh drove straight back to Fort Worth. The only conclusion she could come to was that he wanted to get rid of her. But hadn't she suspected as much? Josh was a player. She'd known that from the start.

He didn't want entanglements any more than . . . than she did.

He stopped the car in front of her apartment complex, but before she could open the door and slide out, he grabbed her hand.

"We need to decide what to do." He spoke softly, but it was like a knife being stabbed through her heart.

"There's only one thing to do—start divorce proceedings." She climbed out of the car and leaned back in through the window. "You have no roots, no ties that bind you. One day you'll just take off."

He opened his mouth, but she raised her hand.

"You might leave tomorrow and I'd never see you again." She stayed calm, even though she felt anything but that on the inside. "Divorcing is the only thing to do. We both know that." She turned and walked away, knowing she was doing the right thing, knowing it also hurt like hell.

He'll break your heart, a voice whispered.

He already has, she answered back.

Every muscle in her ached as she dragged her weary body inside her apartment building and down to the elevator. She pushed her floor number and leaned her head against the wall.

Why the hell had she let him weave his way into her life? Easy, because she'd had the hots for him from the first moment she'd laid eyes on him. Gut instinct had told her she would only get hurt. She should've listened.

The doors swished silently open. She dug her key out of her pocket as she made her way down the hallway. The door of the apartment across from her opened and a little old lady with bottle-bright red hair stepped out.

"Oh, you're back." She beamed a smile in Cody's direction. "We were wondering if you'd been hurt. Me and Aggie." She nodded toward the apartment behind them. "Aggie lives there."

"Huh?" She stopped in front of her door, key aimed toward the lock.

"I'm your neighbor." She pointed to the apartment next to Cody's. "I'm surprised you haven't complained to the manager because of all the noise I make."

Cody cocked an eyebrow. "Wild parties?"

She chuckled. "Don't I wish. No, it's my arthritis." She raised gnarled hands. "I'm always dropping something."

Pity washed over Cody, but she resolutely pushed it away. She didn't want to get chummy with her neighbors, but this one was in a talkative mood.

"My nephew is on the police department. He's always talking about how you kick ass when you bring a bail jumper in. So, did you get your man?"

If she only knew. "He got away."

"Don't worry, dear. I'm sure you will in the end." She started to walk past, but at the last minute stopped and gave Cody a brief hug. "Take care of yourself, dear. We'll have tea soon. I want to hear all about how you capture the bad guys. We all do. Lord knows we don't have that much excitement in our lives these days." With a nod, she opened her door and went inside.

Cody stared at her door for all of two minutes before shoving her key in the door and unlocking it. As she went inside, she tossed her keys on the table.

What the hell was it with all this hugging? It was almost as if God had looked down and decided to make up for all the hugs she hadn't gotten as a child. It was damned creepy and she wished it would stop.

Liar.

She ran her hands through her hair. Damn, she was more tired than she realized. After she called Pearl, she'd take a nap. A guilty flush heated her skin. Why hadn't she called while she was gone?

She grabbed the phone out of its cradle and punched in the

number. When her call was cheerfully answered, she thought for a moment she'd hit a wrong digit.

"Pearl?"

"Cody, you're home."

She closed her eyes and bit back an angry retort. Pearl was drunk. The only time Pearl was this happy was when she'd been drinking, but showing her anger would only make matters worse.

"You have to come over. If you're not too tired, that is. Moji and I are having tea. It's the most wonderful breakfast blend." She chuckled. "Although it's closer to dinner."

Her mother's words gradually filtered through to her brain. "Moji? What the hell is he doing there?"

"Why, looking after me, dear. Just like you asked. We've had some wonderful discussions about you . . ." Her words trailed off. "And me," she finished.

This was great. Just fucking great. He was only supposed to call Pearl and see if she needed anything. She'd strangle him.

"I'll be there in ten minutes." She dropped the phone back in the cradle and headed for the door.

Josh was nearly home when he realized he was making the biggest mistake of his life. He loved Cody and he didn't want to get a divorce. Damn it, the marriage ceremony had been real for him.

He turned at the next corner and headed back to her apartment. Somehow he would convince her that he wouldn't walk out of her life. He would be there as long as she would have him.

No matter what argument she gave him, this was the right thing to do. Maybe their marriage wouldn't work out, but what the hell did they have to lose? A hell of a lot if they didn't at least try.

Maybe Maria had slipped a love potion into the wine. Stranger things had happened. She'd told him it was a very special wine. Right now, he didn't really care. What did matter was getting to Cody and telling her how much he loved her.

He parked in the garage, locked his car, and headed for the elevator. It felt as if a heavy weight had been lifted from his shoulders as he waited for the doors to open. He felt more alive than he had in a very long time.

And he couldn't wait on the elevator. Grinning, he went to the stairs. Hell, he'd probably fly up them. He took the steps two at a time.

He still wasn't out of breath when he knocked on her door. "Come on, open up, Cody. I know you're in there." He knocked again. And waited. "Cody, I love you."

He heard something fall inside her apartment so he knew she'd heard him.

"Cody?"

Silence.

Slowly, he turned and walked away. He didn't need more answer than that. He'd misread the signs and mistakenly thought she cared for him. Hell, why would he even travel down that road? Cody didn't trust him enough not to walk out of her life like everyone else had.

He went to the elevator. As soon as the doors opened, he stepped inside. He'd see a lawyer tomorrow and start divorce proceedings. There was no sense in dragging their marriage out longer than necessary.

Cody knocked on her mother's door, then paced in the hall while she waited for the door to open. She didn't have long to wait, but any words she'd been about to utter were caught in her throat as she stared at her mother.

It was her mother . . . right?

A gentle smile curved Pearl's lips. "I'm glad you're back. We have a lot of things to talk about." She stepped aside so Cody could enter the apartment.

"What have you done to yourself?" Had Pearl gone on an

alcohol binge or what? Her mother wore a flowing blue caf-
tan and her hair had blond highlights. She'd kill Moji. Where
the hell was he, anyway?

"Moji thought we needed time alone so he left."

"You're reading minds now?" She almost hated the sarcasm in her voice. Almost.

"No, I'm your mother. It wasn't hard to guess what you
were thinking or what you're thinking now."

She opened her mouth, but snapped it shut. She wasn't
going to get into a discussion with Pearl about the joys of
motherhood.

"Okay, so what am I thinking?"

"That I've been drinking."

"Have you?"

Pearl squared her shoulders and thrust her chin forward.
"I haven't had a drink of alcohol in five months, twenty-one
days, and I won't go into the minutes and seconds."

Cody couldn't remember her mother ever going a day
without a drink. Pearl was lying.

"I'm telling you the truth. I knew if I told you I'd joined
AA what you would think—that I'd fail, like I'd failed in
everything else I've tried to do. I *am* doing it, though." Her
eyes pleaded with Cody to understand.

It was too much to take in all at once. She shook her head.
"So why are you telling me now?"

"Moji. He helped me see through some things. You have a
good friend in him." She smiled. "Rather odd, but likable."

"So, where do you go from here?"

She walked to the window and looked down on the street.
It wouldn't last, the voice inside her head warned. How
many times had she prayed, hoped for the day her mother
would turn into her vision of what a mother should be. Each
time her hopes and dreams were crushed and they would go
back to the way they'd been.

Maybe that's what had hurt so damn much. It was the

glimpses of the mother she could've had. If she'd never seen the love in her mother's eyes during the sober times, maybe she wouldn't have yearned for it so much.

"I do love you."

The words were spoken so low that for a moment she wondered if Pearl had actually said them or it was just wishful thinking.

"I love you," she repeated.

The words were stronger this time and held more conviction. She flinched when her mother put her hand on her arm.

"Please," Pearl said.

"I'm afraid."

"Of what?"

"Of losing you again." She closed her eyes tight against the tears, but the next thing she knew, her mother was pulling her into her arms and holding her.

"I know. I'm scared, too. I'm scared that I won't be the mother you want me to be. That I won't live up to your expectations. I've been scared all my life, but AA is teaching me how to be strong." She choked back a sob. "I might fall again. But I'm going to try my best not to."

"I'll help you back up if you fall . . . Mama." She tightened her arms around her mother and held on. *Please,* she silently prayed, *let me keep her this time.*

"We have a lot to talk about." Pearl pulled away, but she held onto Cody's hand as she led her to the sofa. "There's a lot you don't know about . . . about your father and other things. It's time you knew the truth."

"It's not so important anymore." Maybe all those years she hadn't been looking for her father, but trying to find the mother she'd lost somewhere along the way.

"It's important to me that you know. It's the only chance I'll have of surviving." She took a deep breath.

"Okay."

"When I was seventeen, I ran away from home. My father

was an alcoholic. He used to beat my mother so badly she'd carry the bruises for days. She'd scream at me to run and hide. One day I did, and I didn't go back."

"If you don't want to . . ."

Pearl's smile wobbled just a fraction. "No, I do. I have to get rid of all the skeletons in the closet or it will be too easy to take that next drink."

She nodded and Pearl began to talk.

"It didn't take long for me to run out of what little money I had. When James, your father, found me, I'd decided to sell my . . . my body. I couldn't go back home."

Cody understood the effort it was taking her mother to tell her everything. She wanted to say it was okay, that she still loved her, but she knew staying silent would help her mother more.

"James was so handsome and so young. He was also from a wealthy family." She looked down at her hands. "And he was married, but I didn't know it at the time. Not that it would've mattered. I was pretty desperate."

Cody forced herself to remain calm. For the first time in her life, she didn't much like the father she'd fantasized about for years.

"He set me up in a small apartment. I loved him so much it made my heart ache whenever I thought about him. I think he loved me, too. At least, for a little while. But then I got pregnant and he didn't come around as much. I think it scared the hell out of him. His parents would've killed him if they'd found out about us. But I kept thinking he might come back. When he didn't, I started drinking to help the pain go away." She met Cody's gaze. "I told myself I'd be a better parent than my parents were, but I wasn't. I might not have physically abused you, but I hurt you in other ways. I'm sorry."

Cody gathered her mother in her arms. Just like she had when she was younger. "It's okay, Mama. Everything will be okay." There was a big difference this time. This was a time for healing.

"I didn't mean to carry on so." Pearl grabbed a tissue from the box on the table beside the sofa and dabbed at her eyes. "I wanted to be the strong one this time. I guess I'm not very good at it yet."

"I think you're one of the strongest people I know." *Please let this last,* she silently prayed. *Please.* She took a deep breath. "You never saw my father again?" Why had she even asked? Morbid curiosity? She was on a roll with her mother. But damn it, she wanted to know if he'd cared enough to keep in touch in some way.

Her mother shook her head. "He did come and see me for a while, but then he stopped. He was going into politics . . ." Her words trailed off and she looked at Cody.

"You mean, he lives here? In Fort Worth?" And he hadn't cared enough to keep in touch. That hurt, but it also pissed her off.

"He's on the city council."

She drew in a sharp breath as a man's face flashed in front of her. Dark hair, green eyes. She'd seen him on television. Son-of-a-bitch. All this time he'd been within arm's reach and she hadn't even known it.

"It's been so long, Cody. Don't stir up any trouble. He's not worth it."

She snapped out of the sudden fog she'd walked into and looked at her mother. "You're right. He's in the past." She squeezed Pearl's hand reassuringly.

"Have I ever told you how proud I am of you? Well, I am. Tell me how your trip went. Did you bring someone back?"

"He got away." Both of them. No, she wouldn't think about Josh.

"So, did you do anything exciting?"

"Besides getting married? No, not a thing." Her mother's mouth dropped open as Cody stood. "Do you have any of that chocolate ice cream left? Maybe some chocolate syrup, too."

Chapter 24

Cody sat in her apartment watching the television, but not really looking at it. Why the hell had she blurted out that she'd gotten married? Must've been all that sharing they'd been doing. Her mother had wanted to know all the details. She had to keep reminding her that they'd be getting divorced as quickly as they'd gotten married.

She leaned her head on the back of the sofa and closed her eyes.

Damn it, why hadn't he contacted her? Sure, she knew that she'd been the one who said it was over, but he hadn't even argued the point. She wished just once in her life that she would mean enough to someone that they would say, "No, I'm not letting you walk away, we're in this together."

Apparently, she wasn't worth the effort.

A deep sigh escaped. At least her mother was trying harder. That was something to be grateful for. If it lasted. Damn, when had she gotten so cynical? Would she forever be waiting for the other shoe to fall?

She opened her eyes and glanced at the television, then grabbed for the remote and turned up the volume when a familiar face came across the screen.

"Adam Sinclair returned to the United States of his own accord yesterday. Though he will face charges, it won't be for murder. Evidence was recently uncovered that pointed to the murdered man's cousin, who stood to inherit the bulk of his fortune . . ."

"I'll be damned," she breathed. She'd known there was something squirrely about the nerdy cousin. Now Adam wouldn't go to trial for murder. Good, she'd rather liked him and Bertrice.

She started to turn off the television, but the next picture that flashed across the screen made her catch her breath.

"In other news, there are rumors that Councilman James Rutledge will be giving up his city council seat to run for the Senate." The newsman turned to the woman on his right and smiled. "I think everyone knew this day was coming. When you come from a family of politicians it isn't hard to guess the Senate will be the next step."

"That's true," the woman said with a wide, very perfect smile. "Of course, we all thought it would be sooner than this."

Cody turned the television off. She'd heard enough, and no matter what she'd promised her mother, she had to end this chapter in her life.

She grabbed the phone book and thumbed through the pages, stopping when she came to her father's address. Of course, he would live in the better part of town. Anger flared inside her. How many times had she longed for something, but knew her mother didn't have the money?

She reached for her keys and left the apartment.

What the hell are you doing?

She resolutely shoved the voice to the back of her mind. Maybe she would only drive by his house. Hell, she didn't know what she was going to do. There was a connection missing in her life. Not knowing was sometimes worse than knowing. If she just saw where he lived, maybe she could somehow fill one of the voids in her life.

As she drew closer to his house, she saw there was a party

in progress. Lights blazed from the windows, and when she pulled to the curb and turned off the ignition, music and people's voices spilled out.

For a moment, she sat there, looking at the two-story brick and wood structure, the manicured lawn. Everything was perfect. What would it have been like to be raised surrounded by all this?

Without really thinking about what she was doing, Cody climbed off the Harley and walked to the front door. Some force propelled her forward.

She vaguely heard a car stop and the sound of a door closing. Her gaze fixed on the entryway. Somewhere behind the front door, her father laughed and talked to his friends. His wife would be at his side.

Her hands clenched.

"Madison?" A voice spoke from behind her.

She turned. A gray-haired man walked toward her.

"Sorry, I thought you were Madison. You have to be related, though. You could almost be her twin." He laughed and reached across her to ring the doorbell.

Madison? Her gaze swung to the door. She'd never thought about her father having other children. She took a step back, but the man beside her put a hand on her back.

"Careful. You don't want to fall off the step and break an ankle."

The door opened at that moment, revealing a butler. One eyebrow shot upward when his gaze fell on Cody, but he didn't say a word about her jeans and T-shirt as they walked past him.

"It was nice to meet you," she mumbled and walked away from the older man. She wormed her way over, but still continued to stand on the fringe.

There were people everywhere. The two front rooms were full and overflowing into the backyard. She heard someone shout something about the new senator. Then more shouts for him to make a speech.

Her hands began to sweat and her pulse pounded in her ears. She followed the crowd out back. As she walked past a tray of drinks, she grabbed one and quickly downed the contents. The alcohol did nothing to warm her insides.

There was more room outside. Tables were set up around a swimming pool, the water shimmering in a kaleidoscope of colors as it reflected the lights that hung from trees, the patio, and the gazebo. It looked like a fairy tale, but she wasn't Cinderella and she was afraid her life wouldn't have a happy ending.

Why had she come? What had she expected to find? A father who actually wanted her? That was a laugh. If he'd cared, he would've attempted to see her. It wasn't as if he didn't know she existed.

She started to turn to leave, but stopped at the last minute as a man stepped up to the microphone someone had placed on the gazebo. He smiled, laughed, and waved.

"Thank you, thank you." His voice boomed across the yard.

Pearl had been right. She did look like her father.

"I'm not a senator yet, though."

"Only a matter of time," someone called out close to her.

"Only with the help of my friends and . . ." When he turned toward the person who'd spoken, his gaze passed by her, then swung back.

Cody watched the expressions that crossed his face. Confusion, like he should know her. Then understanding, followed by fear. His face paled.

He attempted to finish the sentence he'd started. "And the . . . uh . . ."

A laughing woman came up beside him. "I think you've finally made James speechless with your warm outpouring of love and generosity. I think what he's trying to say is how very much we appreciate each and every one of you." She turned and reached behind her. "All our family, isn't that right, Madison?"

A young woman about Cody's age stepped from the shadows. "Yes, we're all very grateful."

Rather than looking at the crowd, her gaze went straight to Cody—and stopped. She'd been watching from her corner in the back and had seen her, maybe before her father had.

And she knew.

Madison's gaze swept over Cody. Did she note the differences between them? That one wore a white gown that sparkled with jewels and had diamonds around her neck? That the other wore a pair of faded jeans and a T-shirt?

When their gazes locked, she saw the sadness reflected on Madison's face. Maybe her life hadn't been much better. Cody looked at her father. Were there other affairs littering his life? Other children?

She shook her head. This was the man she'd wanted to know? The man whom she'd dreamed about? That he would one day walk into her life and tell the world he was her father and how proud he was of her?

Damn, what a lot of wasted hours. He wasn't worth it. She looked at her sister and smiled. The girl returned it with one of her own. Maybe they would meet someday. Who knows, but she damn sure wouldn't hold her breath. They were from two different worlds.

She turned, and with no regrets, she walked away.

Moji looked at her as if she'd grown two heads or something. Cody had no idea what his problem was, but she had no doubt he would tell her.

"You finally met your father during a big, snazzy party and all you did was walk away? Girlfriend, did I not teach you better? That would've been the perfect time for revenge. You could've at least shouted, 'Hi, Daddy.' Oh my god, that would've been priceless." He laughed. "Can anyone say . . . massive coronary'?"

She lifted the dumbbell toward her shoulder, breathing in. "I didn't go there for revenge." She slowly lowered the ten-pound weight, exhaling as she did. "I was only curious. I saw him and I wasn't curious anymore." And it was the truth. There was no sense in wishing for what might have been. Her secret fantasy of a normal family would never happen.

Still, she did wonder just a little about Madison. She hadn't seemed overly surprised, but Cody knew damn well her half sister guessed the truth.

"I don't know, I think I'd have still shouted out *something*." He rearranged some of the weights on the rack. "I spoke with your mother this morning."

Great. She still couldn't figure out why they'd become the best of friends. They were nothing alike. Now they were calling each other every day.

She replaced the weight, grabbed her towel, and wiped the sweat from her brow before tossing it down and eyeing him.

"And?" she finally asked.

"She just happened to let it slip that you and that hunky bounty hunter got married. I would think that since I wasn't invited to the wedding you'd have at least mentioned the fact you two got married."

"Oh, for heaven's sake, we're *not married*."

His eyebrows rose. "So, you didn't get married."

"We got married. We're also getting divorced. End of story."

"Uh-huh."

"And what's that supposed to mean?"

"Nothing. Nothing at all." He waved his arms about. "Oh, look, there's Tim. God, he's so beautiful. I'm thinking about giving him a year's membership."

"Take it out in trade?"

"You got it, honey." He smoothed his hands over the sides of his hair. "Ta-ta, sweetie, and don't make any rash decisions. Maybe fate stepped in to put you two together. Stranger things have happened."

"Not to me," she mumbled, and headed for the dressing room.

But as she stood under the cool spray of the shower, her thoughts turned to Josh. Even if she could have stopped them, she wasn't sure if she wanted to.

She pushed her wet hair out of her face and grabbed the soap. As she ran the bar over her naked skin, she imagined Josh caressing her. His hands lathering the soap over her breasts, circling around her tight nipples.

She bit her bottom lip as her hand slid lower, over her stomach, down to the thatch of dark curls. His hand had parted the folds, exposing her sex. She swallowed past the lump in her throat remembering how his tongue had grazed her before taking her into his mouth and gently sucking.

With one hand raised, she leaned against the wall of the shower, and with her other hand she slid the soap up and down, pressing the bar against her sex.

"Ah, Josh . . ." she groaned as her body began to tremble, but when she reached for him, he wasn't there. The soap landed on the shower stall with a thud. Tears of frustration burned her eyes. If anything, she was more wired than before.

She'd known better than to get mixed up with him. He was a player. Even though she hadn't seen him in the last few weeks, she assumed he'd moved on, and that she'd be getting divorce papers any day.

Damn it, why did it have to hurt this much?

The shrill ring of the phone echoed through Cody's apartment. She sucked in a breath, then chastised herself. It wasn't Josh. It had been a month since she'd last seen him.

As she walked past, she glanced at the black X's drawn through the days on the calendar. One very long month.

She picked up the phone. "Hello?" Did her voice sound anxious?

"Hello," Pearl said.

The breath left her body for an instant. She closed her eyes and dropped into one of the kitchen chairs. Not Josh. Damn.

"Hi . . . Mom." Why did she still stumble over calling Pearl "Mom"? Her mother had been doing great the last few weeks. She was even shopping for herself and had applied for a job at one of the local convenience stores.

"I got the job." Pearl's excitement crackled over the phone.

"Oh, Mom, that's wonderful. I'm so proud of you. We'll have to celebrate. Maybe go to a nice restaurant for supper this week." She smiled. Her mother was going to make it. She just knew it.

"That sounds like fun. We could invite Moji, too."

"Heaven help us if we leave him out."

They both laughed.

When the doorbell rang, Cody went to answer it, asking questions about her mother's job as she looked out the peephole. She didn't recognize the man. Wrong apartment?

"Hey, Mom, can I call you back? Someone's at the door."

They said good-bye and she laid the phone on the table before opening the door.

"Yes?"

He nodded. "Ms. Pierce?"

"Yes." The hairs on the back of her neck stood up.

"I'm with the firm of Jacob and Anderson . . . lawyers. I normally mail papers, but I've known Josh for a while and he wanted this matter taken care of as soon as possible. Since it was on my way . . ." His words trailed off as he handed her a large, thick envelope.

Chapter 25

Cody swallowed past the lump in her throat and took the papers. The lawyer smiled before he turned and left. She closed the door of her apartment and made her way to the sofa, dropping the papers on the coffee table and plopping down.

She sat there, staring at the envelope.

So, this was it. The end of her love affair, her marriage. She choked on a laugh. It sounded more like a sob. "Damn it, Josh, I loved you."

There, she'd finally admitted it to herself.

She fell back across the sofa and grabbed a pillow, pulling it tightly against her, and stared at the offending manila envelope.

All she had to do was sign the papers and mail them back. Her life would be like it was before Josh. No, she knew it would never be the same again.

Reaching out, she fingered the edge before pulling it toward her. What if she didn't sign them?

And where would that get her? A marriage in name only. No, she wanted all or nothing.

With a heavy sigh, she sat up and opened the envelope, pulling the stack of papers out. She began scanning through them.

"What the hell?"

Had there been a mix-up? These weren't divorce papers.

She went back to the start and began skimming through the document. Business on the northeast corner . . . co-owners . . . Mr. and Mrs. Josh Pierce.

She came to her feet. What?

This had to be some kind of mistake. They didn't own a business. She slipped the papers back into the envelope and rushed to the door. Maybe she could catch the lawyer before he left the building. She opened the door—and screamed.

Josh leaned against the frame. "Is that any way to greet your husband?"

"What?"

He looked at the papers in her hand. "I see you got the paperwork. So what do you think?"

She shook her head as he meandered inside. "Think about what?" Think? Hell, she couldn't think about anything except how damn good he looked.

"Our partnership, of course." He turned back and looked at her. His gaze made her skin go from hot to cold and back to hot. "Damn, I've missed you." He walked back to her and took her in his arms. His mouth lowered to hers, his tongue searching.

She melted in his arms, not wanting to think about what this meant. When the kiss ended, they were both fighting for air and clinging to each other.

"I've missed you," he said close to her ear.

"Then why have you stayed away?" Her voice caught in her throat. She hated that she sounded so blasted pathetic, but she couldn't help it.

"I knew you would always wonder if I'd come home each night. Too many people have walked out of your life. So I decided to prove that I'll always be there for you."

"And?"

"The papers. I bought a small building. At least, I paid a hefty amount down on it. Our building, our own agency. Yours and mine." He chuckled. "We're in hock up to our eyeballs so I couldn't leave you if I wanted to."

She looked at him. "How?"

"For one, I sold the Mustang."

She could feel the color leaving her face. His pride and joy. "But you loved that car."

He shook his head. "No, I love you. The Mustang was only metal and rubber. You're flesh and blood. I love you."

She sniffed back her tears. "I love you, too."

He kissed her forehead. "You are my life." He kissed each cheek. "I will always be there for you." He kissed the tip of her nose. "I'll never walk out of your life." He kissed her lightly on the lips. "Because if I did, I would surely die of a broken heart."

She wrapped her arms around his neck. "I love you," she whispered as tears formed. Oh, how she loved this man.

Here's a peek at Lori Foster's
"Luscious" in
BAD BOYS OF SUMMER
Available now from Brava.

With that parting remark, Lucius made his escape, putting much needed distance between him and Bethany.

When he'd first bought the apartment building of six units, he hadn't figured on renting exclusively to women. Yet that's what he'd done. He'd surrounded himself with ladies.

Was he nuts? A masochist? Or too damn partial to those of the feminine variety? Probably the latter. He did love women, all ages, all professions, all sizes and personalities.

Fellow cops ribbed him endlessly over his circumstances. They nicknamed him sultan, which he supposed was better than Luscious. If they knew about the twins, he'd never hear the end of it, because they weren't just twins. They were really hot twins—and one of them currently wore only panties and a T-shirt.

But oddly enough, it was the other twin who had him twitchy in the pants.

The one with the smart mouth and quick wit.

The one with the attitude.

And those big blue eyes . . . Of course, they both had pretty blue eyes. And silky, baby-fine brown hair. Lean bodies with understated curves. Soft, full mouths . . .

On Marci, he appreciated the beauty, just as he liked the scenery in the park. Nothing more.

On Bethany, the combination made him wild with lust.

Lucius held his breath. If he didn't, he breathed her, and he couldn't deal with that on top of no sleep and a traumatized, newly adopted dog. Bethany smelled warm, and spicy, and she left his insides churning.

She also made it clear that she didn't want to get too cozy with him, and just as he loved women, he respected their decisions. Even when it pained him to do so.

Bringing the dog home had been a spur of the moment decision prodded by some inner Good Samaritan heretofore unrecognized. Now, dead on his feet from exhaustion and, thanks to his eccentric neighbor's sister, tweaked by horniness, he . . . still didn't regret the decision.

One look at the dog and he knew he couldn't have done anything else. Hero deserved a cushy life. He deserved regular meals and pats of affection and security. No way could Lucius have left him behind, or dropped him at a shelter.

However, he could ignore Bethany. And he would. Somehow.

She only showed up about once a month. She'd stay a few days, and then take off again. Surely he could last that long.

But . . . this was August. And a school secretary probably didn't work during the summer. So how long would she be around this time? Long enough to make him completely insane?

He'd just gotten another closet door off the hinges when he sensed her presence. In his bedroom. *Real* close.

He stiffened—in more ways than one.

Without looking at her, Lucius asked, "What do you want, Bethany?" And he thought, say me, me, *me*. Tell me you want me, tell me—

"I was thinking . . ."

"Yeah? About me?" He lowered the door and shoved it under his bed then moved to stand right in front of her, as near as he dared without getting smacked. "I figured as much."

"No—"

"Don't fight it, Bethany." He tried to look serious, but the expression on her face made him want to laugh. She riled so easily. "It'll only make it harder on you." And harder on me, too.

"You are so—"

"What?" He made his tone intimate, provocative. "Tell me."

Have a look at
AUSSIE RULES
by Jill Shalvis.
Available now from Brava!

From the other side of the aircraft, the door opened. A set of stairs released. A moment later, two long legs emerged, clad in dark blue trousers, clean work boots, and topped by a most excellent ass. Not averse to enjoying a good view, Mel stayed in place, watching as the rest of the man was revealed. White button down shirt, sleeves shoved up above his elbows, tawny hair past his collar, blowing in the wind.

Yep, there were a few perks to this job, one of them catering right to Mel's soft spot.

Pilots. This one looked more like a movie star pretending to be a pilot, but you wouldn't hear her complaining. And just like that, from the inside out, she began to warm up nicely.

The man held a clipboard, which he was looking at as he turned, ducking beneath the nose of the plane to come toe to toe with her, a lock of tawny hair falling carelessly over his forehead, his eyes shaded behind aviator sunglasses.

And right then and there, every single lust-filled thought drained out of Mel's head to make room for one hollow, horror-filled one.

No.

It couldn't be. After all this time, he wouldn't *dare* show his face.

His only concession to the surprise was a raised brow as

he lifted his sunglasses, his sea green gaze taking its sweet time, touching over her own battered work boots, the dirty coveralls, the fiery, uncontrollable red hair she'd piled on top of her head without a thought to her appearance. "Look at you," he murmured. "All grown up. G'day, Mel."

Yeah, he'd grown up, too. He was bigger, broader, and taller than the last time she'd seen him, but she couldn't mistake the smile—of pure, devilish, wicked trouble.

Australian accent, check.

Heart-stopping green eyes and long lashes to match the long, thick tumble of light brown hair falling in said eyes . . . check and check.

Curved mouth that could invoke huge waves of passion or fury . . . *CHECK.* "Bo Black," she whispered, getting cold all over again.

Cocking his head, he let out a slow smile. "In the flesh, darlin'. Miss me?"

Miss him? Yeah, she'd missed him. Like one might miss a close call with a hand grenade. "Get off my property."

As if he had all the time in the damn world, he leaned back against his plane, slapping the clipboard lightly against his thigh. "No can do, mate."

"Oh, yes you can." Staggering at a strong gust of wind, she planted her feet more firmly as she pointed to his plane. "You just get your Aussie ass back inside that heap of junk and fly it the hell out of here."

"Heap of junk?" Instead of being insulted, he laughed good over that, the sound scraping at her belly because it'd been a long time since she'd heard it.

Of course, she hadn't seen him in ten years, and the last time she had, he'd been eighteen to her sixteen, all long and lanky, not yet grown into his body.

He was grown into it now, damn him, and how. Reaching back, he lovingly stroked the steel of the plane, making an entirely inappropriate thought take root in her brain: *did he stroke a woman like that?*

Clearly she needed caffeine.

And a smack upside the head.

"You know exactly what kind of plane this is," he noted easily. "And how valuable."

"Fine," she granted. "Your toy is bigger than mine, you win. *Now* you can go."

Tossing his head back, he laughed again, and she made no mistake—he was laughing *at* her.

Nothing new.

And finally, here is a portion of
a wonderful new magical romance
that is the first Zebra trade paperback,
WHEN YOU BELIEVE,
by Jessica Inclán.
Available in June 2006.

The men had been after her for a good three blocks.

At first, it seemed almost funny, the old cat calls and whistles something Miranda Stead was used to. They must be boys, she'd thought, teenagers with nothing better to do on an Indian summer San Francisco night.

But as she clacked down the sidewalk, tilting the black strappy high heels she'd decided to wear at the last minute, she realized these guys weren't just ordinary cat-callers. Men had been looking at her since she had miraculously morphed from knobby knees and no breasts to decent looking at seventeen, and she knew how to turn, give whoever the finger, and walk on, her head held high. These guys, though, were persistent, matching and then slowly beginning to overtake her strides. She glanced back at them quickly, three large men coming closer, their shoulders rounded, hulking, and headed toward her.

In the time it had taken her to walk from Geary Street to Post, Miranda had gotten scared.

Now Post Street was deserted, as if someone had vacuumed up all the noise and people, except, of course for the three awful men behind her.

"Hey, baby," one of them said, a half block away. "What's your hurry?"

"Little sweet thing," called another, "don't you like us? We won't bite unless you ask us to."

Clutching her purse, Miranda looked down each cross street she passed for the parking lot she'd raced into before the poetry reading. She'd been late, as usual, Roy Hempel, the owner of Mercurial Books, sighing with relief when she pushed open the door and almost ran to the podium. And after the poetry reading and book signing, Miranda had an apple martini with Roy, his wife Clara, and Miranda's editor Dan Negriete at Zaps, but now, she was lost even though she'd lived in the city her entire life. She wished she'd listened to Dan when he asked if he could drive her to her car, but she'd been annoyed by his question, as usual.

"I'll be fine," she'd said, rolling her eyes as she turned away from him.

But clearly she wasn't fine. Not at all.

"Hey, baby," one of the men said, less than twenty feet behind her. "Can't find your car?"

"Lost, honey?" another one said. This man seemed closer, his voice just over her shoulder. She could almost smell him: car grease, sweat, days of tobacco.

She moved faster, knowing now was not the time to give anyone the finger. At the next intersection of Sutter and Van Ness, she looked for the parking lot, but everything seemed changed, off, as if she'd appeared in a movie set replica of San Francisco made by someone who had studied the city but had never really been there. The lot should be there, right there, on the right hand side of the street. A little shack in front of it, an older Chinese man reading a newspaper inside. Where was the shack? Where was the Chinese man? Instead, there was a gas station on the corner, one she'd seen before but on Mission Street, blocks and blocks away. But no one was working at the station or pumping gas or buying Lotto tickets.

The men were right behind her now, and she raced across the street, swinging around the light post as she turned and ran up Fern Street. A bar that she knew that had a poetry open mike every Friday night was just at the end of this block, or at least it used to be there, and it wasn't near closing time. Miranda hoped she could pound through the doors, lean against the wall, the sound of poetry saving her, as it always had. She knew she could make it, even as she heard the thud of heavy shoes just behind her.

"Don't go so fast," one of the men said, his voice full of exertion. "I want this to last a long time."

In a second, she knew they'd have her, pulling her into a basement stairwell, doing the dark things that usually happened during commercial breaks on television. She'd end up like a poor character in one of the many *Law and Order* shows, nothing left but clues.

She wasn't going to make it to the end of the block. Her shoes were slipping off her heels, and even all the adrenaline in her body couldn't make up for her lack of speed. Just ahead, six feet or so, there was a door or what looked like a door with a slim sliver of reddish light coming from underneath it. Maybe it was a bar or a restaurant. An illegal card room. A brothel. A crack house. It didn't matter now, though. Miranda ran as fast as she could, and as she passed the door, she stuck out her hand and slammed her body against the plaster and wood, falling through and then onto her side on a hallway floor. The men who were chasing her seemed to not even notice she had gone, their feet clomping by until the door slammed shut and everything went silent.

Breathing heavily on the floor, Miranda knew there were people around her. She could hear their surprised cries at her entrance and see chairs as well as legs and shoes, though everything seemed shadowy in the dark light—either that, or everyone was wearing black. Maybe she'd somehow stumbled into Manhattan.

Swallowing hard, she pushed herself up from the gritty wooden floor, but yelped as she tried to put weight on her ankle. She clutched at the legs of a wooden chair, breathing in to the sharp pain that radiated up her leg.

"How did you get here?" a voice asked.

Miranda looked up and almost yelped again, but this time it wasn't because of her ankle but at the face looking down at her. Pushing her hair back, she leaned against what seemed to be a bar. The man bending over her moved closer, letting his black hood fall back to his thin shoulders. His eyes were dark, his face covered in a gray beard, and she could smell some kind of alcohol on him. A swirl of almost purple smoke hovered over his head and then twirled into the thick haze that hung in the room.

She relaxed and breathed in deeply. Thank God. It *was* a bar. And here was one of its drunken, pot smoking patrons in costume. An early Halloween party or surprise birthday party in get-up. That's all. She'd been in worse situations. Being on the floor with a broken ankle was a new twist, but she could handle herself.

"I just dropped in," she said. "Can't you tell?"

Maybe expecting some laughs, she looked around, but the room was silent, all the costumed people staring at her. Or at least they seemed to be staring at her, their hoods pointed her way. Miranda could almost make out their faces—men and women, both—but if this were a party, no one was having a very good time, all of them watching her grimly.

Between the people's billowing robes, she saw one man sitting at a table lit by a single candle, staring at her, his hood pulled back from his face. He was dark, tanned, and sipped something from a silver stein. Noticing her gaze, he looked up, and smiled, his eyes, even in the gloom of the room, gold. For a second, Miranda thought she recognized him, almost imagining she'd remember his voice if he stood up, pushed away from the table, and shouted for everyone to back away.

Had she met him before somewhere? But where? She didn't tend to meet robe wearers, even at the weirdest of poetry readings.

Just as he seemed to hear her thoughts, nodding at her, the crowd pushed in, murmuring, and as he'd appeared, he vanished in the swirl of robes.

"Who are you?" the man hovering over her asked, his voice low, deep, accusatory.

"My name's Miranda Stead."

"What are you?" the man asked, his voice louder, the suspicion even stronger.

Miranda blinked. What should she say? A woman? A human? Someone normal? Someone with some fashion sense? "A poet?" she said finally.

Someone laughed but was cut off; a flurry of whispers flew around the group and they pressed even closer.

"I'll ask you one more time," the man said, his breath now on her face. "How did you get here?"

"Look," Miranda said, pushing her hair off her face angrily. "Back off, will you? I've got a broken ankle here. And to be honest with you, I wouldn't have fallen in with you unless three degenerates hadn't been chasing me up the street. It was either here or the morgue, and I picked here, okay? So do you mind?"

She pushed up on the bar and grabbed onto a stool, slowly getting to a standing position. "I'll just hobble on out of here, okay? Probably the guys wanting to kill me are long gone. Thanks so much for all your help."

No one said a word, and she took another deep breath, glad that it was so dark in the room. If there'd been any light, they would have seen her pulse beating in her temples, her face full of heat, her knees shaking. Turning slightly, she limped through a couple of steps, holding out her hand for the door. It should be right here, she thought, pressing on what seemed to be a wall. Okay, here. *Here!*

As she patted the wall, the terror she'd had out on the street returned, but at least then, she'd been able to run. Now she was trapped, her ankle broken, and she could feel the man with his deep distrust just at her shoulder.